MASCOT° BOOKS

www.mascotbooks.com

Tethered

For more information, please contact:
Mascot Books
620 Herndon Parkway, Suite 320
Herndon, VA 20170
info@mascotbooks.com

Library of Congress Control Number: 2021919278

CPSIA Code: PRV0322A
ISBN-13:978-1-63755-280-3

Printed in the United States

Dedicated to Shana and Megan—thank you for being my biggest cheerleaders and always wanting more. And to my loving husband, Ryan—without you, there wouldn't be a Nathan.

This book contains material that may be troubling to some readers, including depictions of and references to sexual assault.

TETHERED

ARYN WICKA

CHAPTER 1
DANI, PRESENT DAY

One vertical pink line. Negative. I let out the deep breath I'm holding and put the cap back on the pregnancy test. The relief I feel radiates through me; I can't imagine the idea of being pregnant at a time like this. After disposing into the trash the one good thing I have going right now, I wash my hands and head out of the bathroom. People will wonder where the grieving widow is. I have no interest in being in the room with my in-laws and our friends and trying to hold it together while Joel's body is within six feet of me. Letting the door shut behind me, I hear Maureen, my mother-in-law, as she sobs. The whole building feels as though it's shaking from her pain.

Putting one foot in front of the other, I make it to the front pew. I gingerly sit down beside Pat and notice lines have formed across his forehead where his eyebrows are pulled up. My father-in-law looks like he's aged ten years within the last week. His big, burly body is hunched over as he holds Maureen's hand. I don't think they even realize I've sat down next to them. I'm invisible. Was I wrong? Maybe no one *would* notice if I wasn't here. Crossing my right leg over my left, I turn and look behind me for all of the exits, mentally preparing my escape. *Okay, so that's one straight back down the aisle and another to the left through the sitting room. That's two chances to get the hell out of here before I completely lose it.* I turn back around, and my betraying eyes make contact with Joel's lifeless body. His sunken cheeks are a vast difference to the abundant smile he used to beam. His once-tailored suit looks ill-fitting on his body now. Images of him wearing it on our wedding day flash before me. Seeing him like this only adds to my grief. I never understood open caskets, but this was a ceremony for his parents more than for me.

Anxiety prickles my whole body. I can feel my chest growing tighter, and I'm trying not to gasp for breath. I stand on shaky legs and attempt to casually exit the building while my eyes fill with unshed tears. As soon as the Virginia air hits my face, I fill my lungs and turn my head toward the sky. I'm feeling sad, yes, but I'm more angry than sad. Face still toward the sky, I try to block out everything but the sounds of cars driving by, birds chirping, and children playing down the street. I don't know how long I stand like this, but the effort to distract myself from the confusing anger I feel toward my dead husband must work, because I don't notice Nathan approach and stand in front of me. He clears his throat to get my attention. I pull my head back down, twist my long, black hair with my hands, and release it; it's a nervous tick my therapist has pointed out to me.

Nathan nods. "Do you need anything, Dani?" His amber-brown eyes focus on me.

Ignoring his question, I walk toward him and wrap my slender arms around him. Nathan relaxes into my arms. Letting go, I run my hands over my face. "Your parents are inside at the front. I just stepped out to get some air."

He looks like he might say something else but doesn't. Nathan turns around, taking a deep breath. He pulls the door open and walks in, leaving me feeling alone, yet again.

I wonder how Pat and Maureen will feel seeing their dead son next to their living one. I realize then that my thoughts are insensitive. Joel is just very different from his older brother. Where Joel's hair was buzzed, Nathan wears his a little longer on top. They are similar only in size, although Nathan still has a few inches on Joel. I shake myself out of my strange comparison train of thought and walk back through the stuffy funeral home. Again, I make it all the way to the front and sit down beside Pat. Nathan is sitting beside his mother, trying to console her. Joel's extended family and friends fill the ugly, yellow room.

Right about now, I'm wishing my parents were here, but it's a fleeting thought. The Davises aren't the sympathetic type. They would be more appalled at my bare appearance while out in public, lest they forget the fact that I'm in mourning.

Suddenly, my face feels puffy and hot. I reach up and touch my cheek, realizing I'm crying. Mark that down as another thing Greg and Cindy would chastise me for. I wipe the tears away from my eyes, stifling a groan. Getting through the rest of this awful day is all I can do. I'm thankful no one has really bothered to talk to me since I've been here. I have a feeling I won't be as lucky as the day progresses.

After Joel's excruciatingly long funeral, his family and I move to get in our cars. I head toward my Toyota Camry that's parked by his parents' Ford truck. Placing my hand on Maureen's shoulder, I lightly squeeze. "I'm sorry you both lost a son. That's a pain I can't fathom. Is there anything I can do to help you guys?"

She moves away from my hand and closer to the truck. Once she opens the large door, she turns back to me. "No, Dani, there's nothing you could do for us at this point."

This is how it's always been with us. She doesn't see the fact that I just lost my husband. Maureen doesn't hate me; she just doesn't particularly like me. I've never known why. After three years of marriage to her son, I stopped caring. Her indifference toward me always seemed like it was her issue, anyway.

Maureen climbs into the passenger side as Pat briskly walks around to tell me goodbye. His body language tells me he's unsure of what to say. "Bye, kiddo. . . . I'll see you later, I guess."

After a quick hug, I wave goodbye, not having the energy to say anything. Lowering myself into my driver's seat, I hear the truck peel out of its spot. I stare out of the windshield, wondering what disastrous turn my life has taken.

A *knock-knock* gets me out of my trance. As I look up through my driver's side window, I see Nathan. Rolling down the window, I peek my head out.

"That's the second time today you've caught me off guard. I thought you already left?" I say, looking around for his black sedan.

He looks down at his feet, kicking a small rock under my car, his face red from crying. "I just wanted to check on you. I wasn't sure if Mom or Dad had really given you any time to grieve. He was yours too." Nathan can't even say his brother's name right now.

Desperately trying to get out of this parking lot and away from Joel's corpse, I fumble, "I don't know how true that is anymore." Hesitating for a second, I add, "I'm just going to go home, Nate."

Nathan backs up two steps and doesn't say another word. I pull the car out of the parking lot and head toward Joel's and my house. Nathan lost his brother, his first friend; and yet, he was the only one who *saw* me today. I didn't want to leave that feeling.

I head toward my empty home, taking every back road I can to make the drive as long as possible. Being home without Joel will be a reality I'm not sure I'm ready for. Driving through our neighborhood, I see our black mailbox first and turn the car left into our driveway. Once I'm inside, I drop my keys and close the door. The weight of the last ten days crashes down on me. A sob breaks through my chest as I crumble to the ground. My body is too burdened to move, and I sit on the unswept floor.

My husband is gone.

The person I *thought* was my husband is gone!

CHAPTER 2
DANI, FOUR YEARS AGO

"I don't know how many times I have to tell you, Mom, but this is a restaurant, not a bar they get girls to dance on," I say reassuringly to the other end of the phone. The *Closed* sign to Tav's hangs dramatically in the window as I clean wine glasses and set them to dry on the table in front of me.

"It is completely absurd that you moved to Virginia in the first place, but now you're working in a bar? What will people think, Dani?" she adds, cutting me off.

She's not even listening to me. I try my best to get off the phone. "I don't care what people will think. I'm over letting you guys tell me what I can and can't do. That's specifically why I moved away. I'm twenty-three. If you and Dad can't support me and my decisions, we don't have to talk that frequently." There's a long pause.

"If that's how you feel, Danielle," she says, clipped. The call ends there with a *click*.

Cindy Davis: wife, mother, and bitch. She only uses my full name when she's trying to scare me. I guess that response shouldn't surprise me. I'm very aware of my mother's shortcomings—selfishness being one of them. My mother always controlled everything I did when I was growing up. I'm convinced she didn't really want a daughter as much as she wanted a doll. Unfortunately for me, I am an only child, so I received the full scope of my mother's attention, although I wouldn't wish that on anyone. That meant restricted diets, girly clothing with lots of ribbons and bows, and absolutely no sports. I was to act like a lady so I wouldn't embarrass her. My father, Greg, is her polar opposite. He paid me no mind—simply said hi when he saw me and liked to pretend he was the doting father when others were around. I'm not even sure if he knows my middle name (it's Christine). Ignorance or apathy? My guess would be the latter.

Rolling my eyes at the sudden emptiness I feel in my chest, I gather up the clean, drying glasses to put them on shelves behind the bar. My mom has always reminded me what she and my dad can give me. My parents have money, which they have no problem throwing at me as long as I'm obedient. It's more annoying than you would think, having someone pick out your life choices for you, as if you were incapable of doing it yourself. I wasn't lying to my mom: I do work at a restaurant; it just happens to have a bar in it, as well. Tav's—short for tavern—is a decent restaurant, although the majority of the patrons come here for the bar. I can picture the disgust on Greg's and Cindy's faces if they saw their *naive* daughter working here. I'm dressed in blue jeans with my black polo, and I've unbuttoned the few buttons it has. Twisting my hair in my hands behind my back, I look down. I've got enough cleavage that I know will help get me tips tonight. I'll take what I can get, because when I left home, I promised I would never move back.

"Hey, D, you ready up there?" Evan, the day manager, yells from the kitchen.

"I'm good up here. Let me go check my makeup in the bathroom real quick," I respond in his general direction as I rush to the bathrooms. I've been working this job for a few months now, so I know the routine. Fluffing up my hair and readjusting my bra, I take in my appearance. I'm not a conceited person, but I'm aware of my looks. My curled, black hair falls past my shoulders, complimenting my light, olive skin. I get my big, chocolate-brown eyes from my father, and despite my petite frame, I have curved hips that are my mother's. My eyes are lined with dark-blue eyeliner to enhance my dark irises.

The door opens, and in walks Chantal, a waitress with beautiful mocha skin. Coming over to the mirror, she pulls out a mauve lipstick. Before I leave her to it, she says, "How's it going, girl? You still enjoying working in this place?"

"It's definitely better than where I was, that's for sure. I like the fact that each day is a little different," I respond with a smile.

She lets out half of a laugh. "You seem to be handling it alright, and not everyone likes dealing with the public like you do."

That seems to be the end of the conversation. She turns away from her reflection and opens the door. We both walk out and head toward our designated areas. Like clockwork, Tav's opens at four o'clock. The regulars come in and sit sporadically around me. Handing them each their drinks one after the other, I look around to make sure no other staff need drink orders filled. This routine repeats itself. Before I know it, it's eight o'clock. Turning around, I see a new face sitting down. I haven't seen him in here before; he's watching the television screen above me. He's handsome in a boyish way—short, cropped hair and ocean-blue eyes. I move closer and lay down a coaster. "What can I get you?" I ask.

He brings his head down to face me. "Rum and Coke," he says, smiling. Wow, those dimples. This guy is adorable in the sexiest way possible.

Trying to find my voice, I say, "Can I see your driver's license?"

Leaning off the stool to his right, he takes his wallet out of his pocket. I can see the definition of his shoulder muscles through his shirt. He hands me his ID: Joel Stephensen, twenty-four. One year older than me. Cheering goes on down the bar at something that's happened on the television. Looking up, I see that it's a baseball game; the Cincinnati Reds are playing the Baltimore Orioles. They're replaying a foul ball that was hit and caught, resulting in an out.

Joel lets out a sigh. "What kind of swing was that?" he asks, annoyed.

I keep my eyes on the replay. "It's not his swing, it's the fact he can't keep his back foot still. He's all over the place. He needs to stabilize himself," I add, even though his question was rhetorical.

Joel lets out a laugh. "I didn't peg you for a Cinci fan."

I shrug and grab a glass from the shelf in front of me. "I'm not. I just like baseball."

I begin making his rum and Coke. While I'm getting a lime, I can feel his eyes on me. I turn around to place the drink in front of him, and sure enough, he's looking at me. There's a hint of a smile on his lips, and he makes no effort to look away. Trying not to notice, and failing, I attempt to push down the heat from my cheeks. Joel must notice my blush, because his smile widens.

"Are you from around here?" he inquires.

I'm debating how much information to actually give when I answer, "No, I just moved here a few months ago. What about you?"

"Yeah, I grew up not far from here. Graduated high school two towns over," he says with little emotion. "So, do you play?"

"Play . . . what?" I ask, confused by the change of subject. Was I missing something?

"Baseball?" he says, pointing up to the television screen. "Or, I guess since you're a girl, it would have been softball," he adds.

"Not really," I say, although I'm not sure why I tell the white lie. I've never played before.

His attention is back on the screen. I move down the bar to help Phyllis, one of my favorite regulars. Phyllis is seventy-seven and a pistol. Her high-pitched voice is sweet despite the cigarettes she smokes daily. She comes in almost every day with her white hair laid perfectly in curls around her head and in a different color track suit. Today, it's lilac. Right on cue, she points at me and smiles as I walk over in her direction. Giggling to myself, I ask, "Hi, Phyllis, same drink as yesterday?"

"Heavens no, honey, I need something different. You know I can handle drinks and men, but only so much before I need something new." She smirks.

I stifle another laugh. This woman kills me. "Well, what would you like tonight, then?"

"Let's try a whiskey sour," she responds, her face lighting up with excitement.

I hand the fresh drink to the sweet woman and move around the bar, making drinks for other customers. Periodically, I catch glimpses of the cute stranger. Looking at him now, I take in his smooth skin, and my eyes travel up his neck to his lips. They're parted slightly and look like two, soft pillows; it makes me lick my own lips. He must feel my gaze, because his eyes shift to meet mine. Breaking eye contact, I curse myself for getting caught ogling. As I walk in front of Joel to get more ice, he leans over and grabs my wrist. My breath hitches. I stop and look up at him. He's staring at my chest. I'm about to be offended even though I was the one who was just caught staring at him.

"Dani? That's an interesting name." I realize then he was reading my name tag and not staring at my breasts. "I want you to take a shot with me. I'll even let you pick what it is," he says, trying to sweeten the request.

I've worked behind the bar for over a month, and although men have asked me to take drinks with them, I never do. Evan allows it as long as we don't get drunk or make it a habit. I just don't know if this is a good idea.

Pondering the decision, I look up and lock eyes with Joel. At first, his eyes just seem blue, but the longer I look at them, I realize that's an insult to what they really are. His eyes are a deep blue, the kind of blue you would see before a storm. He has mischief written all over his face. He still has my wrist in his hand, and his thumb is rubbing my now-sensitive skin. My heart instantly starts to flutter. Realizing I'm too in my head, I decide it might be a good idea.

"Okay, yeah. I'll grab some Fireball," I respond. I'm not much of a drinker, but I know Fireball will go down easy enough. He lets go of me so I can grab two shot glasses; I fill them to the brim. Smiling over the liquor at Joel, we clink our glasses together in cheers and throw them back. The liquor hits my throat, causing it to burn as I swallow it down. The cinnamon is a lot stronger than I remembered. The heat fills my belly, and I hear Joel laugh. It's a sexy sound. I want to continue to hear it. Desperate to hear his voice again, I ask, "Can I get you another drink?"

"No thanks, beautiful. I've got to get going. Maybe I'll come see you tomorrow," Joel says.

"I'm not working tomorrow," I say a little too quickly. Wow, I am incredibly lame. Ignoring the desire to say more, I print off his receipt, then lay his tab and pen on the bar for him to sign, all the while silently wishing for the floor to swallow me whole for sounding so eager.

"I'll see you soon, don't you worry about it." Joel winks at me slyly.

Doing my best to busy myself so I don't watch him leave the restaurant, I check the time. It's a little before midnight. I turn back around to grab his receipt. He left a ten-dollar bill. I tuck it into my back pocket, but what grabs my attention is his phone number on the piece of paper. Smiling to myself, I pull out my phone and save the number.

Climbing into bed a little after three in the morning, I struggle to keep my eyes open. Pulling the covers up to my chest and rolling over to my stomach, I stare at the phone lying on my nightstand. The saved number is weighing on me. I only got it a few hours ago, but I know it's going to cause distractions. I picture how carefree he seemed tonight, like nothing could bother him. His smile was infectious, and he had this wonderful way of making me feel like I was the only one he looked at. Customers have certainly hit on me at Tav's before, but none of them were nearly as captivating as Joel. Reaching over, I grab my remote and turn on the television. I put on a random sitcom and wish the actors' antics would lull me to sleep.

It's been two days since I've seen Joel, and I'm proud of myself for not cracking under the pressure to text him. Sure, I've picked up my phone more times than I can count, trying to will Joel to contact me or debating whether I should text or call him; but I have refrained. I held it together despite the picture in my head of his dimples and the way it felt when he held my hand. Tonight's shift should keep me occupied from thoughts of the sexy stranger. I don't even know him. What is with me right now? I've never been so hung up on a guy I just met before.

Tonight is a profitable shift. Customers are pouring in, my pockets are full of small bills, and I hardly even think of what's-his-name. *Who are you kidding?* my inner monologue taunts, *You know his name is Joel.* Last call ends, and we're pushing stragglers out. Taking a quick inventory of the surrounding room, I confirm that almost everyone is out, and my coworkers have started taking half-eaten meals and empty dishes to the kitchen. I wipe down the length of the bar, rolling my neck from side to side, and let out a yawn. I am beat, and the drain of running around for several hours has me feeling warm. I can feel my hair sticking to the back of my neck. I flip my head over, coax every strand of hair to the top of my crown, and wrap it in an elastic band. When I stand up straight, I make eye contact with the stranger I can't stop thinking about. He is in dark jeans and a gray T-shirt that fits deliciously over his shoulders and arms. My heart skips a beat; he's just standing there smiling smugly.

"We're closing," I say, feigning indifference.

"I know. I just wanted to see you," Joel says, raising an eyebrow. He walks around the bar. Not feeling comfortable with having a customer in this area, I meet him halfway and block him out.

"What're you doing, Joel?" His name slips out, unfortunately letting him know I remember him.

"Do you work tomorrow? I'd like to take you out." His voice is un-wavering. It's the same steady confidence I heard the first time that enticed me.

Wanting to play a little hard to get, I don't answer just yet. "What did you have in mind?"

He doesn't miss a beat: "How about dinner. I'll pick you up at seven." It's not a question.

His smile alone gives me butterflies. "Okay, great," I add.

Joel walks out the door as easily as he came in. I hold my buzzing body in place until he's gone. I will not embarrass myself in front of him by giving an outward reaction. But once he's out of sight, an excited squeal erupts past my teeth, and my limbs dance as if on instinct.

When he picks me up at my apartment the next night, I'm nervous. Looking down at my clothes, I hope I'm dressed nice enough for wher-ever we're going. I'm wearing my hoop earrings, worn jeans, and a peach-colored top. It's the fourth outfit I've tried on. My hair is in a low, messy bun with tendrils of hair coming out around my temples and ears. I wrap the strands of hair around my fingers while I pace the apartment. I open the door to see Joel in jeans and a black T-shirt. He looks incredible; the simplicity of his attire seems very fitting for him.

We climb in to his silver Honda Civic, and I'm glad he doesn't open the door for me. The act would feel forced. After a few moments of comfortable silence while Joel twists his fingers to find the right radio station, he looks over at me, flashing me his dimples and wreaking havoc on my heart.

"I love this song," he says, thrumming his fingers against the gear shift. My ears flood with the sound of Breaking Benjamin's "Agony." It is a good song—one I haven't heard since high school. I have two of their CDs lost in a box in my closet. I think it surprises him when I say as much.

"I saw them in concert with my brother, Nathan, when I was fourteen. It was the first concert I had ever been to, and I liked that it was just me and him," he gushes.

Angling my head so I can take in his profile, I ask, "Is it just you and your brother? I'm jealous. I grew up an only child, so it got very lonely being just me."

"Yup, just the two of us with our parents. They're still married and live in the house we grew up in. Ah, here we are. Hope you're hungry." There is a lightness in his voice I've noticed, like he's always in a good mood or on the brink of a laugh.

He's chosen a steakhouse. Walking to our booth, Joel grabs my hand and leads me with his other hand behind his back. It's the second time he's held my hand since we met. It feels very intimate for how short of a time we've known each other. The hostess has chosen a secluded booth for us. After I pick a side of the booth, Joel scoots in directly after me. I've never sat on the same side of a booth with someone while the other side was unoccupied. It seems so silly to be this excited to be near him. I look down at my lap, trying to cover my smile. I readjust my jeans. The waiter comes out to take our drink and appetizer orders.

I look up under my lashes and cross my legs. "So, what do you do?"

"I work on cars. I don't have to ask what you do." He grins. Playing with the plastic straw in front of him, he sounds amused. "Are there any other trivial questions you want to ask?"

Rolling my eyes, I let out a half laugh. "Okay, is there anything *you* want to know?"

"Sure." Joel scoots over close to me, bringing his face down into my personal space. He smells like citrus and pine. "I want to know if it's not too early to do this." He doesn't wait for me to answer, because this isn't really a question. He lets his lips fall to the top of my bare shoulder, sliding his warm mouth up toward my neck, and he stays there, lightly kissing my skin. My whole body feels flushed, and I'm covered in goosebumps. I see nothing; my eyes have involuntarily closed. I don't see him move his hand, but I feel it covering and gripping my thigh.

A whispered moan escapes my lips, "Nope . . . not too early." I'm hoping he can't hear how shaky I'm feeling.

Joel ever so slowly peels his mouth up away from my neck and lays his forehead on mine. I can hear our labored breaths. When I open my eyes, there are a pair of ocean-blue eyes staring back at me. The waiter takes this moment to disturb us by bringing our food out.

When the waiter leaves, Joel resumes his seduction. "You taste better than I imagined." His voice takes on an edge that wasn't there before.

He sits up a little straighter, picking up his beer to drink. The restaurant feels much hotter than when we first walked in here ten minutes ago. A shiver runs through my body. I can still feel his lips on my neck.

Dinner passes by, and I learn more about him. Despite his earlier sentiment, Joel tells me that he enjoys his job, his favorite color is red, he lost his virginity at fifteen years old, and he has flames tattooed over his right rib cage that he got on a dare.

The drive to my apartment is short but filled with buzzing sexual tension. It's nearing the end of the date, and I know that typically means a goodnight kiss at my door. The kiss at the steakhouse left me wanting more than just a simple kiss on the lips. We both want more—I can feel it.

Joel walks me to my apartment door with his hand taking up the small of my back. I want to lean back into the warmth. I don't like false pretenses, so when we get to my door, I put the key in the slot. Before I've pushed my front door open, I turn around and put my back against it.

As Joel moves a few loose strands out of my eyes, I ask, "Would you like to come in?"

"Yes." Never taking his eyes off me, he uses his body to push into mine to open the door. Joel closes the door behind him.

"Would you like something to drink? Or . . ." I swallow, trailing off.

"No, Dani, I don't," Joel says with an arrogant roll of his eyes as he runs his hands down my arms. We both know why he's here, and it's not for a drink.

When he reaches my wrists, he lightly squeezes and pulls me against him. Stepping backward, he moves us to the couch. When it hits his calves, he sits down and pulls me on top to straddle him. Looking down at his handsome face, I realize I've never felt like this before. My body feels like it's on fire. I've only known Joel for four days, and he seems to consume me. I close the distance and push my lips against his. His movements start slowly, then quickly, picking up the pace as he goes. His hands move under my shirt and up my back to grip my shoulders. Joel pulls me down so I'm grinding on his body. I can feel his arousal rubbing against me through his jeans. My hands are behind his neck, holding on for dear life. I can't think straight as his tongue is lapping at my mouth.

Joel glides his hands down my shoulders and around to my stomach. I can feel his fingers digging into my hips as he trails his mouth down my jaw to the base of my neck. He's quick to get my shirt off, leaving me in my lace bra that has low-cut cups. He kisses between my breasts, lightly licking at the skin. I let out a small moan as he nips at me unexpectedly. Everything he does feels like heaven. Leaning down, I unbuckle my sandals and toss them to the floor. My hands move down to the hem of his shirt and pull it up over his head. Seeing the flames that cover his ribcage makes him look every bit of the cliché bad boy my mother warned me about.

Joel stands, lifting me up with him. I wrap my legs the rest of the way around his torso and kiss him along his collarbone. After stepping out of his shoes, he carries me the rest of the way back to my bedroom.

Tossing me onto my bed, he unbuttons his pants and pulls them down. Simultaneously, I strip the rest of my clothing off. Every motion we make seems frantic; it's a constant give and take. Joel climbs onto my bed at the same time I pull him up. Our lips mash together again as my hands rake up his arms and into his short hair. Pulling his mouth away from mine, he looks down at my naked body under his hooded gaze. A low growl sounding like appreciation comes from his throat. He moves his hand to my center and rubs in slow, deep circles. The sensation is overwhelming. I whimper as he deepens his movements even more. I'm so distracted by the breathtaking need building up in my body that I don't hear the sound of a condom wrapper.

Suddenly, Joel's hands go to the backs of my thighs to lift my butt off the mattress. He positions himself at my opening before bending down to kiss me. My arms go around his neck. While I open my mouth to deepen the kiss, he bites my tongue. I let out a yelp, and Joel pushes himself all the way in. I almost scream. He doesn't give me any time to adjust to the feeling.

Joel is pounding into me. The feeling is rough and divine at the same time. I can't see through the haze of lust in my bedroom. Raking my fingernails down his hard back, I begin to feel my orgasm peaking. I mindlessly start bucking; Joel puts his hands on my upper arms to hold me down. His strokes continue with no end or signal of slowing down. Pushing himself deep inside me, I cry out. My moans fill the apartment. Riding out my orgasm, I feel his body jerk as he slows down. Thrusting into me one last time, he stills, his body eventually falling onto me. Our bodies are sticky with sweat. When our breaths return to normal, he kisses my cheek and pushes himself off the bed to remove the condom. Joel returns from disposing of the evidence of our tryst. Climbing into my bed, he wraps his arms around me, pulling me down.

"That was an excellent first date!" he exclaims sleepily.

Elbowing him playfully in the ribs, I say, "I'm glad you enjoyed yourself."

Joel kisses the side of my head a few times before pulling the covers out from under us and motioning for me to get under them. While I climb under, he surprises me by standing up. He looks like he's about to walk out of my bedroom, but he's still naked. I don't know where he's going; half his clothes are on my floor.

I tap my phone to check the time. "Are you leaving?" I mumble.

"No way." He winks at me. "I was just going to lock your front door."

I can't contain the smile that's on my face. When Joel enters my room, he peels back the covers again, pleased I'm still naked. He scoots closer to me than necessary, pulling my back flush with his chest. His arm wraps around my stomach and our legs intertwine. His face nuzzles my hair. It feels cozy being cuddled like this. He throws the blankets back over our legs; I don't know how long we lie like this before falling asleep. All I know is this has been the best first date ever.

CHAPTER 3
DANI, FOUR YEARS AGO

CHAPTER 3
DANI, FOUR YEARS AGO

Moths are taking over my stomach. I can't call them butterflies because butterflies symbolize a happy feeling. This is not a happy feeling; this is a scared feeling. Joel and I have been together for a few months. After our first date, that was it; there was no going back for us. We have spent most of our time together, opting to stay in my apartment. I'm not complaining—I've grown accustomed to having him curled around me as I fall asleep. The idea of meeting his parents is big. The desire for them to like me consumes my thoughts.

My light-blue dress hits right above my knees, and my white flats accentuate my tan. Not wanting to seem too overdone, I opt out of my usual hoops and choose simple diamond studs. Pulling the car visor down, I open the mirror and check my makeup for the fifth time. I'm wearing minimal makeup: just enough on my eyes to make them pop, and blush crossing my cheeks to brighten my face. Running my hand through my hair over my scalp, Joel breaks into my thoughts.

"Relax, babe," he says, stressing the vowels. "They're going to love you almost as much as I do."

Joel pulls the car into the driveway, and I take in their modest, colonial home. I'm briefly jealous. This home looks well-loved. There is a worn, dirt path crossing the length of the yard around the house and to the side where there is a wall of trees. The green siding has faded slightly from what I assume is years of direct sunlight. As I step out of the car, the smell of chlorine hits my nose.

"Do your parents have a pool? I thought I smelled chlorine," I inquire, looking around me.

"Yeah, my parents got it when me and Nathan were in high school." Joel opens the front door and steps into his childhood home.

The windows are open, the fans are on, and there is a continuous breeze going through the house. It feels refreshing compared to the August heat. There are pictures everywhere of Joel and his brother, I'm assuming. I'm trying to look around as much as I can while being quickly led around to find the hosts of today's Sunday lunch. Stepping into the living room, Joel finds his parents. Mrs. Stephensen is putting a book back on her bookshelf while Mr. Stephensen is coming in from the back patio with an empty plate and tongs in his hands.

Joel's dad is the first to notice our arrival. His loud voice bellows over the room, "Hey! I'm so glad you guys are here." Putting the plate down, he bear-hugs his son with a loud pat on his back.

"Hi, Dad. Hey, Mom," he says with a softness in his voice while addressing his mother. She kisses his cheek and turns to me. "This is Danielle Davis, my girlfriend," he adds, placing his hand on my back.

"Hi, Danielle. I'm Maureen, and this is Pat," Maureen Stephensen says, smiling, while pointing to her husband. I look at Maureen and decide that Joel takes after her, particularly in her dark-blue eyes and softer features.

"Please, call me Dani," I reply happily.

Pat chimes in, "It's wonderful to meet you, Dani."

"It's great to meet you both. You have a beautiful house. I love how homey it feels."

"Thank you, dear. We've lived here since Joel was a baby. I hope you guys are hungry; I just put the burgers on the grill. Dani, you're not a vegetarian, are you?" Pat looks alarmed momentarily, as if he's just now considered this.

"No, sir. I love meat too much to be a vegetarian," I answer.

Pat chuckles and picks up his plate and utensils, nodding as he walks into the kitchen. Joel has his arm around his mother's shoulders, which isn't hard for him, given her petite size versus his height. She gazes up at her son, and it's heartwarming to see the maternal love she has for him. It's written all over her face. I've seen it with my friend's parents, but never on my own. A dull ache forms in my chest, and I'm instantly annoyed with myself for allowing my parents to enter my mind and possibly put a damper on an otherwise pleasant day.

"Would you guys like anything to drink?" Maureen asks us.

"No, I'm going to show Dani around the house," Joel answers, walking in front of his mom to stand only a few inches away from me.

His body wash wafts around me; he smells like citrus and pine. Joel is in my personal space, his fingers touching my stomach, and I can feel his body heat. The stance is flirty and intimate; I don't feel comfortable standing with him so close in front of his parents. I move backward one step and peek over his shoulder, but his mother has left the room.

Releasing a breath, my hands slide down over my legs, smoothing out my dress. "I don't want to give your parents the wrong impression. We should act appropriately when we're here," I say in a low hush, staring at him to get the point across.

"Appropriate?" Joel asks flatly, like he can't believe I said a childish thing.

"Yes, we've only been together a short while, and things have progressed quickly. I know what we feel is real, but I *also* know that it doesn't look promising from the outside. And I'm sure your mother doesn't want to see her son feeling up his girlfriend," I respond pointedly.

Joel rolls his eyes. I knew he wouldn't take it seriously; he hardly ever does. "Come with me. I really do want to show you around the house." He starts walking away, leaving me to follow.

As I trail behind him, I take in the living room more than I had earlier. The television is the focal point, with a bookshelf to the right of it and brown couches on the perimeter of the room. The cream-colored walls have several family photos hung on them. I immediately see four with Joel in them, ranging in age from what looks like newborn to five years old. There are more of him with his parents, and even more of Joel with an older child. They look sweet together, like best friends. It feels like I'm looking at a timeline of Joel's entire life. I see him in a costume with his dad at a school play, in a soccer jersey on a field, at Christmas opening gifts, and in a suit going to prom. I love all these captured moments.

Exiting the family space, I step upward onto the carpeted stairs and keep climbing. Reaching the top of the staircase, Joel passes the first two closed doors. I place my hand on the white banister and feel the smooth curve in my hand while I walk toward the last bedroom on the left. Joel opens the door, standing back, wanting me to enter first. Stepping into the poster-ridden room, the first thing I notice is the clutter. Joel left CDs lying on his dresser and video games on the nightstand. The bed is unmade, and there are posters on every wall. Most of them are from rock bands, with a good bit of swimsuit models in between. It looks like what I imagine a high school boy's bedroom would look like.

"It looks like you never left," I say, breaking the brief silence. Joel falls on his bed, leaning on his side. I could picture him in here at sixteen.

"Mom and Dad like to keep our rooms the same, in case anything ever happens and we need a place to stay." He shrugs like it's no big deal.

I sit on the bed, leaning back until my head hits the mattress, my raven hair fanning around me. I'm lying next to Joel, staring at the ceiling. "No, it's sweet. You know, my parents changed my room constantly—both when I lived there and after I left. I love how comforting this house feels, and how they don't want to change your old room."

I turn my head to my right to look at him. Joel has his head propped up with his hand and doesn't waste any time. Leaning in, his lips crush mine. I can feel the weight of his hand on my belly. He trails it down my body to the hem of my dress. Once Joel has found it, his active hand slides underneath the blue fabric. He lifts my thigh to lay across his hip while his hand travels higher to my butt. Placing my hands on his chest, as a small protest, I pull my face away from his, looking into his blue eyes.

"We should go back downstairs. I'm here to meet your parents, after all. I don't think they would approve of us staying up here to make out," I say, hoping he understands where I'm coming from. Before he can ignore me, we hear voices downstairs. It sounds like someone else is here.

"All right," he says, a little annoyed. Standing up from his child-hood bed, Joel takes my hand and pulls me out of the room. "Come downstairs. There's someone here I want you to meet."

Walking back into the living room, I see a tall man with his back to us talking with Joel's dad. Hearing our footsteps, the man turns around. He's an older version of the other boy in the photos. This must be Joel's brother, Nathan. I'm surprised by the height difference between the brothers. Even though Joel's only a few inches shorter, the difference looks staggering. Maybe it's the way Nathan carries himself. They seem like polar opposites. Joel's eyes are a deep blue, where his brothers are that of melted caramel. They look completely different in the face, but they're equally attractive.

"And such a handsome face," Maureen adds what I was thinking as she playfully grabs his chin and kisses his cheek. Nathan just smiles at his mom's antics. You can tell her sons love and truly adore her just as much as she does them.

Pat interjects, "Does everyone want to go out on the patio and eat lunch? Food's almost ready." Then, he clicks his tongs twice, exits the house, and beckons us to follow him.

Sitting down outside at their black patio table, I watch the family get their burgers on buns. Then, I grab the ketchup Pat just put down, meeting his eyes for the first time. They hold the same amber tones as Nathan's. He breaks eye contact with me to stare lovingly at Maureen, something I never witnessed between my own parents.

Maureen guides the conversation, "So, how did you two meet?"

"He came into the restaurant where I work," I answer before taking a bite.

Joel pats my knee under the table, smiling at the side of my face. "Saw the cute bartender and couldn't stop myself from walking right over."

"Have you worked there long, Dani?" Pat asks as he takes a big bite from his sandwich, grease dripping over his fingers.

"A few months. This back patio is gorgeous!" I say, really looking for the first time. The warm, beige tiles of the patio almost look like stone, and the white awning keeps us shaded from direct sunlight. "I would spend all my time out here if I were you. The stone looks new. Did you just have it done?"

"Thank you. Yes, Nathan took care of this for us," Maureen answers with pride in her voice.

"I'm glad you and Dad like it," Nathan says, looking down at his plate and grinning.

"Of course we love it!" their dad says before he takes a drink of lemonade.

Looking around the patio once more, I admire Nathan's craftsmanship. It really is impressive. All the lines are even, and everything looks level. This must be his day job. "It really is beautiful. Is this what you do for a living?" I ask, picking up my burger to take a bite.

"Thank you. I enjoy it, but no, I'm actually a teacher," Nathan answers around a bite of food.

"Wow, that's incredible. You have a wide array of skills."

Joel pipes up next to me, "Yeah, what *can't* Nathan do?" He sounds sarcastic, but maybe I'm imagining it.

Maureen makes a joke of the question, setting her glass down. She pretends to be deep in thought, "Well, he's not good with cars, or as much of a charmer as *you*, Joel."

The rest of lunch goes smoothly enough. I can tell they're a close-knit family. Joel is very lucky to have them. When the meal comes to an end, I'm full. The burgers were delicious; Pat's mixture of garlic and ground beef tasted amazing in every bite. I wonder if his culinary skills have passed down to Joel. I wouldn't know, since I'm the one who cooks.

We all gather our plates, silverware, and anything else left on the table to take into the kitchen. Once his parents' arms are free from dirty dishes, they go to the living room. The television wails. I hear the crack of a wooden bat and the high-pitched cheering of the crowd. Baseball must be a familial hobby for the Stephensens. Putting away condiments in the fridge door, I turn around to notice Joel has disappeared. I keep myself busy by helping Nathan clean up lunch.

"How long have you been teaching?" I ask Nathan as I bag up the rest of the hamburger buns.

He rinses the dishes before sticking them in the dishwasher. No longer leaning over, he tilts his head up to the ceiling, calculating in his head. "I'm twenty-seven, so that would mean five years."

"Is that how you keep track? You have to think about how old you are?" I ask, teasing.

Laughing at the question, he says, "Sometimes I forget how old I even am. It's harder than it seems." He closes the dishwasher and brushes the crumbs into the sink.

Looking around once more, I ask, "Where is Joel? I thought he'd come out and help us clean up."

"I wouldn't hold your breath if I were you. It's fine; I can take care of the rest in here. It's not much more, anyways," Nathan responds, a little disappointed.

"Are you sure? That doesn't seem fair," I say with uncertainty.

"The thing about my brother is he's never really fair. It's okay, honestly. I'd rather you go out there and get to know my parents."

Nathan turns his back to me to wipe down the rest of the counter. I don't like the thought of leaving the rest of the mess for him to clean up. I helped with the majority, but why should he have to clean up the rest? I'm disappointed in Joel for leaving the mess for someone else. I reluctantly leave the kitchen and go to the living room. I see him sitting on the opposite couch of his father, watching the game.

"There she is. Where'd you go?" Joel asks, his hand in the air waiting for me to take it. I walk over and sit next to him.

"I was in the kitchen cleaning up lunch. I thought you were going to come help," I answer, no longer looking at him.

Joel picks up on my tone that I'm not happy. Wrapping his arm around my shoulder, he pulls me in to him, replying at a low volume, "I'm sorry, babe. I didn't realize. I wanted to come out here and watch the game with my dad."

Maureen must have heard part of our conversation. I see her glance toward us and look back down. I don't want to talk about this in front of his family, so I don't push the conversation. His mother is flipping through a *Better Homes and Gardens* magazine. "So, did you have fun in there talking to Nathan?"

Looking up from her magazine once more, she stares at me. I think she might be glaring, but that would be foolish. I haven't done anything.

"Yes, both of your sons are incredible. Thank you both for having me over today. Lunch was delicious."

When I come out of the bathroom in my pajamas that night, Joel is in bed flipping through TV channels. I walk around to my side of the bed and take out my earrings, setting them on my nightstand. "I don't think your mom likes me," I say, voicing the worry I've had since we left his childhood home. Slowly, I shift my body onto the bed and cover myself with the blankets.

"She might just be worried because of how much I like you," he says, draping his arm around me as I lean into him.

Joel slides his arm around me. This is my favorite time of the day—when it's just me and him in our own little world. Nestling into the crook of his arm, I lay my head on his shoulder and look up at him. "I mean, we're living together, and it's only been a few months." He makes a good point.

"That's true, I guess . . ." Trailing off, I draw my shoulders together in a stretch and yawn. "Things just seemed fine at the beginning of the day, but by the end, it felt tense."

Tossing the remote, he turns his entire body toward mine. "I don't want to talk about my mom anymore."

Joel pushes down our blankets. Gripping my thigh, he pulls my body down the length of the bed so I'm no longer sitting up. He rolls toward me, and I open my legs so he can lie in the middle of them. He props himself up on his elbows, dipping his head to kiss the tops of my breasts through the light-pink fabric of my tank top.

"Doesn't that feel good?"

I ignore his rhetorical question. Joel leans his head down to take control of my mouth. As his lips push firmly into mine, I feel his hand snaking its way to my neck. With his palm on the side and his thumb on my throat, Joel pulls his mouth from mine. "Doesn't this feel right?"

The answer comes out in a rush, "Yes."

He's gazing at my face when his eyes widen with an idea. "Don't you want to feel like this for the rest of your life? It could always be this good with me, Dani." There is a finality to his statement.

"Yes . . . wait, what?" Trying to replay the last thirty seconds, I place my hands on Joel's biceps and scoot upward to a slightly sitting-up position. "What are you asking me?"

Staring into my eyes, not missing a beat, he says with conviction, "Marry me, Dani. Marry me! I know it's fast and probably seems—"

"Impulsive?" I finish for him, my voice going up an octave.

"That too. But this feels right. *We* feel right. From the night we met, you could feel this energy between us—don't deny it. Marry me, Dani. I love you, and I want it to always be this good with you." He sounds like he believes this is a great idea.

And he's right. I felt this spark between us almost immediately. Is it crazy to get engaged after only knowing and dating Joel for two months? Probably. Do I love him? Absolutely. The entirety of our relationship has been a little odd. We've been living together since practically a few days after our first date. If I marry Joel, how different would our life be? Joel is different from everyone I've ever known. He makes me feel seen and adored, like I can have an opinion about something.

I squeeze his biceps lightly to give myself the courage I need. "Okay," I say, hesitating. A small smile breaks out over my lips. "Yes, I'll marry you."

Joel's lips are back on mine, pushing me into the bed. His lips are everywhere on my face. It's sweet and innocent how he's peppering kisses across my forehead, down my nose, on my cheeks, back to my mouth. Breaking our kiss, he rests his forehead against mine as his smile takes up his face. "I love you." He sighs, elated I agreed.

On January seventh, a short five months later, the day has finally come. I can't believe Joel and I are getting married today. I'm putting the finishing touches on my hair and makeup in the back room of the small chapel, not far from our apartment. It's a small, white building, perfect for the intimate ceremony we have planned this afternoon. To say everyone was surprised, and a little wary, that we had decided to get engaged and then married so quickly would be an understatement. Our families tried for two months to convince us of the benefits of extending our engagement, making sure we weren't rushing into the marriage. The outside pressure never bothered Joel; he let the arguments go in one ear and out the other. Eventually, the comments dissipated as time drew nearer to our nuptials.

I'm already dressed in my white, long-sleeve bodysuit that looks like a leotard. I step into the light-champagne tulle skirt. Bringing the waistline up over my hips, I run my hands down my stomach and grab the material to fluff the skirt. I've smoothed my raven hair to rest down my back with one side tucked behind my ear. Chantal, my friend from work, did my makeup; the colors are all natural, but my eyes stand out. I don't know what sorcery she performed, but I see a shimmery gold color on my lids that make the dark brown pop. I look like a bride. My appearance embodies romance.

I can't believe I was able to get this shirt and skirt at a consignment shop for fifty bucks! Joel and I kept this wedding as cheap as we could since we were more excited to just be married. My mom and dad offered to pay for the wedding, but they wanted it to be their way. The whole thing would have been a circus. I decided paying for it ourselves was worth making sure we got what we wanted.

Maureen and Pat are here already helping Joel get ready somewhere else in this tiny church. My parents should arrive any minute now. Chantal is in the room with me, dressed in a maroon sheath she's chosen to be her bridesmaid's dress. The lace sleeves look gorgeous in contrast to the ruched bodice. I'm getting ready to compliment her on it when my parents walk in.

Standing up, beaming, I walk toward them. I'm surprised they didn't make an excuse to not come. "I'm so glad you guys could make it!"

My mom looks me up and down, holding my arms out to her sides. "You look so pretty." I wrap my arms around her, inhaling her coconut shampoo. The thought occurs to me that maybe I don't give her as much credit as she deserves. "Despite the dress you've found. What did you do, order this online?" The disgust rolls off her tongue so easily.

My face falls, and I immediately move away from her. I'm quickly reminded why I don't give her any acknowledgement. "Don't start," I say, annoyed, passing her to give my dad a hug.

"Why couldn't you let us throw you this wedding? It would have been much more lavish than this," she says, looking around the small, red-carpeted room.

A part of me can't believe she wants to argue about this in front of Chantal, a stranger to her. "We didn't want to have a big Davis wedding. We wanted it to be small and simple. Can we not do this? Just for one day?" I've resorted to begging. I make eye contact with my father to signal for his help.

"Leave it be, Cindy," he says with no emotion. Good try, Dad. Way to put an effort in. "You look beautiful, honey," he adds, kissing my cheek lightly.

My father's feigned affection is all for Chantal's benefit. Even an audience of one is enough for him to put on his Father of the Year act.

"I don't understand," my mother says over him, throwing her hands up in the air and huffing. "You just met this guy. Why are you getting married? He can't give you anything. He's a mechanic, Danielle!" *There's* her real issue.

"I am fully capable of getting myself anything I need; that is not why I'm marrying Joel," I retort.

She crosses her arms at the same time her eyes roll back into her head. She doesn't hide the condescension in her tone. "Yeah, on a waitress's salary?"

Giving up on the argument, I meet her eyes. "Why did I even invite you here? Seriously, I should have known you couldn't keep your opinions to yourself."

Turning my back on them, I pick up the leftover makeup that's on the table, needing to busy my hands, and distract myself from talking to them further.

My father steps behind my mother, taking her arm in his hand and pulling her in the direction of the door. "Cindy, let's go find our seats. You've said what you wanted."

I don't see them leave, but I hear the door shut. I didn't realize I was holding my breath, but as soon as I know they're not there, a loud *whoosh* comes from my mouth. Chantal comes and stands beside me. "I always thought you were exaggerating about your parents. Wow, was I wrong."

Not wanting to discuss the train wreck she just witnessed, I keep my response short: "You're telling me."

"How you're normal, I'll never know."

When I don't respond, I think she understands I don't want to talk about them.

Chantal continues, "Ignore them. You and Joel are the cutest together. And you look so amazing!" Her gaze lands on my skirt. She is genuinely fawning.

This is the subject change I need right now. Turning to my closest friend, I squeeze her in a hug. "Thank you for being here for me today," I say with nothing but sincerity.

"Of course, girl. I'm so happy you asked me," she says, pulling out of my arms and winking at me.

The family meeting I shared took up more time than I wanted, so now it's about time for Chantal and me to make our grand entrance. I grab my bouquet from the table and make sure Chantal's ready to go out. Bringing the flowers up to my nose, the red and white rose petals are soft against my face and smell heavenly. Nathan opens our door slightly, sneaking in. He looks handsome with his disheveled hair and clean-shaven face.

Luckily, the men didn't need to buy anything for today. They both had black dress pants and red ties. Chantal takes Nathan's offered arm, going out the doorway and walking down the aisle. Once they're standing at the altar, the church of forty people stands to face me. I had decided early in the wedding planning I would give myself away as opposed to letting my father do it. I'm thankful I've made that decision now. As I descend the aisle, mine and Joel's eyes lock. This is it.

We stick with traditional vows, and I stare into his eyes while he holds my hands. It all passes in a romantic blur. Our wedding is short; we didn't see the need for making the ceremony drawn out.

Tav's is holding our reception. Entering the mahogany bar, I'm in awe. My coworkers have set up twinkly lights up over the ceiling and around the windows. It looks rustic and trendy while the dim lighting adds a dreamy touch. Music filters out of the speakers, half our guests are dancing, and the other half mingle. Joel brings me a glass of champagne, a beer in his other hand. Bending down, he kisses my temple. Maureen and Nathan approach us.

"Congratulations, brother! The wedding was beautiful, guys," Nathan says, sipping his drink.

Maureen wraps one of her arms around Joel's side, and they continue to stand that way. "I can't believe my baby is married," she says incredulously.

"It's not that hard to believe," Joel says, winking at me.

"You look beautiful, Dani. Joel is very lucky," Nathan says, looking at me and then turning his direction to his brother, toying with him.

"Yes, she does," Maureen adds, turning to stare at Nathan with something that looks like distrust. I don't understand where this is coming from.

"Joel, can I steal your wife for a dance?" My new brother-in-law asks.

"Go for it, man. I'll go have a drink with the guys," Joel says before turning to his mom.

I head to the dance floor with Nathan as the song changes to Snow Patrol's "Chasing Cars." I put one arm around his neck, and he takes my hand in his, holding my back in his opposite arm. He's so tall and feels warm against me. We move slowly back and forth. I like Nathan; he's always been friendly and easy to talk to, but dancing like this feels too intimate for my liking, especially because neither one of us has said anything.

As if reading my mind, he looks down at me. "So, officially, welcome to the family."

His comment makes me smile. "Thank you. I'm happy you and your parents are here supporting Joel and me. How come you didn't bring a date?"

"I'm busy with school and don't have anyone of interest," he says blandly.

"Well, Chantal can't seem to take her eyes off you, if you want to give that a try." I nudge him to look in her direction. She's talking with someone I work with, but her attention is torn between the girl and us. Chantal is beautiful and confident; she would look good with Nathan.

He shakes his head, laughing. "I don't know. We'll see how the night goes."

The song ends, breaking us apart. "Thanks for the dance, *sis*," he says with amusement.

I stride toward the bar to get a soda. Turning around, I glance around the room and take in our reception party. It looks like everyone is having fun. Sipping from my bottle, I watch our guests. Friends and family members, most of them Joel's, come up to say hello and talk about the wedding.

After an hour of no sign of Joel, I decide to look for my new husband. I spot him coming out of the bathroom, stumbling. I rush over to him, trying to catch him before he falls. "Hey, baby," he slurs.

"Hey, babe. You drink a little too much?" I ask, giggling. I help him stand a little straighter.

"Nah, I'm good," Joel says, bending down and pressing his lips to mine.

"Let's go home. I'm tired," I suggest.

Joel drapes his arm over my shoulders as we make our way to the door, telling our guests goodbye. Guiding Joel outside, Nathan comes out to help me get him in the car. Opening the door, he lowers Joel into the passenger seat. I climb into the driver's side and start the engine. "Thanks, Nate," I say, clicking my seatbelt.

"Any time, Dani. Make sure he drinks some water before bed," he says, his mouth a hard line as he taps the roof of the car.

Joel passes out on the drive home. I wake him up just enough to coax him upstairs and into our room. Leaving him for a minute to undress in the bathroom, I find him fast asleep lying on his stomach. Watching my sleepy, drunk husband's back rise and fall, I get in bed and lie next to him. I end up falling asleep with a smile on my face, replaying our wedding day over again in my head.

CHAPTER 4
DANI, TWO YEARS AGO

"**D**id you grab the last of the boxes?" I yell toward the blue Jeep down the sidewalk from me.

"Yeah, all in the car," Joel says, slamming the door then leaning back against it.

Closing the mailbox slot, I turn, walking toward the vehicle, my winter boots crunching in the leftover salt. I put the junk mail full of coupons under my arm. It snowed two days ago, and it's warmed up enough to melt the majority of it. Everything looks wet and soggy.

Leaning into him, I stare up at the building. "It's weird. I'm going to miss this old apartment."

"It was a good place to live this past year, but the house is going to be better. You know that." Tucking a strand of hair behind my ear, he nudges me and opens the driver side door, letting me know he wants to get going.

"I know. This was just the first place I'd ever lived on my own."

I pace around the car to the passenger side. I peek over my shoulder at him, and he's getting in the driver's seat and starting the car. Opening my door, I toss the mail onto the floorboard and continue, "I know you're right. The house will be better. It's just bittersweet."

I glance at my apartment one last time, then look back and smile at my husband over the middle console. "All right, let's go."

We're in the car for twenty minutes when we approach an intersection. Joel makes a right turn, and the speed limit decreases. We enter the neighborhood. Sidewalks and a strip of grass line the streets in front of the passing houses. It looks much colder than it is, with clouds billowing in the sky. I'm not surprised to see kids bundled up playing basketball and people walking their dogs. It's a sweet neighborhood—the kind where you can ask your neighbor for sugar or some eggs, if you need. It feels safe.

Joel pulls the car into the driveway. The gray siding of the house matches the empty trees. It is almost camouflage if not for the navy shutters. Grabbing a box from the trunk, I follow my husband into our new home. Walking over the threshold, I'm grateful that it's warmer inside. All of our furniture is here, haphazardly set up around the house. Yesterday afternoon, Pat, Nathan, and Joel brought in all the big furnishings with Chantal's and my guidance. I walk past the living room to the kitchen and set the box labeled *Plates* on the butcher-block countertop. A few more trips, and we'll have all of our belongings inside our twelve-hundred-square-foot house.

I get ready for work, slipping on a new pair of jeans and my long-sleeve black V-neck. It's a bummer I have to work tonight; I'd much rather be home unpacking. Luckily, I have tomorrow off so I can focus my attention on unloading the boxes and setting the house up the way we want it. As I line my eyes with eyeliner, Joel walks into the bathroom and leans on my back, resting his chin on my shoulder.

Sliding his hands over my hips, he pulls my body back to his. "What time will you be home tonight?"

I feel my eyebrows pinch together. "Umm, probably eleven, same time I usually am. Why? What're you going to be up to?" I ask, curious about his unusual question. Swiping a tinted Chapstick across my lips, I spin around in his arms to look up at his face.

"Unpack some more boxes, that's all," he responds, loosening his grip and walking out of our bathroom.

Following him out, I call, "Don't worry about unpacking. I can help tomorrow. I would get some rest; give yourself a peaceful night. You seem tired." Bending down to where he's sitting on our bed, I kiss his temple and head out the door. My car is parked on the street where Chantal had driven it over yesterday. I try to absorb all of the views of our pleasant neighborhood as I leave for Tav's.

A month ago, I was promoted to manager. It didn't surprise anyone but me. I love this place and work hard, but I've only worked here a little under two years. I'm not the oldest staff member—not by a long shot—nor have I been here the longest, but everyone respects me.

I've been working on staff schedules and payroll for two hours when Chantal walks in and plops down on the brown couch to the left of my desk. I don't even need to look up from my papers scattered around me to know it's her. She comes in fifteen minutes before her shift starts for every shift that we share.

After crunching in a waitress's hours, I swivel in my chair to face her. "Hey, is it four o'clock already?" I ask.

"Just about. How long have you been here?" Chantal responds, crossing her legs.

"Since one o'clock. I came in and checked the inventory stock, made sure all the bathrooms had enough toilet paper, paper towels, and soap.

Then, I started paperwork," I answer, turning back to the desk and straightening up the papers I've already gone over.

"What're you and Joel going to do for your anniversary? I can't believe it's already been a year!" Chantal says, beaming and running her hands through her hair.

"Two days will be a year, I know! It doesn't feel like it's been that long. I don't know what exactly we're doing. Joel said he's surprising me." I smile to myself. "We'll probably go to dinner. We both agreed no gifts since we bought the house."

"That's adorable. And when can I come by and see the house again?" she asks.

"Give me two weeks to get it in order before you come, or you can come over the next time we're both off. You can bring wine and help me unpack." Focusing back on her, I smile at my best friend.

"We don't have the same days off for a while. Maybe you can fix that, *boss*." Chantal stands up, pulling her arms behind her back in a stretch.

Before she exits the office, I interrupt her. "See if anyone can switch shifts with you. Otherwise, I'll just see you at my house in two weeks."

Chantal puts her hand up at her forehead in a mock salute. I laugh at her as she walks out into the kitchen. I finish entering hours for payroll and move on to kitchen ordering. Once I complete all of my usual job duties, I walk through the restaurant and ask everyone how their service has been. This is my favorite aspect of my job, talking with the customers. It's what I miss the most about being a bartender.

After a few hours, I'm able to lay my head down on my pillow. I fall fast asleep waiting for Joel to come out of the bathroom.

Opening my eyes, I see light streaming in through the window shades. I roll over to check the time; it's a little after nine in the morning. Joel is on his way to work by now. Kicking off the covers, I hear paper crumple. I stand up and search inside the covers, finding a note:

Happy anniversary, babe. I'll see you later tonight. Dress nice! I love you. —J

Excitement fills my belly. I place the note on my nightstand and go into the kitchen to make some coffee. Once I have a mug in my hand, I go throughout the house gathering empty boxes, piling them up by the door leading to the garage. As I'm moving about the house, unpacking as I go, I think about how lucky it was to find this house right as our lease was ending. And in the dead of winter, no less. Normally, people hold them till the spring.

When I've gotten most of the kitchen set up, I move toward our bedroom to organize my clothes and decide what I'm wearing tonight. I've put away most of my clothes on hangers or in my dresser when I pull out a navy, floor-length sheath dress. I only have a little while before Joel gets home. He'll still have to shower and get ready, but he can get ready in no time. Feeling eager, I begin applying my makeup, going for an easy yet glamorous look. The eyeliner comes to a perfect point on the outside of my eyes. I'm putting my diamond studs in my ears when Joel gets home.

"Wow, you look beautiful," Joel says, kissing the top of my hand like they do in movies from the fifties. "I'm going to take a shower and get ready, and then we'll go on our date."

I turn the shower knobs on for him. "Where are we going?"

Stepping out of his boxers he wears a smug smile on his lips. "Why don't you guess?"

I make a show of rolling my eyes at his playful attitude and let a laugh pass through my lips. Watching him step into the shower spray, I guess, "Well, if you tell me it's Tav's, I'm going to be upset. But Claire's is the nicest place in town."

"That was a good guess. I guess we'll see tonight where we're going, won't we?" he teases, the water muffling his voice.

I'm not used to surprises, so I don't know whether to be excited or annoyed. I continue to get ready, resuming my final task of curling a few pieces of my hair to give it a slight wave that looks natural. When I hear the shower turn off, I go to get his anniversary gift that I've hidden. I pull the small box out of the guest room closet, quietly close the doors behind me, and wait for Joel in the kitchen. Eventually, I hear the click of his dress shoes in our hall and see him strut up to the counter shortly after. He looks handsome. He's wearing black pants with a light-blue dress shirt and no tie. I love that he forgoes a tie; it makes him look casual—the best kind of Joel. I'm practically bouncing up in my seat with excitement to give him his gift.

"Happy anniversary, Joel," I say, simply placing the box in front of him. He kisses me on the lips a few times before taking the box in his hands. He opens it, and inside is a gold watch with a brown leather band.

"This—this is my dad's," he says, staring at the watch. "Is this the watch my mom gave him for their first anniversary?"

I nod, smiling, happy he remembered the story. "I replaced the band and had it cleaned. But I thought it would be nice to keep this tradition."

Joel looks up at me, placing both of his hands on the sides of my face. "This is amazing, Dani. Seriously."

Taking the watch out of the box, he puts it on. After we've stared at his wrist for a minute or two, I stand up and pick up my coat that's hanging on the back of the kitchen chair.

"Well, should we head out?" I ask, putting my arms through the sleeves.

"Not yet. Don't you want your gift?" he asks, standing in place.

"Joel, we said no gifts. The reason you got yours was different—I didn't even buy it," I say.

He moves in front of me and pulls a long, velvet box out of his pocket. My jaw drops. No. Velvet boxes mean expensive jewelry, and we can't afford that right now. His hand opens the black box, and inside is a silver, diamond tennis bracelet. It is breathtaking.

"Oh my god, Joel! Oh my god!" Breaking my gaze from the jewelry, I stare at him in shock. "How?"

"Do you like it?" he asks nervously.

"Do I like it?" I ask, dumbfounded. I can't stop staring at the shimmering strand. "It's stunning! How could you have bought this? We can't afford this."

"We can afford anything that you deserve," Joel says, taking the bracelet and wrapping it around my wrist.

I'm speechless. "This is too much," I say, admiring the beauty of the delicate silver that's hanging from my arm.

Rubbing his thumb over my wrist, he holds my gaze. "No, it's not. I wanted to get you something special to show you how much I love you."

"It is beautiful. I love it, and I love you," I reply, gratified. Looking down at my wrist, I spin the bracelet with my other hand and watch the diamonds sparkle. I'm so confused as to how he pulled this off without me knowing.

It's been a few days since our anniversary, and Joel still won't tell me how he kept the bracelet a secret from me. I've checked our bank statements, and I don't see any charges for a jewelry store.

On my day off, while I drink my coffee I go through a list in my head of what rooms I need to finish putting together. When Joel gets home, I'd like to surprise him with having most of the house unpacked. I'm in my pajamas, my hair in a messy bun, and the elegant diamond bracelet is still on my wrist. I've refused to take it off. It's so beautiful: I want to wear it all the time.

Getting enough energy from the coffee, I put on a Breaking Benjamin music playlist and get to work. I get through all of the rooms and am set to finish on ours. I open a box labeled *Joel*, thinking I'll help him get his nightstand organized. I place cologne, extra deodorant, and a few odd trinkets in the drawers. I pull a beautifully carved wooden box from the cardboard box. I've never seen it before. Opening it, I find a picture of Joel and me we had taken on New Year's Eve. My heart warms. We look drunk and in love. Looking down, I see a movie ticket stub. My eyes suddenly zero in on something behind it. The warm smile leaves my face just as quickly as it came.

Putting everything else down, I pick up two plastic baggies. One has a white powder in it, and the other is filled with pink pills. I stare at them, willing them to be my imagination. I'm confused why they're in Joel's things, desperate to deny that they're his.

I have some time before Joel comes home. I pace throughout the house feeling unsettled. *Where would he have gotten these?* I try to ease my mind, wondering if I should give him a chance to explain. The more time passes, the more upset I get. There's a million questions running through my head. I busy my hands and put a pot of water on the stove to make spaghetti. I hear his car pull in, and my heart sinks. Keeping my back to the door, I hear him come in and toss his keys on the side table as he closes the front door. I turn and push my back up against the counter with my arms folded.

He slows his trek toward me but doesn't stop. "What's wrong?"

"I found something today." My voice is deceivingly low.

Joel searches my face for some kind of clue. He grazes my elbow with his thumb. "What did you find?"

I unfold my arms, and in my right hand I hold out his two bags.

It's almost immediate. "I can explain! It really isn't what it seems."

"Really, you want to go with *that* line?" I shake my head, annoyed he would go with such a cliché.

He shakes his head profusely, voice in a panic. "It's not a line. I'm so sorry, that's not mine. A guy from work had it, and he offered it to me because I was stressed about buying the house. I didn't want to come off rude or start issues with work if I didn't take it. I never once took them. I meant to throw them away."

"These aren't yours? You swear to me?" I ask with the hope he's telling me the truth.

"Yes, they are not mine!" he yells angrily.

I raise my voice to match his. "I don't care if it's rude. I don't want this in our house. Never again, Joel! I will not tolerate anything to do with drugs."

He wraps his arms around me. "I never meant for you to worry about this."

I'm confused by his reaction. He was fearful; I heard it in his voice. I just don't know if it's from a fear of losing me or getting caught. Shame creeps up my neck. I should trust my husband. I want to believe him, but I don't know if I do. I leave the safety of his arms and stir the pot on the stove, giving myself a moment to think.

Joel's hand runs up my back, pushing hair away from my neck. He rests the top of his chin on my shoulder; he loves this embrace. "I'm going to go take a shower. Are we okay?"

Turning my face to the side to peek at him, I force a small smile. "I think so."

Joel kisses the side of my head and walks deeper into the house. As I drain the pasta, I make a vow to be more aware of what's going on, keeping my eyes open for anything out of the ordinary. After marrying the pasta with the sauce, I run my hands through my hair, twisting it into a ponytail. I let it go, bracing myself on the counter in front of me. I let out an annoyed laugh. This is ridiculous. This is the first time anything like this has happened, and Joel told me they weren't his. I should leave it at that. Right?

CHAPTER 5
DANI, ONE YEAR AGO

"I'm just going to the shop to set up for tomorrow," Joel says by the front door.

It's four o'clock on a Saturday, the first day we both have off together in weeks. This isn't the first time he's left at an odd time. He's been leaving for various reasons within the last few months. He claims it's been to help a friend, issues with work, or to go grocery shopping. Things have been inconsistent between us since February. It's now April.

"It can't wait until tomorrow morning?" I ask incredulously.

"It won't take long. I'll be back in an hour," he responds, barely looking at me, and closes the door behind him.

To say I'm lonely would be an understatement. I miss my husband. Half the time we talk, it's about nothing meaningful, and that's *if* we talk in the first place. Joel is different. I have been paying our bills by myself; I can't rely on him to remember to take care of something as small as the water bill. He's been secretive, making sure to never leave his phone unattended or allowing me to drive his car without him. I feel as if I'm living with a really crappy roommate rather than my husband. I don't know why I'm even allowing this to continue, but I guess I'm just waiting for us to get back into the groove of things. I know at this point, that's naive. Joel needs to be confronted. I can't let any of this slide anymore.

I end up falling asleep on the couch waiting for him to come home. I wake up to our front door hitting the wall. Joel flicks the switch, and my eyes squint at the intrusion of bright light. I check my phone, and it's nine o'clock—four hours later than he said he'd be home. He's moving about the living room in a way that I can tell he doesn't know I'm here. I watch his movements as he heads to the refrigerator to get a drink. His eyes are red, and he seems on edge. As he tilts the beer bottle against his lips, I take in Joel's every inch, searching his face. He finally notices me.

"Stop staring at me like that," he says, running a hand roughly down his face.

Anger fills me to the brim. *That's all he can say to me right now?* "Why?" My voice is louder than we both anticipated. "Are you afraid I can tell you're high? Do you think I'm an idiot?" The silence swells between us. I can almost hear it ringing in my ears. "It's either that or you're cheating on me. And based on the empty baggies I've been finding in your pants and in your car, I'm guessing it's the former."

"Why haven't you tried to talk to me?" His question stuns me. It feels like an accusation.

"Oh, so this is *my* fault?" My voice goes up an octave. I can feel the tears stinging my eyes, but I refuse to let them fall.

Joel must be able to tell, because he tries to approach me with his hands out in front of him in a comforting gesture. "Dani, baby—"

"No, don't use your sweet baby talk with me right now."

I leave him in the kitchen and storm off to our bedroom, but he follows me. I start taking the throw pillows off the bed and pulling down the covers.

"I'm tired of not knowing what version of you I'm going to get when you walk through the door. Please stop—stop doing this," I plead, trying to make him understand.

He's on his side of the bed, mimicking my actions. "I'm sorry I've been worrying you." His voice is laced with sadness and something else I can't place.

"I want to see you flush whatever else you have. I can't keep doing this with you. I *won't* keep doing this with you," I say, staring into his eyes.

I'm still standing as I watch his moves turn sluggish, and he climbs into our bed. "I don't have anything else," he says plainly.

Knots form in my stomach as I remember what tomorrow is. Not wanting anything else on my plate, I offer, "Maybe we should cancel our family dinner tomorrow."

"They'll want to know why. Besides, it's pointless. I'm fine." He's asleep before I even have time to respond.

I'm as still as a statue watching him sleep unbothered in our bed. Tearing my eyes away, I go into the bathroom, shielding myself. I'm irritated that he's able to sleep so easily after I've been left reeling. Now that I've called him out on his drug use, it feels real. Big. The tears I've been holding onto the last three months fall in fat droplets down my face. Once the dam is broken, there's no stopping it. Sitting down on the cold tile, I cry until there are no more tears left. I'm angry at him for putting us through this. I'm angry at myself for allowing it for so long. Picking myself off the bathroom floor, I check the time; it's almost eleven o'clock. I wipe my face and climb into bed, silently praying for more answers tomorrow.

Sunday evening at five thirty, the doorbell rings, and his parents walk in. I don't know why they still ring the doorbell. We've lived here for a year, and they've been over countless times. After exchanging our usual hellos, we walk away from the front door and further into the living room. I try my best to put aside Joel's and my issues at least for tonight.

Pat chimes in, "The house looks great, guys."

Maureen responds to her husband, "You say that every time we're here."

"Well, I mean it." He chuckles to himself.

Joel smiles at his parents. "Thanks, Dad. Dani, can you go order the pizza?"

I walk into the kitchen to place our pizza delivery order over the phone, grabbing the paper plates to set the table. I hear Pat ask Joel to take a look at his car outside, leaving Maureen inside with me.

I peek over at my mother-in-law while I set the plates down on the table. She is looking around the room quietly. I clear my voice and attempt to make conversation: "So, Maureen, Nathan had mentioned you're planning your next road trip. That sounds exciting! Where will you and Pat be headed?"

"I don't know yet; that's why we're still planning it," she answers somewhat sarcastically. "I didn't know you and Nathan talked that often," she adds, trailing off.

Confused by her sudden change in tone, I respond tactfully, "We don't. He brought it up a week ago when he was over visiting Joel and me."

Maureen stands up, looking out our window. "I'm going to go see what Joel and Pat are up to." She waltzes out the front door after the weird exchange.

As I'm grabbing napkins to place on the table, Nathan walks in. "Hey," I say blandly.

"Hey, everything okay?" he asks with a softness I haven't been given lately.

I avoid eye contact for fear of breaking down. "Never better." I'm obviously lying.

He can hear it in my voice, but he's smart enough that he won't ask me what it is. Nathan has always been perceptive like that. I finish setting the table by placing the napkins next to the plates, and the door swings open to let the rest of the family in. Joel is carrying our pizzas. He gives a curt nod to Nathan, who doesn't return it. It feels like there is tension between the two, but if there is, their parents don't seem to notice.

Dinner passes in a blur. For most of the meal, I don't speak, and I barely pay attention to what is said. I am simply a body in the room, a body who wishes we had canceled instead. I don't notice when Maureen and Pat motion toward the door, starting to echo their goodbyes, until Pat puts his hand on my shoulder to get my attention. I reluctantly stand up to begin cleaning the table. Out of the corner of my eye, I see Joel walk Nathan outside to the front stoop. Loud voices filter in through the thin windows, but I can't make out what they're saying. Are they arguing? Before I can move closer and try to eavesdrop, Joel opens the door.

He stands in the doorway watching Nathan leave, ending their conversation with, "It'll be fine."

Late Monday night when I get home from work, the kitchen light is on, and Joel is sitting at the table waiting for me. "I wasn't expecting you to be up," I say, surprised. It's almost midnight, and he hasn't stayed awake to see me come home in over a month.

"I know things have been hard, but I wanted to make it up to you." He extends his arm across the table and lays a white box down in front of me. I look up at his face, and he's smiling like he can't contain his excitement for me to open it.

I rub my eyes with my hands and withhold a groan. *Is a gift supposed to fix everything?* I open the tiny box, revealing a delicate, single diamond on a gold chain. I wonder how he managed to pay for this.

"It's beautiful," I say flatly. He doesn't say anything to my lackluster compliment. Joel rakes a hand through his hair as his lips turn upward. It looks too much like he feels he just won this fight; he'd have to be clueless to think that. "I'm still mad," I add, staring across the table.

Disbelief covers his face. "I know. I was just trying to soften the blow." He recovers quickly, punctuating his reply with the boyish smile I fell in love with.

I leave for work earlier than necessary in hopes of burying myself in paperwork. Arriving at Tav's at noon, I enter my office, closing the door behind me. I take a few minutes to myself to just feel safe and calm within the four walls around me. Sitting down in my rickety chair, I start going through the week's receipts, welcoming the distraction from my personal issues. After three hours, I have about a half hour before my employees start showing up to set up for their evening shifts.

Standing up, I stretch my arms high above my head, twisting my body in opposite directions. I can feel the pull in the side of my body. My phone rings loudly, breaking the comfortable silence. Sifting through my stack of papers, my hand slips around the small cell phone. Looking at it, I recognize the number; it's Joel on his shop phone. I almost don't answer, but I decide against it. "Hey, Joel."

"Dani, it's Rick. Sorry to bother you, I wanted to let you know I had to fire Joel," Joel's boss says apologetically. My breath hitches, but he continues, "I felt I needed to call you and let you know he's been stealing money and doing drugs in the shop." I can't catch my breath. I can't see my office anymore.

Oh my god, how much more of this can one person take? I feel like I'm going to be sick. Emotion is thick in my throat. "I'll come and get him right now. I'm so sorry! Thank you for calling me, Rick."

"I was trying to keep him here, but he took off in a hurry. I don't know where he went," he adds to what is probably our last conversation.

Hanging up, I blink past the tears pouring down my face. I call Joel three times, and each time, it goes straight to voicemail. Panic lights a fire in my gut, and I text the only person I can think of.

Something is going on with Joel. I need your help. I don't know where he is.

I call Chantal and let her know there's an emergency, that I left the restaurant, and that I will call her when I can. When I reach my car, I hear my cell phone ping. Nathan has replied to me:

Not at mom and dads. I'll call around and let you know if I get anything.

I quickly type back: **I'm headed to Molly's pub. Will check there.**

The ten-minute drive to Molly's feels like an eternity. The bar is relatively empty when I get there. I spot Joel's car and send Nathan a quick text to stop his search:

He's at Molly's.

His text comes in almost immediately: **On my way.**

Bars always seem skeevy in the daytime. The brown paneling looks drab, and there are signs against the windows to block out as much sun inside as possible. I open the door, and everyone looks up except one guy in a back booth. Marching my way over to the only one who refuses to look at me, I see several shot glasses in front of him. They're all empty.

My voice is frantic. "What're you doing?" He still won't acknowledge my presence. I touch his face and turn his chin in my direction. He looks dirty. "Joel, look at me!"

"I took the day off," he replies, bringing the glass to his lips and throwing the amber liquid back into his throat.

He's been here for no more than fifteen minutes, and he's already drunk. I can tell based on the red flush across his cheeks and his bloodshot eyes. He's descending to rock bottom; I can see it. The secrets, the lying, the betrayal right in front of my face—it all hurts. I've been looking at him too long, my eyes burning with unshed tears. I feel like I've been staring at the sun. *How many times did he come home with gifts without an explanation of how or when he had gotten them? How many nights had I gone to bed without him while he snorted pills in our bathroom with the door locked?*

I hear heavy footsteps come up behind me, and a strong hand falls on my shoulder. Looking over, I see Nathan; he's dressed in khakis and a button-up shirt. Shit, he was at school. I can't believe I bothered him like that.

Nathan's deep voice gets all of our attention. "Let's go back to your house, Joel."

I move out of the way for Joel to slide out of the booth. He leans over too far and almost falls. Both Nathan and I reach for him, catching him under his arms. Nathan is trying to carry the majority of Joel's weight, but Joel's drunken state has him leaning awkwardly on me. I'm trying to keep up and get him to my car so I can take him home where he can sleep this off. I open the back door, letting Nathan usher him down on the seat. This isn't the first time Joel has been escorted and placed in my car because he was wasted. Our wedding day comes to mind. Comparing that to today makes my heart ache. *Was he using then? Has this always been an issue for him?*

Nathan leans down, peering at me through the open driver window. "I'll follow you home to help you get him out." He jogs to his car without a word from me. I'm not sure I could find my voice right now even if I wanted to. For the first time today, someone has made me feel like I'm not alone. And I'm angry that it wasn't my husband.

Pulling into the driveway, I cut the engine and get out, slamming my door. I begin to hear Joel incoherently mumbling. Opening the back door of my Camry, I see he's puked all over the seat. I will deal with that later. I decide to focus on the most important task—getting Joel inside. Right on cue, Nathan pulls up, running in our direction. I step out of the way for the second time today, and he moves into the car, gently pulling Joel out and getting him on his feet. Joel doesn't say anything while we walk him up the stairs and into the house. Nathan takes him back to our room while I get him a glass of water. When I enter our bedroom, Nathan walks out. I set the glass on Joel's nightstand and notice Nathan has taken his shoes and puke-covered shirt off for him. I watch Joel fall asleep, just staring at him. How could he do this? No longer wanting to be in the same room as him, I leave, clicking the door closed. Nathan must have already left, because he's no longer in the house. Remembering the mess in my back seat, I grab some cleaning supplies from under the sink of our guest bathroom.

Now that I'm outside, I look up at our yard, into our neighbors', and across the street at all the cookie-cutter houses. It all seems fake now. It's not the perfect, cozy little neighborhood I thought it was when we moved in a year ago. The events of this afternoon and the unknown of my future weigh on my shoulders. I suddenly see movement in the corner of my eye. My gaze moves and lands on Nathan. He's bent down, cleaning the backseat of my car.

"What're you doing? Stop. I can handle this," I say loud enough that he can't ignore it.

He peeks over his shoulder, then goes back to work. "It's fine, I'm almost done. You have your hands full. I wanted to take one thing off your plate," he says with sympathy.

"You don't need to. I said I got it," I retort, even though I can see he really is finished.

Changing tactics, he turns around, crossing his arms, and stares at me. "Tell me what's going on, Dani."

I don't want to throw Joel under the bus with his family, but this is serious. And I had thrown not telling someone out the window when I texted him for his help. Taking a deep breath, I run my hands through my hair and begin: "Joel has been stealing money from the auto shop he worked at and has been doing drugs. I don't know for how long, but my guess is for a while. The past few months, things have only gotten worse."

Nathan's eyes are closed, and he tilts his head down. He looks heartbroken for his brother. I know the feeling. Opening his eyes, he pushes away from the car and begins pacing around the driveway. I look up at the sky, trying to enjoy a sliver of peace at the feeling of the sun's warmth on my cheeks. Peace—something I haven't felt in months. The thought has tears stinging my eyes. I bring my head down when Nathan starts to speak.

"What're you going to do?"

I lick my chapped lips and wipe the tears from under my eyes. Hoping I sound more confident than I am, I say, "I'll get him help. I'm sorry I bothered you today. I didn't mean to pull you out of school." I look at his white button-up.

"You didn't bother me. He's my brother, and you're family. You needed my help," he says with certainty. "And my classes get out at two-thirty, so I was already out of school."

This simple fact makes me feel better. Walking the distance between us, I hug Nathan. He smells like sweet cologne and spearmint. He hesitates for a second. Afraid that I'm making him feel uncomfortable, I'm about to pull away. Before I'm able, he wraps his arms around my back. His tight grasp is for my benefit. I know that, but it doesn't take anything away from this moment. I'm exhausted over the stress of the last few days. I can feel my resolve breaking, my life in tatters. Humiliation pushes my spine straighter, and I turn my back toward Nathan while trying to get my emotions under control.

"Thank you for your help today. I'm going to wait for Joel to wake up to talk to him," I tell him, hoping he'll take the hint that I want to be alone now.

"Call me if you need help again. Promise?" he asks with urgency.

I've already started walking backward toward the house. "Promise."

Sitting down on my couch, it's extremely quiet. Nathan's gone. Joel's asleep. I'm alone. Pulling my phone from my pocket, I see several texts from Chantal.

Made it to Tav's.

Thinking about you.

Is everything okay, Dani?

Text me when you can!

I don't want to ignore her, but I don't know what to say. I still need to talk to Joel.

I send a quick reply: **Thanks for covering for me tonight. I'll call you when I can.**

After a few hours of stress cleaning and aimlessly walking around our house, I decide to check on Joel. When I enter our bedroom, I see that he's awake, staring at the ceiling. Leaning against the doorframe, I wonder how long he's been awake. Is he trying to avoid me or the elephant in the room? We stay like this—him lying, me standing—for several minutes. Neither one of us knows what to say, the epitome of the last month.

Tired of the silence and the secrets, I cut through the quiet: "What's going on, Joel?" My voice is low. He doesn't answer me, just continues to stare at the ceiling, barely blinking.

His avoidance is unbelievable. I can feel the resentment in my bones. Pushing off the doorway, I kneel on the bed. "Joel, I'm not doing this anymore. If you refuse to talk to me or get help, our marriage is over! I am done playing these games." My voice is a loud plea.

Joel sits up slowly, like his whole body aches. His bare chest glistens with sweat. "I'm not playing games. Dani, baby, what's the problem?" he asks, reaching over to stroke my face. He's distracting me; he's always been good at this. I haven't felt this sweet, intimate touch in so long that I almost lean into it.

"You know what the problem is, Joel. You were fired today. You've been lying to everyone around you, especially me."

"Everything will be okay. I'll get another job," he responds, missing the point entirely.

"That isn't what this is about, and you know it. Hear me now: the stealing, the drug use—it stops *now*. I can't force you to get help, but if this continues, you can pack your bags." I stare into his eyes making sure he knows how serious I am.

Heaving a deep sigh, his head drops back to his pillow. "It stops now. Everything will stop. I'll make it right, Dani. Please don't leave me."

Climbing into the bed, I kneel beside him. Putting my hands on either side of his face, they slip under his head. My desire to believe him is reckless. Lifting his head, I brush my lips against his. They're warm against mine. *How long has it been since we've kissed?* I'm saddened by the fact I'm not sure. Wrapping my arms around his shoulders, we lay on the bed together, holding on to each other and to the hope that this is the worst it'll ever be.

CHAPTER 6

DANI, TWO WEEKS AGO

The room feels cold. Why is it always cold in here? It's like it sucks the life from your body. The air smells stuffy like a dusty, old church. I'm in my rightful seat on the couch with a pillow laid across my stomach like a security blanket. Listening to the hum of the white noise machine, I begin to wring my hands. This will be the sixth time I've seen Maggie. Looking up, I see she has her trusted pen and pad of paper. Glancing around the room, I see that everything is the exact same as it was the first time I came in. Books are stacked on the floor even though they could fit in the spaces on the bookshelves if she rearranged the picture frames she's used to decorate. Two overflowing potted plants are in the windowsill, and there are children's toys in the corner.

She breaks me out of my inspection of her office; I haven't been paying attention. I think she asked me how I've been since she last saw me. Looking back in her direction, I reply, "Things have been good." I hope my guess is right.

Maggie has been consistent, soft, and understanding since I started seeing her over a month ago. Her graying hair is in its signature ponytail. She's waiting to see if I'll add more. I don't. It takes me a little bit to warm up each session. "Is Joel still refusing to come?"

I run my hands through my hair, playing with the ends. I sigh. "Yes. He says he's fine. He says he goes to meetings once a month."

"He says?" Maggie asks, repeating me.

"He says he goes. I just don't know if that's true. Everything has been good between us for the past eleven months. Really. It took him some time to finally agree to get some form of help. I guess I'm just waiting for the other shoe to drop."

"Letting go and trusting is a difficult process for everyone. I wonder," she says, trailing off while jotting notes down on her pad, "if it's reminiscent of being at home with your parents?"

I'm not sure where this is going. "What do you mean?"

"Well, you've told me previously you couldn't rely on them. They were always focused on themselves. In a lot of ways, I think Joel has made you feel like you couldn't count on him either. And since you were young, you've been taught only to trust yourself. But asking for help is necessary in order to be a healthy adult. You coming to therapy is a big step, Dani. I'm really proud of you," she answers with pride in her eyes.

"Thank you," I say quietly, smiling to myself.

"Have you been practicing asking for help in other ways?" Maggie inquires.

I shrug slightly. "I'm not sure in what other ways I can ask for help. I have everything under control."

Putting her pen down, she rests her hands in her lap, looking directly at me. "Why did you originally decide to come in for therapy?"

I can't get away from her stare; I feel she can see right through me. The concern in her tone is evident. "I wanted Joel and I to work through issues regarding trust." She nods her head, signaling me to keep going. "But then, he felt it was unnecessary for him to go, so I decided to come in anyway. I was hoping it would help me to help him."

"And just like that, we're back to you helping others with disregard for yourself," she adds with a small, triumphant grin. Lifting her wrist, she looks at her watch, "And that's our time. Dani, I want to say I understand wanting to help your husband. And you should, but that doesn't mean you can fix him. You do not have to carry Joel on your back. It is not up to you to fix everything. Your homework for this week is to look for chances to ask for help, and then take them."

Maggie rises from her faded, peeling, pleather chair and gives my shoulder a light squeeze as I walk out of her office. I'm walking to my car, listening to the snapping sound of my flip flops while trying to decipher how I'm feeling. The feeling I have after therapy is always strange. It's contradictory. I feel lighter from getting things I've held in off my chest, yet heavier from analyzing those very issues.

I roll down the windows on my drive home. It's June, fourteen months after I found him at Molly's. The air is warm but not sweltering. The drive home has me thinking how Maggie's right. I can and *should* help Joel, but it is not up to me to fix him. I think back over the last year and remember all the efforts he's taken to right his wrongs. Joel got a job with a local construction company, and he checks in several times a week while at work to let me know where he is. He's affectionate again. I've missed that so much.

I pull into our driveway, parking behind his car. Sitting there with the car off, I stare at our house. I can't keep holding on to this. Joel is making every possible effort to make me trust him, and I've been afraid this whole time. I make a promise to myself that once I walk through our front door, I will let go of the past.

I hear music playing low on the speakers. When I walk into the kitchen, I see him cooking, his back to me. I stand there staring. I feel some of my resentment slip away. A tear slides down my cheek at the same time he turns and catches me staring at him. I don't wait for him to ask me what's wrong. I rush into his arms, my lips seeking his. The moment my lips touch his, it's like our hearts break all over again. The feeling is so great I can't ignore how long I went without it.

Deepening the kiss, we become two frenzied people eager to forget everything but ourselves. Hungry for his touch, I pull my shirt over my head. I'm standing in my jeans and bra in the kitchen, and his hands run down my sides. Breaking through our moment, he leans over to turn off the stove before throwing me over his shoulder.

Laughter bubbles up, pouring out of me at his playfulness. He tosses me down on the bed, and I land on my back. Joel crawls over me, taking over where we left off. My arms snake around his neck, keeping him close to me. Our lips are mashed together with such force it almost hurts. He licks into my mouth and then surprises me by pulling away. Joel stares down at me with a hesitant smile on his face.

"I've missed you," he says with grief.

Looking into eyes the color of the ocean, I feel content. "I've missed you too."

He lies down next to me, draping his arms around my naked torso, keeping me pressed to him like I'd run away otherwise. "Can we just lay like this for a while?"

"Sure," I respond, laying a blanket over our legs.

My head is next to his. I lift up slightly to get even closer and lay it back down on his shoulder. Closing my eyes, I take a deep breath, smelling him. I don't know how long we lie there in silence, but it feels like it's mending something in us. I must've fallen asleep, because when I open my eyes, the sun has started going down. Joel is peeling his arms from around me so he can stand up. Before he leaves the room, he bends down and kisses my lips, and he softly says into the dark room, "I love you."

Over the next few days, we fall back into sync with one another. It feels like it used to. Even his family has noticed. We're grocery shopping for the week, and Joel is on the phone with his dad next to me. I'm putting pasta sauce in the shopping cart when he ends the call and sticks the phone into his back pocket. He lays his arm over my shoulders as we walk. "Dad was just calling to make sure we still want to go to the baseball game this weekend before he orders the tickets."

I glance over at him while I continue my trek down the canned goods aisle. "Of course."

He chuckles in agreement. "Yeah, that's what I told him."

His phone rings, interrupting the rest of the conversation. As I turn a corner to continue shopping, I notice he's a few steps behind me, looking down at his phone with concern. I stall to wait for him to catch up, but he stays grounded where he is. Phone raised to his ear, he fiddles with the label on a jar of pickles. It feels like he's avoiding my gaze. Deciding not to make a mountain out of a molehill, I push the cart back in his direction. His eyes meet mine, his lips turning upward slightly. He looks embarrassed.

"Yeah, I'll come meet you and take care of it." Joel presses the screen, ending the call. "Sorry about that. After we unload the groceries, I have to meet Dave at the job site to clean up some of the tools we left lying around."

"Okay, well, we're all done. We can check out and then hit the road."

The car ride home is comfortably quiet. The only thing making a sound is the crooning air conditioner. I intertwine my fingers with Joel's, and he lays our hands on his thigh. Leaning my head back on the headrest, I turn to face him. My eyes trace the lines in his profile. Joel has gotten more handsome as he's aged. Before I know it, the car is in front of our house, and he's pushing the gearshift into park. Getting the grocery bags in the house takes two trips. I open the bags, pulling out the perishable food to be put away first. Joel begins heading back toward the front door. "I shouldn't be long at the job site. As soon as I grab my tools, I'll head home."

"Okay," I say, smiling and waving him off.

We've had a good day. The house is basically clean, and the groceries are put away. I resolve to keep dinner easy. We'll have hot dogs and watch whatever baseball game is on. Until then, I turn the television on and tune in to a game show. Bliss washes over me. Peering out the windows, I see big, gray clouds rolling in. I open the windows in the house to let the stormy air waft in, creating a breeze. The clouds are full of rain, but it never comes. Time passes quickly, and I haven't heard from Joel. Muting the TV, I pick up my phone from the coffee table, press his name, and wait for it to ring. It rings once, then goes to voicemail. Weird. Attempting not to read too much into it, I send a text: **Just checking in. Do you know when you'll be home?**

Turning my attention back to the contestants, I feel myself check the time every few minutes and watch every vehicle that passes down the street. This goes on for another painful hour and half. I'm debating calling Pat and Maureen when a loud knock on the door startles me. I jump up from the couch, rushing to let him in. *Why would Joel have locked the door on his way out?* I wonder. But as I approach the door, I notice it's unlocked. Twisting the handle, I open the door and see a police officer standing there. Any hope I had falls. *Dammit, I thought Joel was home.* Shaking off that he hasn't come back yet, I speak to the officer, "Hi, how can I help you?"

He tips his head in a silent nod. "Ma'am, I'm Officer Campbell. I'm with the Sheriff's Department. Are you Danielle Stephensen? Do you know Joel Stephensen?"

Dread fills my gut. Oh god, what has he done? "Y-yes." I'm gripping the door for dear life.

Pain briefly flashes over the officer's features, but he manages to compose it quickly. "There has been an accident." I'm squeezing the doorframe so hard I'm afraid I might break it. "Joel was in a car accident this afternoon. I'm so sorry. He didn't make it."

TETHERED

Letting go of the door, I leave it hanging open and collapse on the first chair I find. Taking the open door as an invitation, Officer Campbell steps in, closing the door behind him. He comes to stand in front of me. Denial rises in my throat, and I want to yell at him. No! Joel is not dead! He can't be. My body is burning with a blind torment. How can this be happening? Palming my hands over my eyes, I begin to sob. Tears drip through my fingers. Lifting my head up in a desperate plea, I ask, "Are you sure?"

"Unfortunately, yes, ma'am. But we'll still need you to identify the body. It's procedure," he answers reluctantly.

I feel stuck. I don't know how to get past this moment in time. The agony is consuming every inch of me. I can't see anything past the hot tears streaming down my face. This doesn't feel real. I think about what this means. I will never hear Joel's voice again. I will never speak to Joel again. I've missed him so much over this last year. I felt like we were just starting to get back to our normal. More pain ensues. Bile rises in my throat, but I choke it down. "What do I do now?" I whisper, defeated.

"Is there anyone you can call to be with you during this time?" Officer Campbell asks. His hands are tucked behind his back.

Looking up through wet lashes, I see his discomfort. How awful it must be to have his job right now, to tell strangers of their loved one's accidents. He's right, though. I'll need to call our family and friends. Raking my hands roughly through my hair, I stand and pace the living room. I take a deep breath through my nose, letting it out, and struggle to reel in the sobs. "How did the accident happen?" I ask, clenching my mouth at the end of the question, gathering as much control as I can.

Clearing his throat, Officer Campbell explains, "He was speeding and lost control of the car." Lifting my hands, I wipe under my eyes. The officer begins speaking again, "I'm sorry to ask, but can you go down to the coroner's office this week?" He hands me a card with the address on it.

Missing the feeling of Joel's embrace, I wrap my arms around myself and nod. The officer, having delivered his message, leaves. The silence rings in my ears. I look around our home, and I see a pair of sneakers Joel left out by the door and a jacket hanging on the coat rack. He's everywhere, and yet I can't reach him. I search for my cell phone. When it's in my hand, I want nothing more than to throw it at the wall. I end up staring at it in my hand, unable to call anyone. The option slips through my hands as my phone screen lights up. Nathan's calling me.

I answer his call, "Hello?" My voice is shaky.

"Hey, I was just calling to ask if you could tell Joel to call me back. He's not answering," he says with brotherly annoyance. He must hear me crying because he continues, "Dani, hey what's wrong?"

"Joel was in a car accident, Nathan. He didn't make it," my voice cracks, unable to mask my sorrow.

I'm hunched over in my seat with my head in my hand. The remainder of the conversation is a painful blur.

Maureen and Pat rush over to our house after Nathan tells them the terrible news. They ask the same questions I've already gone over in my head. Striding into the kitchen, I pour two Ibuprofen onto my counter and fill a glass of water. My head is throbbing from the crying and the constant questions. Drained from the day, I resign myself to bed, not caring about the company I leave in the living room. Opening the door to our room, I stare at the bed we shared. I turn on my heels to go into the guest room. I slink down in the bed—the one no one has slept in yet—and allow the tears to fall. Sleep does not come peacefully, nor does it stay for long.

Chantal offered to ride with me to the medical examiner's for moral support. I declined; it didn't feel right to allow anyone else to see him like this. My feet pound into the ground, and with each step, the knot in my stomach grows tighter. I'm scared about how he'll look. Sitting down on a wooden bench, I close my eyes, silently wishing to wake up from this nightmare. A loud, raspy voice calls my name. Blinking my eyes open, I see a balding, chubby man in a white coat standing by an open door.

Rising to my feet, I walk toward him. "I'm Danielle Stephensen."

"I'm Dr. Langley. Follow me," he says tersely.

He leads me into a lab that feels twenty degrees colder than the waiting room. There is a substantially large body bag on the table. Panic racks my body as I process that Joel is in the bag. My legs continue toward him on their own accord while my body shakes. Dr. Langley pulls the zipper down just enough that Joel's face shows. My chest aches, and I can't catch my breath. His skin is gray and gaunt. I can feel the doctor's eyes on me. I bow my head, wiping the snot that's beginning to drip from my nose with my sleeve. "This is my husband." I'm unable to contain myself anymore; a cry releases from my throat. "How could this have happened?" I ask out loud for the first time since I first saw Officer Campbell.

"Mrs. Stephensen, your husband had cocaine in his system," he says mechanically.

The room begins to close in on me. My heart shatters. He was lying to me. Again. Closing my eyes to steady myself, I'm distraught as I think over the past week and how I promised myself to stop looking for things that weren't there. I gaze down at his face and no longer see my loving husband. It's someone I don't think I ever really knew.

The monotone gentleman cuts off our appointment. "Thank you for coming in. We'll be releasing the body in a few days so you and your family can finish making arrangements for his funeral. If you'll excuse me, I need to tend to the family of the second victim of the crash." He heads toward the door when I process what he's just said.

"*Second* victim?" I ask, following him out like a puppy.

"Did the officer not tell you?"

"I was told Joel was in an accident and lost control of the car."

"Your husband was speeding and lost control of the car, yes. But when he spun out, he hit another car and pinned it against a tree. The driver was seventeen." He holds the door open for me and points to a woman sitting on the bench I had occupied. She looks utterly broken. Her hair is a mess, her face is red, and it looks like she hasn't slept in days. I can only imagine how I fare next to her.

It's like a punch to the gut. It's more than his family and me; he's taken another life with his selfishness. That poor woman lost her child. I cross the hallway, taking the seat next to her. It hurts to know we're shackled together through this horrendous event. I watch as Dr. Langley calls for her, and she makes her way toward him. When they disappear, I decide to sit for a little while longer, not quite ready to go home to an empty house.

Leaning my head back on the cement wall, I stare at the ceiling. Disappointment and blame consume me. There's no denying that Joel is at fault here. But what about me? Had I pushed him harder, maybe he would have gotten help. Maybe that mother's child would still be alive. I feel nauseous realizing I could have done more. My eyes sting, and my breath quickens from my chest growing tighter. I'm on the verge of a panic attack.

Not wanting to cause a scene, I rush to my car. Once I've planted myself in the safety of my Camry, I place both hands on the wheel and let the dam burst.

A wave of anger crashes over me. I throw my hands at the dashboard in front me and allow it to drain from my system. After slamming my right hand on the hard surface repeatedly, I begin to lose steam. My knuckles are throbbing, and my breathing is labored. *When will this horror end?*

By the time I get home, my hands are red, and faint, blue speckles are scattered across my knuckles. They'll be bruised by tonight. I hear my phone signal a text message has come in. Sliding my hand carefully in my back pocket, I pull it out to read. I'm surprised to see my mother-in-law's name.

Let me know when you are back. We need to plan Joel's celebration of life.

I am in no mood to plan Joel's *celebration* of life. The thought of being buried in a casket makes no sense to me, anyway. A comfortable, pretty box being lowered into a giant hole in the ground is a waste. But Joel would want the fuss. He loved having attention on him. My eyes roll at the thought.

I enter a quick response: **I can come over tomorrow and we'll make the arrangements.** I click send. I send a silent prayer that Maureen will grant me the evening to myself to adjust to all that's happened.

Scrolling through my phone, I see dozens of text message alerts and missed calls from family and friends. I feel exhausted looking at all the names of people who want to be updated and want to know what's going on. Half of them are just nosy. The accident will be in the paper; they can get their information that way. I can feel animosity settling in my bones. Tired from the whiplash of my emotions, I pour myself a generous glass of wine, trying to numb the wounds Joel caused. When the sweet, red liquid touches my tongue, I tilt my head back, gulping the rest. I pour myself another, and then another, until the bottle is gone. Shrugging off my cardigan, I leave it in the kitchen, sluggishly walking back to our bedroom. The hallway feels like it's tilted on its axis. I have to brace myself on the wall to slow down. Slowly entering the room, I push my jean shorts down and kick my sandals off. I end up falling on the bed in just my tank top and underwear. I'm too drunk to care that this is the first night I'm sleeping in our bed without him or that I'll have a nasty hangover tomorrow. I'm just grateful I'm not feeling anything right now. My eyelids are heavy, and I let them slam shut as I lick off the stickiness of what wine remains on my lips. I hope this distraction lasts.

CHAPTER 7
DANI, PRESENT DAY

I'm a widow. *I'll have to check a whole different box when I fill out paperwork now,* I think as I lie in bed, staring at the ceiling. Making the decision to get up and leave my room the morning after Joel's funeral takes the majority of the day. When my feet hit the floor and my body is straight, I feel the stress I'm carrying so tightly, like a rubber band waiting to snap. My shoulders ache. Rolling my head from side to side to work out the soreness, I walk aimlessly around my house. I don't have anywhere to go today. The staff at Tav's are being accommodating and are covering the restaurant for a few days until I'm of sound enough mind to go back to work. Although, I would rather be there dealing with paperwork than looking at all of my dead husband's things. *What the hell am I supposed to do?* Stopping by the sink, I smell the dirty dishes beginning to pile up. Instead of putting them in the dishwasher, I elongate the process, scrubbing each dish with soap, turning the water as scalding hot as it'll go. The pain on my hands takes my mind off the emptiness I feel. Unfortunately, washing the dishes doesn't take as long as I'd like it to. Checking the time, it's only 2:45 p.m. I still have at least four hours and fifteen minutes until it's a respectful time to go back to bed.

Weak, unmotivated legs carry me to my couch. I lean against the back, pulling my legs up to cross them under me. I stare out the window ahead. I'm angry, but I'm beginning to get past my anger and just miss Joel altogether. I wish I could talk to him one more time. I have questions that I don't have answers to. I contemplate what hurts worse: that Joel wasn't who I thought he was, or that I'll never have answers to my questions. A shudder rakes through my body as my eyes take in the room, seeing the remnants of someone who's no longer here. My heart falls in my chest. *I wish it would stop doing that,* I think, annoyed with my body's innate response. I know he's not coming back. This isn't a surprise; it's a fact of life and death, so why does my heart feel like it's falling from a cliff every time I see something else of his? Deciding then and there, I pull out my phone and call Nathan. It rings twice.

"Hello?" he asks, answering the call.

"Hey, sorry to bother you," I answer, not concerning myself with announcing who's calling.

"You're not bothering me. What's up?" Nathan inquires, not missing a beat.

"I want to clean out the house, go through Joel's things, and I figured you would want some of it . . ." I respond, trailing off. My voice gets softer as I continue to speak. Maybe he'll think it's too soon. Fearful of being judged, I begin to backpedal, stuttering in the process.

Nathan cuts me off, "Yeah. I'm grading papers right now, but I'm almost done. Do you mind if I come over in a half hour?"

Heaving out a grateful sigh, I feel lighter. "Sure, no problem."

While I await his arrival, I decide to take a shower—a task I've skipped for a few days. The hot water cascading over my face, coating my hair, and running down my limbs absolves me from my grief. Focusing on the sensations of the water, I squeeze the shampoo bottle into my hand. Smoothing the gel over my scalp, I begin lathering it in. Tipping my head back into the spray, I let the water wash away the bubbles. I stay under the waterfall for much longer than I meant to, not wanting to get out. I feel like I'm somewhere else entirely. I feel so warm. Despite it being June, I've been cold since the accident. I'm reluctant to turn off the spray, but Nathan will be on his way.

Wrapping a towel tightly around my middle, I leave the bathroom a foggy mess to get dressed. Throwing on black yoga pants and an oversized, navy T-shirt, I feel comfortable, but most of all, I feel clean. The shower was a good idea. Throwing my hair up in a messy bun to keep it out of my face, I make my trek back into the kitchen to get trash bags. We have some cardboard boxes in the garage, too, so I go to get those as well. Coming back into the house with the boxes, I hear Nathan come in the front door.

He's dressed casually in jeans and a baseball T-shirt. His eyes race around the room. "Where do you want to start?"

I answer honestly, "Anywhere. Take anything."

Nathan isn't quite sure about my response. He hesitates, then asks, "You don't want me to check with you first before I take something?"

Meeting his eyes, I can feel his stare trying to read me, see through me. "I want it all gone. I can't look at it anymore." My eyes break from his, and my voice betrays me by faltering.

I can tell by Nathan's motions he doesn't know how to proceed. We each gather items left in the living room or coat closet by Joel, placing them in a trash bag. Moving through the house, we end in the hardest room: our bedroom. Standing in our closet, Nathan respects my wish and starts taking down Joel's clothes.

"Can you leave two of his shirts hanging up, please?" My voice shakes.

"You don't have to do this, Dani. I can leave this all here if you're not ready," Nathan says, his voice low, like he's afraid the sound will hurt me.

I look up at his face and see softness there. It's in every line and every freckle of his appearance. I'm grateful for his compassion. "I know, but I want to do this." Returning my gaze to the clothes before me, I reach my hand up and feel the fabric. It's worn and comfortable. Taking a step forward, I pull the hem to my nose and inhale. It's a shock to my system; Joel is in my senses. Dropping the shirt abruptly, I back away, leaving the closet quickly. Nathan sees all this and asks me what he's been wondering.

"How are you doing?"

"Honestly?" I ask, waiting for his confirmation. "I've been blaming myself for not pushing Joel harder. I constantly wonder if that kid would still be alive if I had." My chin falls slightly in shame.

"Joel made his own decisions. You know he wouldn't have listened." He sounds firm, but there's something in his voice. It's like he isn't sure if he's trying to convince me or himself.

Lifting my face toward the ceiling, I blink rapidly, warding off the tears. Sniffling, I say, "You're right; I know that. It's just what keeps me up at night. How are you doing with it all?"

"I feel like I lost my best friend," he answers sullenly.

Embarrassment creeps its way into my mind. He's lost his brother, his first friend in life, and I'm making it about me. "I'm an only child, so I can't even imagine. I'm so sorry, Nathan." Sympathy floods my voice.

"Stop apologizing!" he booms loudly, the sheer volume surprising both of us. "I'm sorry. . . . I'm just tired of hearing you apologize or accept blame for things you couldn't control."

Wanting to get past the awkward moment, I start moving again, picking items up and putting them in a box. We move in silence for several minutes. Opening Joel's nightstand, my fingers reach out and wrap around the family watch. This is something Nathan should definitely take with him. But I feel a connection with the accessory and am apprehensive to give it up. I think back on the memory of when I gave it to Joel and how surprised but happy he was over the small gesture.

"You can keep it," Nathan says, touching my elbow softly, assuring me.

My fingers squeeze around the leather band, unaware Nathan had noticed my dread of handing the watch over. Twisting my neck, I peek behind me, feigning a smile. Everything about me feels weak in this moment. "You should take it. It was your dad's. It should stay in the family." Turning around to face him, I open my hand for him to take it from me. Nathan steps forward, placing his rough hand on mine and closing my fingers. He doesn't say anything, nor does he need to. He simply walks out of my bedroom, continuing to clean up more of Joel's things and picking up the mess I've left as he goes.

When Nathan leaves, the sun has started to set. I'm still an hour away from my allotted bedtime, but reflecting on the events of the day, I allow myself to crawl into bed early. As the light fades from my windows over the next few hours, I lie beneath my blankets, listening to the crickets outside. Their chirps seem to get louder and louder as the night grows. I toss and turn, trying any position to get comfortable, but sleep slips through my fingers. I feel so alone in my house now; it's no longer a home. *Is this just grief or my new normal?*

Rolling onto my back, I heave out a breath, feeling grateful I had Nathan over today. At least he provided a distraction and helped me clean out most of Joel's things. It dawns on me that he didn't take everything; an idea springs up. I kick off the covers and hop out of bed, aiming for our walk-in closet. I flip the switch and open the door, scanning the much emptier space. Pulling one of Joel's T-shirts down, I shrug out of my own clothes and into his. Closing our closet door, I hit the light switch and head back to the bed. Lifting the neckline up to my nose, I breathe it in. It smells like sweet mint, just like Joel. I hold his pillow to my body and temporarily allow myself to feel like I'm not utterly alone.

The sunrays are creeping in through my blinds, and opening my eyes feels like an assault. They both burn from exhaustion. Sleeping in a Joel-scented shirt didn't help like I thought it might. Closing my eyes against the assailant doesn't relieve the sensation. Pushing my palms into my eyes and rubbing, I get up, deciding coffee is the only answer. When the pot is brewing, I choose to call my mother. This will be the first time I've spoken to her since the accident. My parents were on vacation when everything happened, so they couldn't be reached in a timely manner. I ended up leaving the news that my husband had died and his funeral information over voicemail. It's probably better that I didn't speak to them in the long run.

"Hi, honey," my mother's voice rings innocuously.

"Hi, Mom."

"How are you doing?" Her question seems selfless.

Leaning into that, I answer, "I don't know. I'm really confused." I can hear the pain in my own voice.

"I'm sorry, Dani. I just, I don't know what to say to help you," her discomfort is palpable. "Oh! Did we tell you about the next trip we're taking?"

Disappointment aches in my chest, but there is no surprise left in me in regard to her selfishness. Frustration is etched on my face; I can feel it in my clenched jaw. I take a sip of my hot coffee and contemplate the standards I've already set so low for my parents. *My life feels like it is falling apart beneath my very feet, and she can't take the time to hold a meaningful conversation for more than two minutes.* The pain from the past two weeks is like a double-edged sword dug deep in my back. Its point scrapes against my spine. I've lost the person I thought Joel was, and I don't have any family who cares. Letting my head fall back, I realize the painful truth: I'll be mourning them both.

After not working for two weeks, I'm desperate to go into Tav's. I need to get out of my house but within the space of somewhere I feel safe. That's Tav's. When I make it in, all of my staff stop what they're doing and stare in my direction, making me feel like a walking train wreck.

Looking around the room, I decide it's now or never. "Hey, everyone," I say loudly, projecting my voice so everyone can hear me, even those not on the main floor. "I want to thank all of you guys for holding down the fort while I was gone. I need things to continue normally. What I don't need is for you to tiptoe around me! Got it? Thanks, guys," I say when I see most of the staff nod. I continue making my way to the office. I step into the room, noticing it's slightly cooler, and close the door behind me.

After a while, I check the time and deduce it's halfway through the shift. Glancing down at the desk, I take in the lack of work I've done. Most of my time was spent staring off into space, analyzing my unknown future. Pushing my chair away from the desk, I leave my office, wanting to talk to some of our patrons. I spot my favorite older lady in a yellow sweat suit. She sees me before I've made it all the way over to her. Turning in her stool, Phyllis opens her arms, waiting for me to walk into them. She's happy to see me, and the feeling is mutual.

"My girl! How are you holdin' up?" Phyllis releases me from the tight hug, holding my upper arms with her strong hands.

"I'm fine." I paste a smile on my face, not wanting to make a commotion.

She shakes her head at me. Phyllis releases my arms and motions for me to sit down at the bar with her. I comply. "Don't give me that crap, Dani. I see right through you. Why are you here?" She's asking why I am working so soon after the funeral; an ordinary widow would need more time than I've taken.

"I needed to feel normal. I'm tired of sitting at home wondering what else I could have done."

She takes a long pull from her drink before speaking again, but I see Chantal has stopped serving others to join our conversation from behind the bar. "What else could you have done, sweetie?"

"I just keep thinking I could have changed the outcome. Saved the boy, saved Joel, I don't know." I look down in guilt.

Phyllis's fist slams down on the bar, snapping my head up. "I knew that boy was trouble as soon as I saw him that night. He had selfishness and charm written all over him. A dangerous combination."

Chantal's raspy voice chimes, "Phyllis, that doesn't help her." She holds her with a pointed stare.

Phyllis returns her look. "I don't reckon how it doesn't," she says to only Chantal. Turning her attention back to me, her voice is softer than before. "Joel only did what Joel wanted to do. There was nothing you, or anyone else, could have done, Dani. If it wasn't that kid, it would have been someone else. I can't stand to see you beatin' yourself up over something that's not your fault."

Chantal leans over, takes my hand in hers, and squeezes it. Looking up at her face, I can tell she is trying to comfort me. "She is right about that."

Shrugging, indifference heavy on my shoulders, I mutter, "Thanks guys. I appreciate it. I should probably head back to the office and finish the mountain of paperwork."

Several weeks go by, and each week is the same as the last. I pick up around the house, go to work, go home, try to sleep, wake up, and do it all again the next day. Chantal has been begging me to go out with her, even if it's just grabbing dinner or shopping. I don't have the motivation to do anything outside of the basic needs I have to sustain in order to stay alive.

I'm typing in receipt amounts when she barges through the office door, capturing my attention.

"Hello to you, too," I retort, watching her fall onto the couch.

"What're we doing for your birthday? And don't say nothing. You're turning twenty-eight. We still have another month, and we *are* going to do something," she says, exasperated.

"You pick; I don't care." My attention returns to the restaurant's tickets.

"Danielle, think about it and get back to me." Her use of my full name makes me stop what I'm doing. She's serious. If I don't think of something, I'll never hear the end of it, or she'll plan it. And although we're close, we don't enjoy all of the same things.

"Okay, I'll think about it," I respond. The heel of her foot is bouncing aimlessly on the floor. Glancing up, I make eye contact. "I promise." Chantal's nerves must be soothed, because she smiles and leaves my office to wait the rest of her tables.

I love my birthday, but this year will be different. I usually made Joel and our friends celebrate the whole week. She's right, though. I still have another month till September. I rack my brain for ideas, but nothing sounds appealing. Shaking it off, I conclude it's a worry for another day.

Checking my watch, I realize I'm going to be late. Tonight is the first night we're doing family dinner since Joel's passing. A little piece of me is surprised I'm still invited, but I'm sure that was Pat and Nathan's choice, not so much Maureen's. I drive over to my in-laws' home. *Should I still call them my in-laws?* Moving past my brain hiccup, a small part of me has missed this feeling—the feeling of warmth and comfort of being in the company of family. I'm grateful they invited me over; at the very least, it's one fewer meal I have to make for myself.

Upon entering the house, I hear voices in the living room. I walk deeper into the family home, not sure what mood will welcome me. Maureen is standing, and Pat and Nathan are sitting on opposite couches, but they're all engaged in what seems like a bland conversation. Giving them the benefit of a half smile, I raise my hand in a wave. Pat stands up, making his way over to embrace me. It's familiar, but most of all, it's comfortable. Yes, I've definitely missed this. Nathan nods in my direction while Maureen doesn't say anything, deciding the kitchen needs her attention more. She exits the living room without a second glance. I move around the furniture to sit on the couch next to Pat. It's strange how at home I feel given the awkward tension Maureen pushes on me. Ignoring it, I lean back into the couch. The original conversation has come to a halt, and the men are staring at me, silently assessing how I'm holding up. I loathe the attention being on me like this.

My hand raises and runs through my hair. Clearing my throat, I reassure them, "I'm fine. Can you please stop staring at me like I'm going to break."

They immediately look down at their hands, at the floor—anywhere but at me. After a beat, the conversation resumes. They're discussing what upgrades Nathan is trying to complete in his home. I end up gawking at him while he shares his details.

It occurs to me this is the first time since we lost Joel that I've made and followed through with plans outside of working. I'm basking in my surroundings, allowing myself to enjoy being around people. I stand up and excuse myself from the ongoing exchange, heading into the kitchen to offer Maureen any help. My body stops when I enter the archway of the room. Maureen is wiping her eyes by the sink. Her shoulders are rolled over from grief; she's suffering alone. Walking slowly toward her, my arms open to take her in, wanting to console the weeping woman. She turns her back to me, and my body falters. I know she is probably silently blaming me for her son's death and is refusing to come to terms with the fact he had a drug problem. I shrug it off, trying not to take it personally. Looking around, I can conclude dinner is almost ready.

"Is there anything I can do to help you? Could I make the salad?" I ask.

Sniffling with her back still to me, she pretends to mess with the dishes in the drying rack. "Yes, thank you."

Grateful she's allowing my help, I take the salad out and mix it into the bowl, adding feta cheese and vinaigrette dressing.

When we sit down together for our meal, it's quiet. The knowledge that one of us is missing lies heavily on all of us. Eventually, Pat gets the conversation going and tells a story about his week, to which Nathan responds and gives anecdotes about his students. Maureen barely says anything. I chime in when appropriate with lots of *yeahs, okays,* and nodding. The truth is, I don't really have anything to give. But that doesn't stop them from attempting to pull me into their menial discussion.

Midbite, Pat ropes me in, "How are you doing, Dani?"

This was what I was afraid of. I chew slower, buying time to come up with something that doesn't sound as sad as "I go to work to avoid being home alone." Staring at my plate, waiting for it to give me an idea, nothing comes to me.

Stabbing a piece of my lasagna, I answer, "Fine. Just busy working." I shove my fork in my mouth to avoid saying more. They all quietly tend to their own plates and drinks, not pushing for more.

After the dining room has been cleaned up, we say our goodbyes. Leaving at the same time, Nathan and I walk down the driveway together, our cars parked single file behind his parents' cars. Instead of peeling off to get in his car, he walks me to mine.

"Have you been talking to anyone about Joel?" he asks.

I don't know why he's asking. *Probably because he knows you're a wreck, and he saw how much of a mess you were when you asked for his help after the funeral,* I think. I look around. I can still make out most of our surroundings despite it being dark outside. "Not really. No, I haven't gone back to therapy yet." My answer is truthful, although *yet* implies I will, and I haven't decided what I'll do.

Nathan's looking at me intently. I read understanding on his features. "I know it's not my business, but you should. You seem like you're just going through the motions, like you're not all there. Even if your body is." He's coming from a place of concern, that much is clear. He keeps going, "Dani, you have to take time for yourself and not distract yourself by working every day."

How would he know I've been working every day? Confusion turns to surprise. "Have you been talking to Chantal?"

Nathan avoids my gaze. "She mentioned it."

"Well, thank you for your concern, but I don't need anyone to worry." I open my driver door, agitated.

"Hey, hey, hey," he says behind me, gaining my attention. Both his hands are up in a sign of surrender. "We just want to make sure you're okay. That's all."

I turn to face him, putting the subject back on him, my anger simmering under the surface. "And how are *you* doing? Are *you* talking to anyone about Joel?"

Shoving his hands in his pockets, I can tell I'm making this harder. I don't know why it's bothering me so much to have people check on me. Eventually, Nathan answers my questions, "I talk to people. I'm trying to find a new routine. It's not easy, but at least I'm trying. But I'm not ignoring my pain by working and shutting people out."

Raking my hands through my hair, I pull them back down over my face. "Again, thanks for worrying, but I'm fine!" I raise my voice over the last word.

"Yeah, you seem like it," he says, finishing the conversation. I close my door at the same moment he walks to his car.

On my drive home, I play back our conversation repeatedly. I'm mortified I responded with anger over his general concern. By the time I get home, the evening has left me feeling drained. I don't go to my bedroom; the memories in that room are too loud to fall asleep. Instead, I lie down on my couch and pass out almost immediately.

CHAPTER 8
NATHAN, PRESENT DAY

D
riving home, I turn my rock music up loud, tapping my hands on
the steering wheel. I think about how that conversation should
have gone. I should have approached that more delicately, not
giving away how Chantal spilled the beans that Dani's been working
every day for the last month. The last thing Dani needs is to feel like
people are talking behind her back.

As I pull my car into my driveway and come to a stop, I move the
gears to park and lean my head back against the headrest. I refuse to take
all the blame for tonight. *She could have opened her eyes and tried to
see where I was coming from.* Frustration twitches in my jaw. *I wasn't
trying to put her down. Dammit, I've made a mess.* A yawn escapes past
my lips, reminding me of my long day. Tomorrow is Saturday; I'll get to
sleep in. I'll try to make things right later, but right now, I want to get
some sleep.

I wake with my head and shoulders buried under my pillow. Lifting the pillow from my face, I can see it's light outside. Checking the time on my phone, I see I've been able to sleep in a few more hours than normal. Tossing the covers away from my legs, I get up, slipping on some basketball shorts. Walking into the kitchen, I make a quick breakfast of a bagel and eggs. I make a mental to-do list of things I need to get done. *Grade tests, work out, text Dani.* As I'm looking down at my bare chest, I add laundry to that list.

As I'm shoveling a forkful of scrambled egg in my mouth, I hear my phone ping in the other room. Walking back to grab it, I check the alert, resuming my breakfast.

It's Travis, my friend from college. **Gym at 10:30?**

Yeah. I hit send.

We both live nearby, so it takes us no time at all to get to the gym. I've kept the same gray basketball shorts on, throwing on a fitted, white T-shirt over my shoulders. When I enter the gym, cool air from the fan overhead hits my face. Moving forward, I spot my friend in the back doing pull-ups. I pick up my pace, seeing he started his warmup without me. Travis and I met our sophomore year. We didn't share a dorm room but were on the same floor. He wasn't as big as he is now; he used to be scrawny. But his mop of blond hair is still the same. Travis didn't have many friends growing up, but you wouldn't know it given how laid back he is. He clicked with me and my friend group and started coming to the gym with us regularly. Now he can lift more than me and doesn't let me forget it.

Coming to stand near Travis's equipment, I begin stretching. After ten more pull-ups, Travis drops himself on to the floor and stands by me as I take a drink of water.

"Nice of you to join me." Sarcasm coats his voice.

"You said ten thirty." I lift my phone from my pocket. "It's ten thirty-four, jackass."

"Come on, man, we're doing arms and chest today," his husky voice replies as he points to the dumbbells.

Good thing; I don't think I could do legs again today. They're still a little stiff from two days ago, but I can't tell him that. "Alright, man, let's go."

A long hour of lifting various weights goes by, and my body is slick with sweat. My arms feel loose, and my mood has improved. I'm feeling motivated for the rest of the day. Before we call it quits, I signal for Travis's attention as he's coming out of the bathroom.

"Let's finish today with some basketball." I'm already walking toward the doors to the basketball court. He keeps up with me. Jogging onto the court, I let Travis get a ball from the rack in the corner. I hold my hands open, and he tosses me the orange ball. I dribble a few times before I shoot. Travis catches it under the net. He pounds the ball into the ground as he runs out from under the basket and turns around to shoot from the free throw line.

Throwing his arms out toward the basket, he asks, "How are thing's going for you, man?"

Jogging toward the ball, I catch it mid-bounce. "I'm okay. Really, it sucks I don't have Joel, but I'm getting by."

He watches me shoot a layup. "Have you guys picked back up with family dinners yet?"

Tossing Travis the ball, I charge him to change the game from simply shooting hoops to one-on-one. While I defend the net, I feel sweat dripping from my hairline. "Yeah, we had our first one last night. It went as expected until Dani and I got into an argument in the driveway." While I wipe my forehead with my shirt, he takes the opportunity and sinks the ball into the basket.

I chase after the ball, and he stands there watching me. "What did you have to argue with her over?" he asks with interest.

"She's just not taking care of herself. I don't feel like getting into it," I say with nonchalance, hoping he takes the hint.

"Dani's hot! If she needs some help taking care of herself, I'll gladly help," Travis says, a devious smirk taking over his face.

Without thinking, I heave the ball at him. Distracted, he doesn't catch it, and it ends up hitting his shoulder. Ignoring the bouncing ball behind him, my friend stares at me. "What was that?"

"What was what? Sorry you can't catch," I say in mock apology.

Travis gets the ball back, aimlessly dribbling and watching me. "Did I hit a nerve, Nate?"

I roll my eyes, trying to pretend he's off base. I don't even know what to respond with without giving myself away. Then it comes to me: "No, but she just lost my brother. Show a little respect."

"Alright, fine. But don't pretend you're not hot for her for my sake; you always have been. I can see through that bullshit from a mile away," he says, throwing the ball back at me with the same force I did to him.

Sitting down in my living room, I have a baseball game on with the sound off and a stack of paper packets on my coffee table. Lifting a few of my seventh graders' tests, I go through, checking their answers. It becomes more tedious as the task goes on. I reach into my jeans pocket and pull out my cell phone. Scrolling past unread text messages from Chantal, Travis, and a woman I work with, I find Dani's name and begin typing.

Sorry about last night. Meant for that to go different. I click send

Tossing the phone onto the table in front of me, I attempt to put my focus on the game on the screen. My thoughts flicker back to Travis's comment. I can still hear him saying, *If she needs some help taking care of herself, I'll gladly help.*

Irritation causes the hair on my arms to stand up. I've always known men look at her like that, but hearing it from my closest friend sounded like nails on a chalkboard. Of course Dani is attractive; she has big, round, chocolate eyes with full, heart-shaped lips and the softest-looking skin. She is more than that, though, and she's in a dark place. It's not right for men to be ogling after her. *Yeah,* I think. *That's why I was defensive. It had nothing to do with what Travis thinks I feel for her.* The game does little to capture my full attention. Picking my phone back up, I text my friends, telling them we're going out tonight. I get dressed quickly in jeans and a short-sleeve button-up. Replies start pouring in with suggestions of where to go. Even though I'm thirty-one, only a few of my friends are married, so it makes it easier to set plans in motion.

Opening the heavy, wooden door to the bar, I scan the neon-lit room. There's a steady flow of customers. I see I'm not the first one of my friends to arrive at Molly's. Paul and Ken are sitting on their respective stools and drinking beers. Striding up to my buddies, I raise my hand to get the bartender's attention; he comes over to take my drink order.

"Bud Light, please."

He hurries off to get the bottle, twisting the cap off in front of me and setting it down on the coaster.

"Where's David?" I ask the guys in front of me.

"Kara's sick, so they couldn't come out," Paul answers lamely. My friends like to poke fun at David for how he dotes on his wife, Kara. Truthfully, I think David's lucky. It must be nice to come home every day to the one person you love.

"You still need some help tiling the bathroom in your house?" Paul asks, shifting the conversation.

"Yeah, that'd be great. I've already got the tile; do you think we could get it done tomorrow?" I inquire, hoping he'll say yes. I know a lot about fixing little things, but anything being done in a bathroom is out of my element; Paul does this for a living.

Taking a long pull from his beer, he seems to contemplate my request. "Yeah, that should be fine. I'll head over to your house after I wake up. Just don't expect it to be early."

"Wouldn't expect anything different."

"How're the brats?" Ken asks, his face lighting up with humor.

I chuckle down at my beer. "School just started, so we haven't gotten to know each other well enough, but I'm sure they're great. It's only seventh grade."

"That's such an awkward age. Do you remember what it was like in middle school?" Ken asks with a grimace.

"All I remember is Penelope Sawyer. She got even hotter in high school," Paul says, practically drooling.

"Too bad she didn't know who you were," I respond around my beer. Ken breaks out into a laugh. Paul has a decent enough sense of humor to not take it too personally. Travis walks up to our group right at that time. The guys all share their hellos.

Travis chimes in, "Sorry I'm late. I was busy with an early *date*." He says the last word smugly. As if we didn't already know he was out hooking up with some girl.

Paul, Ken, and I grew up together, having met in middle school and high school. Travis went to college with Ken and me, and we've had an easy time merging our friend groups. The guys either congratulate or scoff at Travis. I choose the latter, rolling my eyes. I tilt my head back and swallow my beer.

"Do we really have to hear about this every time?" I ask, feeling a buzz flow through my body.

"What's the matter, Nate? I figured you'd enjoy all my details since it's been so long since you've gotten any."

Ken and Paul don't attempt to hide their laughter. "Ha, ha," I say sarcastically. At that moment, I feel a small hand run against my lower back. Turning to see who is touching me, I see Chantal. As I wrap my arm around her shoulders, she smiles up at me. She looks great. Her dark skin peeks through slits in her white jeans, and the pink top she's wearing sits low on her shoulders. She looks like a model. Running her fingers through her hair, she glances at my friends and then back to me. Pulling me a few paces away, she positions herself between me and the guys.

"So, a little heads up that you mentioned to Dani I told you she was working every day would have been nice. I swear you men blab more than women do," Chantal says, staring up at me while trying to hide her grin.

I chuckle at her comment. "I'm sorry. Did I get you in trouble with the boss?" I ask, staring down at her face and watching her chew on her lip. Things are starting to change between us. It's been nice to have this female attention, but something is off. Right on cue, my eyes catch movement behind her. Lifting my gaze from her bare shoulders, I freeze. It's Dani.

She's wearing ripped jean shorts and a loose-fitted, black shirt with her hair up in a messy ponytail. Everything about her right now looks effortless. Gorgeous. Chantal must catch my distraction, and she follows my gaze. Turning her body, she sees who I'm staring at.

"What's she doing here?" I ask with sincere curiosity.

Chantal turns her attention back to me, pride evident in her tone. "Can you believe it? I got her to come out."

Yes, that must have been a hard feat. Paul turns most of his attention toward Dani, putting his arm around her shoulder in the process. He says something to make her laugh. A twinge of jealousy jolts through my system. Trying to focus back on Chantal, I attempt to make out what she's talking about. My gaze keeps flickering back up to the one woman I can't have. I inch toward the group, wanting to be closer to her, to hear her laugh. It's wrong to want my brother's wife. This isn't lost on me. It's been almost three years since I've admitted my desires to myself. Dani meets my eyes as I approach the group, giving a polite smile—nothing else. It occurs to me she never responded to my text. *Is she still mad?*

Paul's voice is the first one I hear: "Nice of you ladies to join us."

Chantal smiles and answers with a wink, "We thought you guys wouldn't mind if we just came over to say hi."

"Why leave? Stay and hang out with us," Ken implores, downing the rest of his drink.

I see Paul's eyes travel down Dani's slim body. Travis catches the action, turning his gaze silently to me. I don't want to give away what I'm feeling, but I'm afraid it's written all over my face. Clearing his throat in an effort to signal Paul to knock it off, Travis gains more attention than he meant to. Everyone looks at him. An awkward pause fills the space between us.

Patting Travis's upper back, I take over, needing a minute to think to myself. "Does anyone need drinks?"

We're pretty close to the bar already, but as more people flow into the building, I decide to get our drinks a little farther down the bar to distance myself. I only received two requests, so carrying them back will be no problem. Leaning forward on my elbows, I order our drinks, willing the customers around me to fade into the background. It's nice that Dani came out; she needs to get back to her life. She seems lighter tonight. Thinking back to how Paul has been ogling her all night does not sit well with my nerves. Grinding my teeth, I see Dani move up next to me. I push myself up, standing upright, but she doesn't look at me. She fidgets with her hands instead. The bartender brings our drinks over. Neither of us move to head back to our friends.

"Sorry," we both say at the same time.

We both emit a small snicker. Dani raises her hand to stop me from continuing so she can speak first. "I'm sorry I snapped at you. I know you were coming from a good place. But I'm listening. I'm out right now." She reaches up, idly touching the back of her neck. "I'm just worried how people will react to me being out so soon after Joel died," she trails off.

"You've been through hell. Joel put you through the ringer. No one is going to condemn you for going out or trying to get past all of this," I respond earnestly.

I watch Dani's ponytail bounce as she shakes her head. "You're right, and I am enjoying being out. It feels nice to look good for once." She sounds reluctant.

"You do look very nice," I add, as detached as I can muster.

She takes a sip of her beer, and I notice a blush from the alcohol has taken over her face. "Thank you. I'm glad we can still hang out even after everything that's happened."

Turning my head toward her, my stomach flips over seeing her delicate, dimpled smile. "Me too."

The next morning, Paul walks into my kitchen a little after eleven. He must have been serious when he said he would roll right out of bed, because his hair is pointed in several different directions, and his face still has indentations from his pillow and sheets. Getting started on the bathroom floor, we manage to finish in the late afternoon, making small talk and a mess along the way. When it's all said and done, Paul and I move back into the kitchen to clean ourselves up. Pulling out leftovers from my fridge, I start warming up food for us to eat.

"Thanks for your help today, man," I say, shoveling a cold bite of casserole into my mouth before setting it in the microwave.

"No problem," he says as he scrubs the dried grout off his hands. The microwave beeps loudly. I open the door to take out the container, and Paul begins to speak again. "It was nice seeing Dani last night."

"Yeah." I grit my teeth.

Grabbing a kitchen towel, he dries his hands slowly, thinking. "How's she doing?" He's aiming for nonchalance, but I know he's fishing for any information or opening I'm willing to give him.

"Fine, I guess, all things considered," I reply halfheartedly. Staring at Paul, my hands gripping the counter behind me, I'm quietly daring him to spit out what he really wants to say.

"I was thinking about stopping by her place some time to see if she needed help fixing anything around the house," Paul answers my question without my having to ask.

Ice fills my veins. He's going to be biding his time and laying down groundwork before she's ready to date. So when she is, she'll look to him first. It's smart, I'll give him that. It still has me seeing red. My brother has only been in the ground a little over two months, and Paul is already trying to move himself into her view. I knew guys would be coming out of the woodwork to be with her, but I wasn't anticipating it'd be this fast. Or my friend.

My stomach twists in a knot thinking about Dani being involved with Paul. Swallowing past the lump in my throat, I resolve to shove down whatever feelings I'm having for Dani. I've seen her with Joel and everything he made her endure for the last four years. Watching her with someone else should be a piece of cake by comparison.

I think back to the moment I knew she was different. The air was hot and sticky; it was going to be brutal to be outside for the baseball game. Dani rode shotgun while my dumbass brother was comatose in the backseat nursing a hangover. I pulled the car into the gas station, needing to fill up. As soon as I put the car in park, Dani jumped out. Confused, I got out and followed her to the pump.

I watched her lift the lever from its handle. "What are you doing?" I wasn't hiding my disbelief.

"Um, I'm putting gas in the car," she responded somewhat obviously.

"Why? You don't need to. I got it."

"You're driving today; it's only fair." When I didn't say anything and continued to stand in front of her, unsure of what to do, she added, "Don't you want to go inside and get snacks for the road?" She punctuated the question with a cute smirk.

I contained my amusement. "Would you like anything?"

"Sour Patch Kids, please. Oh, you might also want to grab a ginger ale for Joel."

As I walked into the air-conditioned gas station, I was taken aback by her thoughtfulness. She pumped and paid for the gas without my even bringing it up. And I hadn't planned on it; I had no problem doing it myself.

I considered how opposite Dani was from Joel. She was sweet and considerate. I was shocked when she offered to help me do the dishes at my parents' the first night we met. I loved my brother, but I knew his faults. How did they become a thing? I knew what drew him to her—she was hot. Her round, dark eyes had green speckles in them when the light hit her face; her tight body flowed like a river, rhythmically, when she walked. Her complexion, smooth, looked like it was kissed by the sun. Dani might not have been aware of her beauty, but no man was blind to her.

After paying for our snacks, I headed back toward the car. Dani pushed her hair back on her damp forehead and placed the pump back in its original place. I took the big, yellow candy wrapper out of the plastic bag and held it out for her. She smiled from ear to ear as she reached for it.

"Thank you!" Two excited dimples shone up at me.

Our fingers brushed one another, causing our eyes to linger. We stood like statues in that moment for one millisecond longer than we should have. She broke contact and opened her car door to climb in. I did the same, got comfortable, and continued toward our destination. If she had felt anything in those two seconds we were outside, she hadn't let it show.

CHAPTER 9
DANI, PRESENT DAY

Vegetable cans line the shelves in front of me. Scanning each label, I reach for the green beans. The mundane chores are getting easier to do with each passing day. They're almost enjoyable. Pushing the wobbly cart toward the checkout line, my phone buzzes repeatedly in my pocket. Looking at the screen, I smile to myself.

"Hello?"

"So, I was thinking about your birthday," Nathan's deep voice rings.

"You were," I say absentmindedly as I load my groceries onto the conveyor belt.

"Why don't we have a barbecue at my place?"

Reluctance spills out of my mouth. "That's okay. I wasn't really going to do anything for my birthday this year."

"That's not an option. Would you rather have a low-key party at my house or let Chantal drag you around?"

"Damn, I was hoping she forgot about that."

"Not a chance. So, which one will it be? It's your call, but you *will* be celebrating your birthday, not sitting at home alone," Nathan responds with authority.

I take a moment to dread the impending spectacle of my birthday as I move closer to the cashier. I let out my breath, unaware I was holding it. "If I have to choose, I'd rather it be a backyard party versus whatever Chantal would make me do."

Throaty laughter fills my ear. "Good choice. I'll take care of it."

When I slide my phone into my back pocket, appreciation resonates in my bones. Nathan has been a surprisingly crucial part of my life this past year. Guilt rests on my neck as I think about our . . . I wouldn't call it a fight. Disagreement? Our *disagreement* after the family dinner. The conversation felt like an accusation, like he was suggesting I wasn't grieving properly. And why would Chantal be relaying what I do or don't do to Nathan? *Probably because they're just worried about you*, I think. In hindsight, I shouldn't have reacted so poorly. I've included him in so much of my life by needing his help with Joel, it made sense that he would check up on me after the fact.

I wake up the following Saturday wishing my birthday would pass. To my luck, the first half does in the blink of an eye. I slip into my yellow sundress, the hem hitting me mid-thigh. The color gives my skin a glow like I've spent my weekends outside instead of being a recluse. I opt to leave my hair down and curl a few pieces, giving it a messy, beach-waved look. Pulling out the plug of the curling iron, I hear my phone ping. Walking into my bedroom, I lift my phone to see two texts from my parents, both with the same sentiment: **Happy birthday D!**

That's it. Nothing more, and a stupid nickname I never liked, no less. They can't even pick up the phone and call. They're probably too busy with whatever plans they've arranged today. My birthday was never a big deal growing up. My parents always dragged me along to whatever party or function they had that day, and that was deemed celebratory enough. It's why I always made a big deal of my birthday after I moved out. This year doesn't have the same excitement—for obvious reasons.

I head into the kitchen in search of my purse. As I slow my pace toward the butcher-block counter, I eye the flowers on my kitchen table. The white and pink lilies that were delivered the day before brighten up the small space. Grabbing my keys, I take a quick turn and walk to the table to appreciate the pollen-speckled petals. Their scent is strong, filling the adjoining rooms. Joy simmers beneath my skin as my fingers briefly touch the card.

"Happy birthday, kiddo. Love, Pat," I whisper, smiling at the sweet gesture.

Getting to Nathan's house is a little harder than I thought it would be. My wedge sandals slip on the car pedals. As I pull up to the beige brick house, I can't tell how many people are already here. Cars line the street, but I'm sure some of them aren't for his gathering. Upon entering the house, I hear noise coming from the backyard, filtering in through the screen door to the deck. The acoustics in his house make it seem much louder than if I were outside. Striding toward the commotion, I slow, taking in the decorations surrounding me. Nathan's living space has transformed, with light-colored balloons and flowers everywhere. It's subtle and beautiful. It dawns on me that Nathan could not have done this himself. He's a very handy man, but he doesn't have this type of touch. It has to have been a woman. The answer becomes obvious: Chantal did this.

Looking down, a large coffee table with varying snacks is in the middle of the room. Bending down, I grab a pretzel and toss it into my mouth, then step over the threshold onto the deck. The deck is filled with our friends and some other people I don't recognize. I descend the wooden stairs, nodding and saying hello to the few people I pass. My goal is to find the host. I spot him by the cooler talking to someone; he lifts his gaze and sees me. I watch him close the lid and excuse himself without ever looking away from me. Nathan approaches me, wrapping his big arms around me.

"Happy birthday!" his throaty voice rasps.

"Thank you. Say, who are some of these people?" I ask, peeking around to point out groups I don't know.

"I made today a casual thing. Not everyone knows what today is. I figured it would make it a little easier on you than having everyone's attention."

A grateful sigh leaves my chest. "I appreciate that. Maybe next year I'll be up for my regular shenanigans."

"Help yourself to anything; you know where it all is. Chantal should be around here somewhere. I have to go get the meat ready to be put on the grill," Nathan backs away from me and turns, climbing up the steps to the deck and talking to his guests as he goes.

As the party goes on, I begin to relax and enjoy the small attention I'm getting from my friends. I remind myself I'm allowed to enjoy being recognized today. Standing in a circle with Chantal, Paul, and another one of Nathan's friends, the conversation flows naturally. It feels wonderful to be outside with the sun's rays warm on my face. Sipping the third fruity drink Chantal has handed me this evening, I lightly sway to the music coming from the speakers.

"Someone looks like they're enjoying themselves," Paul says, his eyes roaming up from my bare legs and hesitating on my chest.

Stifling an uncomfortable laugh, I remove my mouth from the straw. "I am. This drink is delicious. No wonder you're my bartender," I add, directing my attention to Chantal.

"Here, let me get you another one," she answers, seeing I'm almost done.

"Nu-uh, I'll be too drunk to get home," I say, already feeling my words start to run together.

"Don't worry about it. I can drive you home." Paul doesn't miss a beat, sounding eager to help me. He has a nice, warm smile, but it doesn't reach his eyes. It's such a minor detail, but it's one that I immediately notice.

The purple liquid floating in the clear, glass cup is all but shoved into my hands, or at least that's what it feels like. "Thanks," I reply, the manner ingrained in me even though I didn't really want the drink. I remind myself to drink this one slower.

As the conversation continues, Paul migrates closer to me, eventually putting his arm around my shoulders. The evening has started to cool, and I've thoroughly enjoyed another birthday. Chantal shares a story about a pesky customer at the restaurant, but I lose focus when Paul bends his head down and whispers, "You look beautiful tonight."

Turning my head in his direction, he mistakes my uncomfortable expression as approval and slides his hand down off my shoulders to around my waist, squeezing my hip. Knots begin to tie in my stomach. Excusing myself from the group, I head inside Nathan's house. Passing more people in the living room, I move down the dark, lone hallway. Shame shows its ugly face as soon as my back hits the wall. I shouldn't have drunk anything tonight. Now I'm relying on Paul to give me a ride home. I'm not interested in him. The idea itself is complete nonsense to me. Palming my eyes, it occurs to me he's been nothing but nice this entire evening. Maybe I'm making a big deal out of nothing.

"Is it becoming too much?" Nathan says, appearing from his room and closing this door behind him.

I feel my soul jump out of my skin. "I didn't know you were back there." Placing a hand on my chest to steady my erratic heart and trying to make him out in the little light leaking into the hallway, I can only see his general stature. "I just needed a little break."

Nathan peers down at the cup in my hand, then back up to my face. "I'm not trying to stick my nose where it doesn't belong, again, but let me know if you need a ride home."

"Paul offered to take me home, actually." The knots pull tighter.

Looking up at his face, I can't see any of his features. I can't see his warm, amber-brown eyes or his expressive mouth, but I think he might be angry. The energy around us has shifted. Maybe I'm imagining things.

"Great, he'll see to it that you're taken care of." His words come out clipped. Pushing off the wall he'd been leaning on, he trudges forward, trying to leave.

Lightly reaching forward, my fingertips grasp his forearm in protest. Nathan stops in front of me, giving me his full attention. I don't know what to say, guilt leaving a fog in my head over one of his good friends. Should I tell him how uneasy Paul makes me? "Can I be honest with you?"

He nods.

"Can you or Chantal drive me home, please?" I chicken out, unable to tell him the truth.

"S-sure." He doesn't ask why, or if anything happened.

When I don't say anything else, he walks away into the heart of the party. I allow myself a few more minutes of solitude in the hallway. This sliver of the house is getting darker by the minute as the sun descends. Feeling more settled and a little less buzzed, I stride over to the snack trays. Once I've eaten a handful of assorted snacks, I wander into the backyard as people are dwindling down. There's a chilled breeze in the air. Wanting to warm myself up, I begin to help Chantal and Nathan pick up the empty cups and anything else lying around.

"You ready to go, Dani?" Paul asks behind me, his voice elated.

Fearful of the sheer awkwardness, I try to come up with an excuse.

Before I can say anything, Nathan interjects, "I'm going to give her a ride home tonight."

Paul looks confused, then downright defiant. "Are you sure?" He's not asking Nathan, but me.

"Yeah, I've got to pick up a few of Joel's things, anyways. Right, Dani?" Nathan adds, helping me.

"Right! Thanks for the offer, though," I say, trying to soothe the situation.

Paul walks away, leaving us to continue cleaning.

"What was that about?" Chantal asks after the coast is clear.

"He made me feel uncomfortable today, and I asked Nathan to drive me home instead." I try to shrug it off.

"Yeah, I could see he was being a little forward with you today." Her agreement validates my initial concerns.

I catch Nathan looking at me, then quickly look away, tossing the cups in the trash can. I know he heard what Chantal said. I hope he doesn't ask about it.

After the cleanup is done and the deserved thank-yous are given, we wave goodbye to Chantal. It's later than I thought. The clock in Nathan's car shines almost eleven. It was a wonderful birthday. I spent most of the day outside, and between the sun and the alcohol, I feel my body begin to fade. The exhaustion settles in, making my eyelids feel heavy. Yet, I'm still completely aware of how loud the silence will be at home. As each mile passes, I feel desolation encroach my lungs.

As we pull into the driveway, I feel water prickle behind my eyes, burning them. It's no longer about Joel but how alone I am in this world. Wanting to hide the inevitable sadness welling up and out of me, I quickly exit the car.

"Do you mind if I come in and use your bathroom?"

"Sure," I respond without turning around.

Opening my front door, I leave it open for Nathan to follow behind me. My goal is to get to my bedroom before the first tear falls. As soon as I turn the doorknob and open the door, the water hits my cheeks. I slip off my shoes and slide under my covers. The dam has broken; grief floods my system. Every day seems like it's one step forward and two steps back. Knowing someone else is in my home, I suffer in silence, allowing no noise to emit from me. My bedroom door creaks like it's been pushed open. Heavy footsteps fill my ears, then sound like they retreat.

But I was wrong. "Dani . . . are you okay?"

My back is to him. He can't actually see me crying. *Can he feel my sadness? My loneliness?* Nathan stands there patiently waiting for me to answer.

"Nathan? Can you just lie with me and hold me?" Uncertainty is etched in my voice. I hold my breath for the answer. When he doesn't say anything, I feel worse. My eyes slam shut. How could I be so stupid as to ask my dead husband's brother to hold me? I feel so pathetic.

Suddenly, the bed dips. My eyes open wide. Turning my head to the side, I see his long body moving up behind mine to cradle me. He moves in so close, resting his chest on my back, making sure to line his legs up with mine. Our bodies fit perfectly, like two puzzle pieces fitting together. Nathan's compassion does the opposite of calming me down, causing the tears to fall harder instead. Slipping his other arm under my head, he wraps both limbs around my stomach and pulls me to him. His thumbs softly rub small, soothing circles on my arm and hip. I can only hear his sweet reassuring whispers: "It's okay . . . shh . . . I've got you." He comforts me like a parent would a child. The tears subside, and my body absorbs his warmth like I'm standing by a fire.

I lean my head back on his shoulder. His lean face is so close to mine. I look into his eyes. "Thank you. You're always helping me."

Something crosses his face—an emotion I can't decipher. "Of course."

I don't know how long we'll lie like this for, but I'll never complain. I relish the feeling of being in his arms feeling safe and warm. It's the first night in three months I sleep without interruption. When I wake up, it's just me and an indentation of where he was. I should feel weird about what happened with Nathan, but all I can think about is how much I've missed being held by a man I trust.

My mind wanders as I move throughout the week. Memories of Nathan's arms wrapped tightly around my frame pop up like pictures, frozen in time. It transports me back to that night. I can still feel his hard body pressed into mine, his breath on my neck, and his stoic expression not giving anything away. I hit a metaphorical brick wall. *What is wrong with me?* Pinching the bridge of my nose, I rack my brain for any logical excuses I can come up with. I'm lonely, that's a given. I drank more than I had in a while. Yeah! That's got to be it. The combination of the two is playing with my already damaged psyche.

Shopping with Chantal is the perfect diversion for my racing mind. Walking through the maze of clothing racks, I stop and begin to look through the pieces in front of me. I don't need anything in particular, but I wouldn't say no to some new clothes. I push each hanger back to see what is on it, and our conversation picks up.

"It was sweet of Nathan to take you home the other night," Chantal says to me, looking at the jeans she's holding up in front of her.

"He's always sweet." The scrape of the hanger squeals as it's pushed back, and an involuntary smile settles on my face.

"I like that you still have him as a friend," she says, throwing the jeans over her arm.

Should I tell her about the night of my birthday? I haven't even spoken to Nathan yet. *Maybe I should talk to him first to see where his head is at. Or maybe I'm making a bigger deal out of it than it needs to be.* I open my mouth to tell my best friend my secret.

"Do you know if he's dating anyone?" Her question echoes in my ears.

My expression reveals I'm clearly taken aback, and Chantal makes an embarrassed sound. "Sometimes it seems like he's interested, and other times . . ."

"I just didn't realize you were into him. I mean, it makes sense. Nate's sweet, generous . . . handsome." My voice lingers too long, making it noticeable.

"Wow, how did I not see this?" Chantal asks rhetorically.

"See what?"

"You have feelings for Nathan," she says pointedly.

"He's Joel's brother, Chantal. Don't be ridiculous," I retort.

"That's not a ridiculous notion. Nathan has been there for you through all the hard times. It would actually make sense."

"The grass hasn't even grown over Joel's grave yet. So even if I did have feelings, which I definitely don't, it's too soon."

"You know what I think?" she asks with accusation in her tone. "You're denying this a little harder than is necessary. Look, if you like him, you can tell me."

"I already told you it's not like that." My eyes roll to the ceiling.

"Okay, then you wouldn't mind if I ask him out?"

"Sounds like a great idea." My mood plummets.

My phone vibrates in my back pocket at the same time Chantal pulls hers out of her purse. Her face lights up at the screen. "Speak of the devil," she purrs, her voice amorous. "It's a group text inviting us to watch the baseball game tomorrow."

Her fingers fly against the glass surface of her phone, responding to my brother-in-law. I feel a twinge in my chest. I convince myself it's because I feel guilty about not telling her. I'm not even sure why I didn't. *Why can't I let it go?* My brain hangs onto the images of his embrace. I resolve, *I have to talk to him. It's the only way I'll be able to put this behind me.*

CHAPTER 10
DANI, PRESENT DAY

Opening the door to Nathan's house, I lean in and shout a greeting to give a warning that I'm here. Running my clammy hands down the front of my jeans, I continue my intrusion into his home. I've purposefully arrived early, hoping this extra time will allow us to clear the air. Stepping out from the hallway, Nathan comes into view. His hair is wet from taking a shower, I assume. The dark blue jersey he's wearing accentuates his broad shoulders and strong arms.

"Hey, what time is it?" he asks, tousling his wet strands with his fingers while he frantically looks for a clock.

"You're not running late. I showed up early." He graces me with a relieved expression. "I wanted to talk about the other night." My hands find each other, my fingers aimlessly twiddling.

"We can if you want to, but I don't need to." Turning his back to me, he opens his fridge and begins taking several dips and condiments out.

Watching the food land on the counter, I'm confused. "Are you sure?"

Closing the refrigerator door, he turns toward me, making sure I understand. "Look, I know what you're feeling. Joel died a little over three months ago. I know what it feels like to need someone during a time of loss. You asked for my help that night, and I gave it. I'll always help."

His intense sincerity catches me off guard. Breaking eye contact, I look out the window above the kitchen sink and sit down at his breakfast table, absently running my hands through my hair and trying to regain my thoughts. "Phew, that makes me feel better. I was feeling a little embarrassed."

I don't admit to him how often I've thought of that night or the fact it was the first night in a very long time I'd actually gotten a good night's sleep. I shake my head to rid the thoughts that come. Sinking my teeth into my bottom lip, I watch Nathan get ready for his guests. He's concentrating hard enough that he doesn't notice my attention on him. He must be working outside more. I see a light dusting of freckles scattered across his cheeks, and the muscles in his arms look more defined under his shirt. My eyes follow the hard lines of his face. Everything about him screams masculine. All male. If I hadn't been married to his brother, I would have wanted him immediately.

Hopping off my stool, I work around him to help get things set up for the game. In no time, we begin to dance around each other as we move about his house. Travis comes in carrying a case of beer, like I'm sure he's done a hundred times before.

"Hey, man," he says, putting the box in the fridge.

"Hey, we're just setting food out now," Nathan responds to his friend.

"*We're?*" Travis asks. He looks around, noticing I'm in the house as well. His eyebrows go up in surprise. "Oh, hi! I didn't see you," he politely says to me before turning back to Nathan. A look passes between them, one I wish I could be in on.

"Everything okay?" I ask the men in front of me.

"Yeah."

"All good." They both respond, breaking through whatever conversation they had been having through facial expressions.

Walking to the cabinet to get a glass, Travis's voice fills the room, "Did you ever tell Chantal whether you wanted to go on a date or not?"

Turning around to fill my cup, I notice Nathan peeking over at me. "Chantal asked you out?" I hope my tone sounds curious.

His gaze flickers to Travis for a harsh second before it comes back to me. "Yesterday," he answers plainly.

"She works fast." My tongue blazes without thought.

Travis pipes up, "What do you mean?"

Looking between the two, I'm annoyed that I just said that out loud. The two men are peering over at me, waiting for my answer. "Nothing." I feign mere innocence.

As I fill my glass up with sweet tea, the conversation resumes around me. I walk out into the living room, pull out my phone, and sit down on the couch to distract myself from the unsettled feeling that sits in my stomach. It almost feels like jealousy, but I know it can't be. Why would I be? Jealousy implies I want something from Nathan. And I don't!

More people start showing up at Nathan's place. The atmosphere shifts and is no longer awkward, but warm and friendly. The evening rolls on, my uncomfortable exchange forgotten about. When the game ends, I grab my purse and begin looking for the host to say goodbye. I spot him by the sliding glass door enthralled by my best friend. Chantal leans against the wall away from him, drawing him to her. They look too cozy to interrupt, so I sneak out the front door without a word, leaving them behind. Definitely not jealous.

Opening my eyes comes easier this morning. Something's changing. It's small, but I can feel it. My thumb rubs the worn band on my ring finger out of habit. Lifting my hand to look at the simple, silver ring, I'm drenched in indifference. Slipping off my once-beloved piece of jewelry, I take the invisible chains wrapped around me with it. I wonder what my life would be like had I not been tending bar that night at Tav's or if I hadn't gone out with him that first time. *What if I had kicked him out instead? Would I still be a widow at twenty-seven?* Questions on whether I've made the right decisions begin to plague me. It's perfect timing, since I'm headed into my appointment with Maggie.

Maggie welcomes me into her office. Settling into our respective ends of the chilly room, I pull my jacket a little tighter, thankful I remembered one today. I place my hands in my lap, and I see she's looking at me. I've had a lot on my mind the last few weeks: dealing with Joel's death, work at Tav's, and Nathan; now, I'm not sure where to begin. Instead of getting my toes wet and working my way forward, I blurt out what's truly been nagging me.

"I don't want to hold on to Joel anymore."

"Okay," Maggie states simply, encouraging me to continue.

"Things weren't good for a long time. Even in the end, with us working hard to get our marriage back, it wasn't the best. Whenever I think of him now, I just think about the pain he caused. I'm not mad anymore. I just want to let it all go."

"What's holding you back from letting him go?" she asks, watching me intently.

"I just . . . I'm afraid of people thinking I'm not handling it all appropriately. Or that I shouldn't be moving on from him so quickly." I sigh, shrugging my shoulders.

Maggie smiles at me with understanding and compassion before giving me the dose of honesty I need. "You're allowed to let go of Joel and the pain he caused you. You're not obligated to hold on to that forever, Dani. Have you ever thought of telling him goodbye?"

I feel my eyebrows pinch together. "How should I do that? Write him a letter and burn it? I've seen friends do that in high school." The sarcasm is subtle enough to have us both grinning.

"No," she says tactfully, jotting something down in her notebook before looking back up at me. "I think you should go to his grave. Tell him everything you ever wanted to—things you loved about him, things you didn't—and give yourself the goodbye you never got to have."

Could it be that easy?

That million-dollar question dances through my mind the rest of the forty-five minutes I've paid for. With each step I take away from her office toward my car, it feels like I'm moving in slow motion. It's surreal that I'll visit the cemetery today. It'll be the first time since we buried him. I make my decision quickly as I close the exterior building door behind me. I can't think about whether I'll go to Joel or not, because if I allow myself to question it, I won't do it. Sliding the key into the ignition, I start the car. The engine kicks to life, and my hands dampen for the remainder of the drive.

Finding the correct tombstone takes a little longer than I thought it would. The grass has grown back already—something I wasn't expecting. It surprises and slightly bothers me. The green beneath my feet reminds me life is moving on, with or without me present. I end up standing in front of the large, gray stone and am speechless for several minutes. Not sure what to say to someone who is not there, an annoyed huff of breath comes out, and I sit down, anchoring myself to the ground above him. My fingers playfully toy with the grass between us as I think about the passionate yet unstable years I had with my husband.

"I don't hate you." The words begin to flow naturally, wanting to explain myself and the feelings I never got to share. "I just wanted to say that out loud. Make sure you know." My voice breaks, betraying me.

"Do you remember our first vacation together? How we argued that whole first night about which route to take?" I smile at the memory of us in my car, bickering in traffic, wanting to get to the beach as fast as we could.

"I often try to remember our good days, like when we went camping. And it was colder than we thought, so we cuddled close the whole night. Those fun memories have little holes in them now as I think back. I remember we left late because you had to go to the shop and grab something. It took you two hours to come back home, and when you did . . ." My voice falters, no longer wanting to relive a memory for a ghost. "I often wonder if we were doomed from the start. If maybe this was always our destiny. I'm not angry anymore. I just think it's time for me to say goodbye. Through it all, I wish this wasn't your outcome." Standing up, I kiss my two fingers and press them to the granite for one final goodbye.

I hear leaves crunching behind me. Turning around, I spot Nathan. "I wasn't expecting anyone else to show up today," I state, surprised by his sudden appearance.

"This is our standing date every month. Am I interrupting? I can wait," he asks, stopping short.

"No, that's okay. I was just telling him goodbye," I respond, turning back to Joel's grave.

Nathan walks up beside me. "Sit with us. I think he would like it if we both were here together."

His offer is so innocent and sweet as he thinks of his brother's possible wishes. I sit down again, this time not alone. I don't know what Nathan usually shares or if he even speaks out loud when he comes to visit Joel.

"I miss him," Nathan says.

I peek over at him. He's stone-faced, simply stating a fact.

Feeling my gaze, he looks over, making eye contact. "I miss him, but I'm glad he's not hurting anyone anymore."

He's talking about me. "I'm sorry you lost your brother." The wind picks up and blows my hair across my face, breaking our contact.

"I'm sorry you lost your husband."

Picking the hair from my face and tucking it behind my ear, I think about what I had said moments before Nathan arrived.

"I loved Joel very much, and I'm happy I had what time I did with him. But I'm not sure he was ever supposed to be my husband."

He turns his attention away, taking in the truth of my words. I've kept this blunt realization hidden for months. Today is the first time I've ever let the confession spill out of me aloud. His face is still obscured from view, and I can't decipher what he thinks of my slip of the tongue.

"I'm sorry. Maybe I shouldn't have said that," I say, filling the silence with my retraction.

His attention turns back to me as he speaks, "I'm glad you can be honest with me. I don't want you to ever feel like you have to hide what you're thinking or feeling from me."

Staring at the hunk of rock in front of me, my eyes linger on the reflection of him. It's so quiet between us that we can hear the breeze rustling through the trees. Will he always be there to tell me exactly what I need to hear? Brushing my hands together, I move to prop myself up, putting them on the ground on either side of me, and my fingertips lightly graze the hand next to mine. My gaze flickers down. Neither one of us moves away. Nathan's forefinger gently lifts over mine to graze across my knuckles. My heart threatens to beat out of my chest at the small touch. I don't have to peek to know he's looking at me, but that doesn't stop me. Warm, brown eyes find me. They suck me in, and I can't look away. We're at an impasse, unsure of what to do, what to say, or what's even going on.

Abruptly breaking contact, I start to stand. "Well, I'll leave you and let you have your visit in peace."

"I'll see you later," his deep voice penetrates my ears. For some reason, I get the feeling his statement is more of a hopeful promise than a farewell.

Kicking off my shoes and dropping my belongings onto the entryway floor, I move through the house. The wood feels cold beneath my bare feet. Heading in the direction of my room, I stop at the thermostat and turn the heat on for the first time this year. Slinking further down the hallway, I hear the vents begin to hum. Getting ready for bed, I feel distracted. I reach over, grab my remote, and click on the TV mounted on my wall. The characters on-screen are in a deep discussion, but I don't make out what they're talking about.

Thoughts of Nathan from over the years fill my mind. He's always been a secure place to ask for help. I shouldn't have been surprised by his lack of judgement at my confession regarding my marriage. But I was. He didn't just hear my words—he seemed to understand them. Earlier, when his fingers brushed mine, it felt like a test. I couldn't look away from his face. His amber-brown eyes pierced into mine, and his full mouth parted. Heat rushes to my cheeks as I recall the feeling. I almost kissed him. I wanted to kiss him, and I didn't want to stop. My heart pounds loudly in my ears. Before I lose my nerve, I text Nathan: **I almost did something crazy at the cemetery today.**

His response comes after a minute or two: **Like what?**

Moment of truth. **Kiss you.**

I stare at my phone after I press send. Minutes seem to tick slower as nothing comes in. The silence from my phone sends me into a panic. It's been fifteen minutes of nothing. What have I done? How on earth can I take it back? It's in writing; it's permanent! Suddenly, I hear loud banging. Tiptoeing forward closer to the sound, I realize it's coming from the front door. I peer through the window to see who it is, then pull the door open wide. Nathan's here, standing tall even though he's leaning slightly forward. His hands grip the doorframe, as if to hold himself off from me. He's breathing hard; I can see it with the lift of his chest.

Nathan's eyes bore into mine as I stare at his handsome face. He looks like every girl's dream: strong arms and a bulky chest.

Without a word, he moves forward into my space, delicately reaching out to graze my arm with his hand. When he finds my wrist, he slides his hand into mine, pulling me directly to him; all the while, he's snaking his opposite arm around my waist. He dips his gorgeous face to mine, seeking out my lips. Wrapping my arms over his shoulders, I squeeze myself closer to him. His hand drops mine and wraps itself in my long hair, controlling the kiss that's coming to life. Our mouths are in perfect sync as they move frantically. Kissing him feels like I've been drowning in the darkest lake, and I'm finally coming up for air. His lips slide over mine. I feel it all the way down to my toes. He's everywhere.

Nathan reluctantly breaks the kiss. Resting our foreheads together, trying to catch our breath and steady our racing hearts, I feel years' worth of stolen glances, little comments, and many memories fill the small space between us.

With his eyes still closed, he looks pained by what he's about to say. "There's something you should know."

My body begins to fade. It feels like the great abyss has opened up and is swallowing me whole. I'm suspended in a freefall. I feel my heart lodged in my throat as my body crashes to the ground.

Shooting up out of bed, I see movie credits rolling. Checking my phone in a panic, I see what I was expecting. Nothing. No text was sent. I fell asleep. I allow my body to fall to the bed with an exasperated *thud*. I'm alone. It wasn't real. Nathan was never here. Emotions roil in my stomach, forcing me to lie awake in the dim light of the TV. I can still imagine the trail he left with his hands and the taste of his lips on my tongue. I don't know where my head or my heart is going with Nathan, and I'm not sure I can stop it.

CHAPTER 11
DANI, PRESENT DAY

A month has passed since my dream. It's felt longer, since I've had to listen to the details of Chantal and Nathan's relationship—if you can even call it that. From what I know, it's still pretty casual. They've only kissed, which makes me happy, although I could have done without a play-by-play. Listening to Chantal describe every second with Nathan has me wanting it to stop, yet I yearn for more information. I've been avoiding him because of it, ignoring messages and phone calls. I even skipped a family dinner with the ruse of work. It's becoming harder to be around him with the faulty images from my dreams and the desire they spark. I can't take it. Jealousy has popped up and shown her ugly, green face. She's like a relative who's overstayed her welcome. And that bitch won't leave.

Coming back from making bank deposits, I pull into the relatively empty parking lot at Tav's. We're not open yet, otherwise it would have been too full to notice Nathan's car parked in front. *He's probably just here to flirt with Chantal,* I think sourly. Before I've opened the door, I feel my heart flutter inside my chest. I'm surprised by the excitement I feel in anticipation of seeing him. It dawns on me that I've missed him more than I'd like to admit. Walking past the hostess station, my eyes catch a glimpse of them talking by the high-top tables. An ache fills my chest. It's worse than I thought. I forgot how handsome he is, his full lips pulled back in a smile I could gaze at forever. My memories don't hold a candle to the real thing. My body still doesn't know the difference between my dreams and my reality.

I feel the familiarity pulling me toward him. I want to walk over and throw myself into his arms. Seeing him now after being apart for this long makes it harder on me. I duck back into my office to avoid any more discomfort over the situation. Sinking in my chair, I empty the contents of the bank bags on my desk. Rolled coins and a deposit slip fall out. While double-checking the amounts listed with what I had written, there's a knock on my door. Nobody comes in. Strange. No one knocks at Tav's without entering at the same time.

"Yeah?" I ask, waiting for them to come in.

A broad, strong body emerges, taking up my entire doorway. The same body that's been haunting my thoughts. Nathan's movements are fluid as he walks into my office. Amber eyes scan the ordinary room we occupy until they inevitably land on me.

"Hey, haven't seen you in a while." His deep voice invades my ears.

"I know, things have been busy around here. What's up?" I try to bluff my way through the possible awkward encounter.

"I've missed seeing you around. Do you want to come over?" The question is so tempting spilling from his lips. "Trav and I were going to order wings and pizza," he adds, sweetening the deal. He knows how much I love wings.

I have to stay strong. "Thanks, but I'm probably just going to go to bed after I leave here tonight. I'm exhausted," I add sheepishly, faking a yawn.

"Did I do something wrong?" Nathan's voice is firm as he shoves his hands into his pockets.

I'm saddened by the fact that he feels this is an issue with him and not me. "What do you mean?"

Taking a step forward, he grips the back of the chair in front of him. "You didn't come to Mom and Dad's for dinner, and you and I haven't talked in weeks. Are you avoiding me?"

"That seems like a stretch. Besides, I'm surprised you even noticed with Chantal keeping you busy," I huff too quickly, my real feelings starting to poke through my façade.

There's a brief pause. It's quick, so quick I wonder if he misses it, but it was there. Lines are pulled up on Nathan's forehead. "That's why you've been avoiding me? Because you're jealous?"

Mayday, mayday! "I am not! Why would I be jealous?" I roll my eyes at the beautiful man in front of me, trying to show him how preposterous the idea sounds.

"You tell me." His response is calm.

I try to regain control of the conversation. "I think the topic got away from us. I'm not avoiding you."

Standing straighter, Nathan looks more at ease. "Well then, come over and hang out with us."

In an effort to prove him wrong, that I'm not jealous or avoiding him, I agree. "Okay, I'll come over after work."

The smile he rewards me with makes it all worth it. "Thank you. Was that so hard?" He chuckles, gives me a quick wink, and exits the way he came.

Knowing that I'm going to Nathan's after my shift has me constantly checking the time. *Get a grip, Dani.* When I run into Chantal, she mentions tonight is Nathan's guys' night, so she's free if I want to do anything. I decline, purposely not mentioning that I was invited to said *guys'* night. I enjoy the idea that I'll have his full attention without Chantal there, and that alone leaves me with a layer of guilt hanging over me.

Before I get out of my car, I check my sun visor mirror and wipe away any smeared makeup from under my eyes. *Why am I doing this? Why am I here? Is this a good idea?* The questions begin to steamroll through the rest of my thoughts. I'll have to get used to being around him again. *This is why I'm here*, I answer the unspoken question. Blowing out a nervous breath, I walk up to the solid mahogany door, twist the knob, and enter without a warning, like I always have. I hear male voices coming from the living room. It sounds like they're talking at whatever's on the television.

"Hey, Dani," Travis says, seeing me first as I approach the coffee table.

Looking between the two men, I sit down on the floor in front of the short table, making myself comfortable. "Thanks for letting me crash your evening. I heard it was supposed to be guys' night."

"Don't worry about it. You're practically one of the guys, anyways," Nathan says, elbowing my shoulder.

The wind deflates from my sails, and the playful jab leaves me feeling disappointed. There have been instances lately and in the past where I thought he felt differently about me. Clearly, I'm delusional. I'm practically family. I inwardly cringe so hard I'm surprised they can't see it. I need to shake this little crush or whatever it is.

"Alright, well, I'm starving," I respond, pulling the take-out box of wings in front of me.

Digging in, Buffalo sauce coats my fingers as I work carefully not to get it in my hair, on my shirt, or make any other mess than what's on my hands. Conversation flows effortlessly between the three of us over the sound of the TV in the background. I'm having such a good time with Travis and Nathan, listening to them share old stories about each other in college, that I'm not even sure what game we're watching. Eventually,

Travis steers the conversation in a different direction, shocking both Nathan and me.

"Have you thought about dating any?" Travis asks.

Looking around, confused as to whom he's asking, I see him looking at me curiously. "Why? Do *you* want to date me?" I retort, making light of the question between us.

Humor fills his voice between bites of pizza. "You know it. You just call me when you're ready." He exaggerates blowing me a kiss.

Letting our laughs subside, I decide to give a real answer. Clearing my throat, feeling more serious than before, I announce, "I guess I've been thinking about it. I don't want to just date anyone random." Shrugging, I backpedal. "We'll see how it goes; I don't know," I add, shaking my head and feeling foolish. Sneaking a glance across the table in the other direction, I see Nathan is staring at me. He doesn't look happy. *Hmm, I wonder if he doesn't like the idea of me dating, or if maybe he just wasn't expecting my answer.*

My hand flies out to my nightstand, haphazardly feeling around trying to turn off whatever is causing the earsplitting madness. I don't remember setting an alarm. What time is it? My eyelids are heavy, and I feel like I just went to bed. I stayed much longer at Nathan's than I was expecting. But being near him again reminded me of how much fun he is. I smile to myself. The loud ringing stops for mere seconds before starting again. Groaning, my hand finds the loud culprit. Grabbing my phone, I see it's not an alarm, but my mother calling. For the second time in a row. It's 9:48 a.m.—later than I thought, but not late enough for me to feel guilty about. You would think since I didn't manage to answer the first call, she would leave a message. What could she want? My thumb hovers over the talk button. Do I really want to answer this, this early, when

I haven't even had my coffee? Before I can decide it's a bad decision, I answer the looming call.

"Hello?"

Her frantic voice fills my ears, "Finally! You're not still in bed, are you?" I'm about to respond when she keeps going. "Heavens, Danielle, is this what you do every day? Just sleep in till whenever? You should have more structure than that."

I was right; it's too early for this. I need my coffee if this conversation is going to continue. Making my way into the kitchen, I tilt my head to my shoulder, holding my phone with my face while my hands mechanically set up my morning fuel.

"I was sleeping in a little. It's not the end of the world," I respond with little fight.

The crackling sound of the coffee pot filters throughout the kitchen at the same time the warm smell of the Arabica beans washes over me. Her voice goes on and on about nothing important. I try to interrupt, "Mom? Why'd you call?" Realizing my question could be interpreted as rude, I follow up, "I mean, I doubt you wanted to talk to me about my sleeping habits."

"Oh, it's . . . umm . . ." Her voice suddenly gets serious.

"Is everything okay?" My mind goes to the worst case scenario, "Is it Dad? Are you guys okay?"

"Well, we were just wanting to know if you were coming up for Thanksgiving?" she asks blandly.

"That's it? Your tone made it seem like it was serious," I say, relieved.

"It is serious! We need to know how much food to tell the caterers."

I roll my eyes. "Yes, I'll be up for the holiday." It's just like Cindy Davis to make a big deal out of a meal she isn't even making.

"Wow, I'm surprised," she says somewhat coldly.

Pouring the black, energizing liquid into my cup, I take her bait. "What is?"

"I just figured you would want to be with Joel's family, since you favor them more than us," she answers passive-aggressively.

I set the coffee carafe back in its place. I didn't think it was possible to roll my eyes this much before ten o'clock in the morning.

"Mom," I say in warning.

"Well, it's true," she retorts with indignation.

I try to contain myself so I don't snap at my mother, but I can't contain my irritation. "If you thought I wasn't going to come, what was the purpose of calling me? You could have easily sent a text."

A dramatic gasp sounds over the phone. "So now I can't want to talk to my only daughter?" she asks with fake hurt.

I've learned my lesson for today. "Okay. I can see this isn't going anywhere," I say, refusing to respond to her rhetorical question.

"Stop being so dramatic, Danielle. I was only saying."

"Me, dramatic?" The irony of her statement is not lost on me. "Okay, Mom, I've got to go. I'll call you later," I counter as lightly as I can muster.

"See you, dear," her voice rings.

Running my hands down my face, I consider my options for the holidays. I sip my hot coffee, savoring the strong flavor. I can't not go, but I'm already feeling like this is going to be a disaster. Thinking more on the conversation with my mom, I wonder if I *should* have talked to Nathan and Pat about it. I definitely can't talk to Maureen. Shaking my head, I gather my dark hair into my hands and push it all together to tie it in a bun. I can tell it's a wreck, but that's okay since I'll be my only company today.

Halloween at Tav's is always interesting, and this year won't be any different. The staff and patrons dress up—it's one giant party. Walking around my restaurant to check in with the customers, I'm thankful the music is louder than usual, otherwise I'd be able to hear my clunky combat boots hitting the floor. Circling the room, I stop when I get to Chantal, who's filling drinks in a cheerleader costume—a rather short cheerleading costume. Chuckling to myself, I decide not to comment on it. I ask her how her night is going. She's got to be busy, since the restaurant is packed.

"This costume sure is helping my tips," she says with a waggle of her eyebrows. "I'm slammed right now, though. Do you mind taking these drinks over to Nathan's group?" She asks, nodding her head in the direction of his high-top table. Following the line of her eyes, I spot him staring.

His eyes rake over Chantal, and I feel myself deflate. I grab the tray of drinks, take a deep breath, and begin my trek into the lion's den, puffing up my chest. *I will not let their relationship get to me*, I think on repeat. Weaving my way through the aisle, I notice I was wrong. Nathan's eyes are on me, not Chantal. And they've started moving over me again, up my bare legs, over my stomach, and lingering on my chest, before ultimately landing on my face. No part about my costume is skimpy; every part of me that should be covered, is. Yet the fire in his gaze makes me feel like I might as well be naked. Setting the tray down on the edge of the table, I attempt to be unaffected and greet the men in front of me. My eyes betray me, focusing on only him.

"Hey," his deep voice floats around me.

"Could it be? Lara Croft?" I loved that video game as a kid," Travis tells me.

"I'm just glad someone recognizes who I'm dressed as," I respond, looking down at the simple, gray, high-neck tank top, black shorts, and fake gun holster on my thigh.

"Even if they didn't, they'd just assume you were dressed as a hot chick," Paul announces with a flirty tone.

"True," Travis says, nodding in agreement while Nathan scowls down at his drink.

"Well thanks, guys. Let me see who we've got. Paul in no costume. Joker"—I point to Travis—"and Clark Kent," I say to Nathan as I take in the fake glasses and white button-down left open to reveal a Superman emblem. His white shirtsleeves are pushed up to reveal his strong forearms.

Pulling my French braid to the front of my shoulder, I watch them take the first sips of their drinks. "Alright well, if you guys don't need anything else," I say, getting ready to excuse myself.

Before I can make a full turn, Nathan's hand shoots out, grabbing my wrist. "Stay. Hang out with us for a little while."

There's no tone in his voice to give him away, but I feel his thumb drag lightly back and forth on the underside of my wrist. He's doing it again. This is deliberate.

I answer while trying to hide my blush, "Okay, I can sit for a little while."

Pulling up a seat, I put myself between Nathan and Paul. The playlist over the speaker flows from song to song. There are certain times in our conversation where I feel like they're both vying for my attention. Eventually, I scoot closer to the table, resting my elbows on the top as I laugh at a crude joke Travis makes. As our laughter begins to subside, I feel Nathan's knee touch mine, lingering, not moving. Peering over at him, I see he's smiling to himself, then at me. I think he's flirting. Warmth fills my body, surprising me with rising goosebumps. I've never been so giddy over such a minor contact. As I'm reeling over Nathan's innocent touch, Chantal comes over. Leaning down, she lightly presses her lips to the side of Nathan's face. I immediately pull my knee away from his, cutting off all contact. I'm surprised no one at the table can hear the crack of disappointment move through my chest. My heart sinks to my stomach.

"Hey guys! Sorry, I've been busy, or else I would have been over sooner. What'd I miss?" Chantal asks with enthusiasm, her ponytail swaying back and forth.

"Not much. Here, you take my seat. I was just about to get up, anyway," I say to my friend as I get up with a fake smile placed on my face. Praying she can't see the guilt I feel inside over flirting with her boyfriend, I hold out my warm chair for her. Watching her slide in, her eyes locked on Nathan, my heart crumples like a piece of paper.

"Alright, see you guys later," I respond with mock fervor as I back away.

Paul breaks through my trance. "Dani, save me a dance?"

"Sure, just come find me," I answer robotically. My eyes look between the men and land on Nathan, who is watching me leave.

Walking straight to the bathroom, I push the door closed behind me. Ducking down, I check to make sure the stalls are empty. Once I know I'm by myself, a breath heaves out of my lungs as I place my hands on the sink and grip it hard. *What the hell am I doing? Why am I playing a secret flirting game with Nathan?* Shaking my head, I regroup my thoughts. It's nothing. We're not doing anything wrong. And even if we were, which we're *not*, we couldn't do anything about it, anyways. Splashing cool water on my neck, I reprimand myself over my wanting and make a promise to make it stop. Quickly leaving the bathroom, I head back to my office. My head is so busy trying to organize my swarming thoughts that I'm unable to pay attention to my surroundings, and I walk right into someone.

Embarrassment shades my cheeks. "Oh, sor—" my voice cuts off. Looking up, I see I ran into Nathan. Glancing around, I realize he's in the back of the restaurant near my office—not where he should be.

Speaking softly, I remind him, "You're not supposed to be back here."

"I was looking for you," he says, as if it's obvious.

"Whatever you need, I'm sure Chantal can help you." We're still only inches from each other. Neither one of us has moved since we collided.

Reaching his hand out, he delicately intertwines our fingers. His other hand reaches up to the side of my neck. It's firm as he tugs me forward slightly. My tongue runs across my bottom lip before I bite it between my teeth, restraining myself from saying anything stupid. Having this much contact with him is making me lightheaded, but I can't get enough. Lifting my free hand, I run the tips of my fingers on the outsides of his. I want to feel those hands everywhere. Staring into his fiery eyes, I stand on my tiptoes and lightly kiss him. It's so soft, and surprisingly unreciprocated. I pull away, more embarrassed than I was when I ran into him. I don't get very far.

Nathan leans in the rest of the way, pushing his mouth onto mine. His tongue parts my lips, flicking its way in. My body explodes. Instinctively, my hands go to his hair, tugging backward. The hectic movement of our lips combined with the taste of beer is heady. As I lap my tongue into his mouth, he lets out a groan that sends thrills down to my stomach. *He likes this. He wants this just as much as I do!* Pride rises up and spurs me on, and I deepen our already frantic kiss. His big hands move to my waist while his fingers grip my sides tighter, like he's afraid I'll slip away. I haven't been kissed like this in so long.

I'm instantly jealous of every girl who's ever been with him in this way or has experienced more than what I'm taking right this second. That thought and the way he nibbles on my lips down to my jaw make me wonder what it would feel like if we allowed ourselves to lose control. But that can't happen. Because anyone could walk down this hallway.

Reality crashes down on me. Anyone could see us. Breaking the earth-shattering kiss, I step back, wiping my mouth of any evidence. Panicking, I look around to make sure no one has seen us. The hallway is empty. We're still alone. *Thank goodness!* Nathan rests his forehead on mine in a sweet gesture, making my heart want him even more. I can practically hear his heartbeat.

"You have no idea how long I've wanted to do that," his voice rings breathlessly.

Listening to our breaths return to normal, I state the painfully obvious, "We shouldn't have done that."

Nathan steps back, searching my face. "Why not?"

"Well, you're dating my best friend, for one."

"Chantal and I aren't exclusive."

"Do you think that would matter if she found out? It wouldn't. It wasn't fair of me to kiss you behind her back," I say, taking the blame.

"What's the next point?" he asks, eyes no longer on me.

"Huh?"

"You said 'for one;' was there a second point?"

Apprehension sits on my tongue. I don't want to point out the next reason we shouldn't be together. "Second point being . . . you're Joel's brother."

Nathan blows air out of his mouth, making a sound like he doesn't believe me. "You're making excuses right now. That kiss was not a *brotherly* kiss." His annoyance is evident as he says the word.

"It doesn't matter. This was a mistake. I'm sorry I kissed you. I won't let it happen again." When he doesn't add anything, I insert my foot further into my mouth. "I hope we can eventually get past this, so our . . . friendship can return to normal," I add, trying to compose myself.

"I don't know exactly when you stopped viewing me as your brother-in-law, but I know that was a while ago. I'm not your husband's brother anymore. He's dead, Dani. It's time to move on." His voice rises in frustration.

A pang of hurt stings my chest as he mentions his brother's death so casually. "I may have been confused for a little while, but I know my mind is just blurring the lines of my loneliness and our friendship. That's all," I say, trying to convince the two of us. "It was a good kiss, but let's not make this worse than it already is. I'm sorry if you thought it meant more to me than what it did," I reply carefully, watching his response like I'm in the hallway with a crazed bear ready to attack.

"Me too." Nathan's curt reply hangs in the air as he stalks off.

What a mess I've made. Raking my hands over my temples, I attempt to regain my dignity. Letting my arms drop to my sides, I think positive. *It'll be okay. Nathan will eventually get over it, and Chantal will never know because it was a stupid mistake. Tonight was a fluke; no reason to bring it up to anyone,* I lie to myself to cover the overwhelming guilt rising in my throat. I'm just going to lock myself in my office and throw away the key.

Sitting down in the beat-up chair, I can't think straight. Between the image of Nathan's hands on the nape of my neck, the overwhelming scent of him on my clothes, and the hurt he wore on his face when he left, I don't know where to go from here, physically or mentally. Physically, I refuse to leave this office. He could still be in the restaurant, and I couldn't bear to walk around forcing myself to avoid his eye contact. Although, after what I just did, he probably wouldn't even look at me. That might be worse than if he did. Mentally, I'm mortified. I just went behind my best friend's back and hurt Nathan in the process. Laying my head back in the chair, I make futile wishes. I wish I was leaving for my parents' sooner. I wish Chantal wasn't interested in Nathan. But most of all, I wish his cologne would linger on me longer.

CHAPTER 12
DANI, PRESENT DAY

DANI, PRESENT DAY

"Are you listening to me?" Chantal asks as she bites down on a fry.

"Sorry, I must have zoned out. What did you say?" We're sitting at a window booth in our restaurant eating lunch before we open.

"I was saying, because my parents will be coming back from their vacation on that Thursday, no one wants to cook. So, I was wondering if I could come with you for Thanksgiving?" She stares at me over her drink, clearly eager for an answer.

Warning bells ring in my head. "Oh, Chantal. I don't know if that's a good idea. You've met my parents," I remind her.

"Yeah, but they can't still be that bad. When was the last time you went home?"

"Joel and I went last year. It was supposed to be for a weekend. We stayed one night. I couldn't make it the whole weekend, and I'm their daughter." Hoping she heeds my warning.

"I want stuffing, mashed potatoes, and turkey. Ple-ease," she whines.

"Fine, but just remember you asked for this." Pulling my phone out from my pocket, I type a message to my mother letting her know Chantal will be coming with me. I doubt she'll care. She'll feign inconvenience, but Cindy Davis loves showing off her home with all its fancy trinkets and appliances. She wouldn't miss this opportunity. I'm glad I'll have a friend, a lifeline in their lifeless mansion. It will be the first time in years. Technically, Joel had gone with me, but he wasn't much of a distraction. Now as I look back, it feels more tainted with his drug use.

Joel had woken up that Thanksgiving morning rattling off an excuse to leave me at my parents'. He'd kissed me senselessly in my dreamy state before leaving me naked in our warm bed. "I won't be gone long. I wouldn't leave you alone with the monsters lurking to fend for yourself" he'd promised, raising his eyebrows with humor.

After the first two hours, I'd started to worry. Texts and phone calls were going unanswered. Joel didn't come back until two o'clock in the afternoon, when he waltzed into my parents' home with such energy it didn't seem right. I'd been drowning in the loaded questions from my mother about his whereabouts, worried he was hurt, trying my best to keep myself afloat; then, he'd had the audacity to come in the front door as if nothing was wrong. Joel had many different reasons for showing up late—none of which made sense—but I had been wound too tightly to focus on whether I believed him or not.

My mom had proceeded to belittle my husband for several hours, question my sanity and my ability to make decisions, and pester me about when I would make her a grandmother. Like I would really bring a defenseless child into the devil's den. Joel made incoherent conversation with my father during our early dinner, ending their chat early to run upstairs. I'd found him in our bathroom, hunched over, sweat beaded on his forehead while he expelled the meal he just ate, exhaustion cloaking me. Feeling the remnants of the long day, I'd sat down beside him and rubbed his back in hopes of providing comfort. Voices from the kitchen filtered their way up the stairs. I heard my mother and father talking, questioning why I was with Joel.

Their hurtful comments continued for some time as my sick husband started to come to. The last straw for the evening had been hearing my parents question why they didn't try harder to force me to stay so they could ultimately make my decisions. Once Joel was feeling better, he'd agreed to leave and head back home. I'd offered to drive so he could take it easy, and I began the six-hour drive looking forward to talking to him about what happened during those missing hours. The promise of company fell flat, again, and he'd fallen asleep twenty minutes into our car ride.

The memory makes me sad. Shame clouds my brain, making me wonder the age-old question: how did I let it go on for so long?

The background noise of the bar fades out while I get more lost in my thoughts. I've been doing that a lot lately. Chantal thinks I'm mad at her or something. But that's not the case; I just don't know how to act around her these last few weeks since I kissed Nathan. He calls frequently and texts almost as much. We've only spoken a few times, each time going over the same thing: that we have nothing to talk about. I don't want to keep hurting his feelings, but he's not leaving me any other choice. I'm not going to hurt my best friend over something that won't happen again.

When I step into my childhood bedroom, it's like I never left. The pale, champagne-colored walls are perfectly decorated, just the way my mom liked. There are no knickknacks or identifying picture frames around the anonymous-looking room. It's picturesque, like a magazine, not so much a child's bedroom. Opening my closet doors, I see my boy band posters still stuck to the inside. *She clearly didn't look in here*, I think with a smile. Otherwise, they'd be gone, considered contraband. Tossing my bag on the floor, I bend over to plug my phone into the charger before I show Chantal to her room.

"You're not going to unpack?" Her organization and tidiness amuse me.

"No, unpacking feels long-term, like we're staying. The sooner we can leave, the better. Let me show you where you're sleeping." I walk down the hall two steps in front of her. "It's this door on the right."

I open the door to the guest room. It's a surgical white with gray and marble decorations and furnishings. Over the large, king bed is a gray canopy draped over the four posts.

Chantal looks in awe. "Wow. This will do." A joyous smile breaks out over her face as she runs and jumps, landing on her back on the big bed. This is something I love about her. She's genuine in everything she does. A phone pings, I'm not sure whose, but Chantal pulls her phone out of her pocket to check.

"Oh, it's Nathan," she says, watching the phone intently. "Look how cute," she says, flipping the phone around for me to see. It's him in a turkey hat. Given the background, I can tell he's at his parent's. *Probably would have been easier to stay there*, I punish myself by thinking.

Wanting to get away from seeing her fawn over the messages that come through, I excuse myself. "I'm going to go search for my parents. Pennsylvania was a long drive; feel free to rest up here if you'd like."

"Okay," she says, her eyes never leaving her phone screen.

Exiting the room, I begin to worry. *Am I going to have to listen to her text him and hear what all he's saying the entire time we're here?* I ask myself with regret. Each step down the stairs leads me into the belly of the beast and puts me more on edge. Rounding the corner, I see my dad's office doors cracked. I pop my head in and see he's staring at the desktop screen in front of him. Noticing movement, he looks up at me.

My father waves me off with a flick of his hand, letting me know he's too busy to be disturbed. Normal parents would be excited to see their daughter and would possibly even greet her when she arrived, but my parents aren't normal.

It's been a year since I've seen them, but this is what I expected. The tile under my bare feet is cold like their presence. Striding toward the French doors, I peek out the windows and look out onto the deck. I don't see my mother. Suddenly, she bursts through the garage door, shopping bags in her hands.

Her ageless face creases with a smile. "Oh, you're here!" she says excitedly, reaching out to pat my back.

"We got here a few minutes ago. I wanted to come down and try to find you guys."

Abruptly, her arm gets stiff as she pushes me away and holds me at arm's length. "Have you gained weight? You should really try to wear clothes more suited to your body type." Her words fall effortlessly out of her mouth. "Why don't you go change, dear," she adds, dismissing me.

Ah yes, we will be leaving as soon as we can. Scanning my eyes down my torso, I look at my jeans and striped sweater. Nothing about this looks too tight. My hands form fists at my sides as I try to let go of her unnecessary insult. I will not let her bully me like this, not anymore. I'm an adult.

"No thank you," I defy her, through gritted teeth. "I am comfortable in what I'm wearing." I make sure to punctuate my sentence so it can't be interpreted as uncertainty.

"Where's your friend?" my mother asks, her eyes searching the ceiling like she will be able to see what room she's in.

"Upstairs in the guest room. I told her to rest. Then I came to find you guys. Dad's in his office."

"Well, I'm glad you're here, but you don't have to follow us around the house," she responds, turning her back on me while she floats around the kitchen she's never cooked in.

Staring at her, I don't blink. My voice takes on an edge that's less bewildered than how I actually feel. "We only see each other once a year. Do you think we could keep the comments to a minimum?"

"So touchy." Her response is under her breath, and I know she's hoping I haven't heard.

I stand up straighter. "I don't think I'm asking for too much." She pretends she doesn't hear me.

Closing my eyes in frustration, I resolve not to say anything else. Turning away, I leave to go to my room. Looking in on Chantal, I see she's exactly where I left her, playing on her phone. It's weird that it bothers me how much she's been texting Nathan. A few weeks ago, I was praying he'd stop texting me. And now he has. Maybe he's forgotten about our little kiss, or he's realized what a bad idea it was and is no longer interested.

I keep on in the direction I was headed, closing my bedroom door behind me. Walking into the adjoining bathroom, I twist the shower knob, turning it as hot as it'll go, watching the steam fill the room. Beads of moisture cling to the tiled walls. Stripping out of my sweater and jeans, I leave them on the floor, attempting to leave everything outside of these four walls. Coaxing my body into the hot spray, I let the water fall around me. Needles prick my body where the hot water stings my skin. It doesn't surprise me that it's helping ease my irritation with those I'm trapped in this house with.

Forgetting my father's dismissal, my mother's rude comments, and Chantal and Nathan, I clear my mind. I choose to focus on the silky soap that covers my hands. I guide them over my arms and down my belly. Losing myself in the sensations, I begin to daydream of the one thing I know I shouldn't want. Oh, how I wish it were him here with me and not Chantal. I could have coaxed him into the shower, pulling him in behind me. My hands are suddenly his.

"Mmm." A low moan escapes my throat while he squeezes the tops of my thighs. His long fingertips graze between my legs. Unable to withstand the pleasure, my head rests back on his shoulder. The steam feels like hot breath on my neck.

His deep voice fills my mind. "You like me touching you like this, don't you?" His unoccupied hand trails up my throat, holding me in place with enough pressure. "You're so sexy," he whispers into my ear.

I can practically hear his breath hitch as he watches me come undone for him. His tongue swipes out of his perfect mouth to lick up my neck to my jaw. His fingers are still rubbing mercilessly; I'm already aching. Despite knowing this is my imagination at work, it still feels real to me in this moment. Nathan might as well be here. My whole body feels like it's going to explode. Then, it does.

After the haze of my orgasm clears, I push myself up off the wall I'd been leaning on and finish cleaning myself up. I really need to get a grip on these fantasies. Hopefully, no one has noticed I'm not out yet. Rinsing the remnants of soap and my secret off, I'm disappointed to realize my climax has left me feeling sullen.

Against my mother's wishes, Chantal and I set the table.

"That's something the staff can do."

Ignoring her, we set the grand dining table for my parents, their guests, and us. It doesn't take very long to see I'll be doing the majority of the settings. Chantal is on her phone and has barely helped; but by the thoughtful look she has on her face, something might have happened. She looks serious.

"Everything okay?" I ask.

The only response I get is her fingers ferociously tapping away at her phone. Alright, I'll give her some time. I don't know what could have happened. Maybe she just didn't hear me. Making my way around the table, folding and laying the napkins appropriately, I keep checking on my friend to make sure she's okay. She no longer looks upset, but more entertained. I begin to speak, telling a random story about how I fell off a horse when I was a kid. Chantal doesn't respond or even realize anyone else is in the room with her. When I've placed the last glass in front of its plate, she is putting her phone away, looking at me.

"I'm sorry, were you saying something?" she asks without care.

"Nothing."

"I was thinking, would you want to go on a double date with me, Nathan, and Paul?"

Anger starts rising on my tongue, leaving me dumbfounded. I want to swallow it down. I do not want to argue with her. "No. Thank you."

"What? Why not?" She sounds alarmed, like it would be an obvious yes.

"Well, for starters, you've been on your phone the whole trip up here texting Nathan and pretty much ignoring me while I set the whole table. Why would I want to be subjected to that on a date? Also, Paul gives me the creeper vibes—I told you that!" My anger spills out, getting the best of me.

"Woah, what's with the attitude? You don't usually care when I'm on the phone," she asks, tucking her hair behind her ear.

"Now it's constantly in my face. *Look what Nathan sent. What should I wear on my date with Nathan when I get back?*" I answer, mimicking her.

I can tell she's confused by my outburst. "Fine, I'll stop."

"Fine," I respond with finality.

The drive back to Virginia is long and awkward. Chantal and I don't speak about our dating lives. Or, more accurately, we don't speak about Nathan. It's almost like we both avoided that topic on purpose.

124

After I've been home for the last twenty-four hours, I'm feeling grateful to be back. Curling up on my couch, I start making a grocery list on my phone when my door opens. I didn't invite anyone over. Jumping up, I hear all-too familiar footsteps enter my home.

"We're just coming in uninvited now?" I ask, irritated. He's gorgeous as he stands there in his dark jeans and plain T-shirt. It dismantles me.

"You left me no choice. You don't answer phone calls or texts anymore."

"So, you think you can just barge into my home? Without even a knock?"

Nathan looks down, searching the ground for answers to my questions or the confidence to ask his own. I'm not sure which. "What are you doing?" His voice sounds stronger. "Why are you so hell-bent on pushing me away?"

I push my hands through my hair, combing it out of my face. "Please! I am not; everything's fine."

"Is that why you were rude to Chantal over Thanksgiving? *Because everything's fine*?"

I scoff. "I was not rude. Sorry, I just don't like overhearing every detail about your relationship. It's annoying."

A hint of a smile breaks across his full lips. "You're jealous."

It's the second time he's accused me of that, and I hate it as much as the first. But I don't say anything. I'm not even sure what to say. Why is he here?

Nathan steps closer but still leaves a few feet of distance between us. "You don't like the thought of me kissing her like I kissed you." He's goading me, and it's working. Just his even talking about it hurts in ways I'll never let him know.

"I couldn't care less," I lie through my teeth.

"I haven't had sex with her," he says softly, staring into my eyes. Nathan's hoping this will change something for me. Unfortunately, it can't.

"You should probably go. I know you have a date tonight." Crossing my arms, I attempt to hide the hurt in my voice with ice.

"Fine, have it your way, Dani! Keep pushing me away after all the help I gave you." His deep voice emanates anger at my dismissal.

Irritation forces my eyes closed as I gather my hair together and twist it behind my back before I drop it. "I don't need your help. I could have done it all on my own." I'm lying. Nathan turns his back to me, and I can read in each one of his tense muscles that he knows I'm lying. But my words have hurt him, and that was their sole purpose.

Nathan's tall stature turns around and comes toward me, stopping short before he bumps into me. "Then stop calling on me!"

I could hear a pin drop, it's so eerily quiet. The house has dropped a few degrees since our argument began. I pull my sweater tighter over my chest like it's impenetrable armor. Nathan's pained expression is laced with anger as he turns on his heel again and slams my front door, leaving.

The rise and fall of my chest is so extreme I begin to pace down my hallway to get rid of this energy. It'll be okay. We can take some space from one another, but we can recover from this. Maybe we'll be the type of friends who only see each other once every few months. *I can do that; I can get used to seeing him that infrequently. Right?* Now I'm no longer lying to him. I'm lying to myself.

Coming to the end of the hallway, I pick up a lone book from the table and throw it at the wall in frustration. As the book makes a *thud,* my front door opens much slower than it was shut. He's coming to finish the argument, I guess. Without a word, he climbs the half staircase, meeting me where the foyer joins the hallway. His expression is different this time. I can't place what he's feeling. It makes me uneasy.

Nathan steps toward me. With each step he takes, I take a small one back until my back touches the wall. I'm not sure what's happening or what mood he's suddenly in.

"Tell me to stop seeing Chantal," he answers my unspoken question.

"What?"

"Tell. Me. To. Stop. Seeing. Chantal." His deep voice is a whisper over my face.

His presence is everywhere. I can feel the heat from his body, we're so close. His lips part as his tongue flicks out to wet his lips, and his amber eyes take in my face. We know this can't end well. He's Joel's brother. He was the best man at our wedding. I want to tell him we can't do this, but this feels like a long time coming.

"Stop seeing her," I reply softly. If he were anywhere but right in front of me, he wouldn't have heard.

NATHAN, PRESENT DAY

NATHAN, PRESENT DAY

"Stop seeing her." Her voice is barely audible.

I see her throat bob; she's just as surprised as I am that she actually said it. Looking down at the woman in front of me, I'm mesmerized by how beautiful she is. Her skin looks soft enough to touch as she stands there in her thin, cotton sweater. I comb a loose strand of hair out of her face, and her eyes hold my gaze as she turns her head into my touch. The air between us grows thick. It's immediate, the relief I feel in my gut. Finally, she isn't pushing me away!

Leaning the rest of the way in, I set out to get another taste of this girl who drives me mad. Electricity tingles through my body as soon as her soft lips touch mine. Her plush tongue licks across my lips, making her hunger palpable. Dani tastes so sweet. She's like my favorite candy I never want to stop eating. My arms wrap around her small frame, squeezing her toward my chest. It doesn't take my hands long to find her ass. Squeezing, I lift her up, and her legs go around my waist and grip my sides.

I can't believe I'm here right now. I can't believe Dani is in my arms. I'm ashamed to admit how long I've wanted this, but I can't let that haunt me now. One foot in front of the other, I carry her down the hall to her bedroom, our lips never breaking. It's like we're catching up for the last month. Walking over the threshold, I continue until my knees touch the bed. I bend halfway to lay her down and begin staring at the image before me. Hair splayed out all around her, her fingers reach up to calm her red and puffy lips. She's breathless. I listen to her try to catch her breath, returning it to normal. Mysterious chocolate eyes rake down my torso. It's a picture cut straight from my dreams. Suddenly, my eyes drift to the sheets under her body. The contrast of the dark blue against her gorgeous, creamy complexion is staggering.

Something in my mind makes a shift. My eyes lift up, taking in the bed in its entirety. A dangerous thought has wedged itself into my brain, one I desperately wish I could let go of in this instance. This is the bed she shared with my brother. Joel slept in this bed with her, his wife. Daggers stab my chest, causing me to falter slightly. I lean back, stabilizing myself against their—her—dresser, I correct myself. I aim to compose my thoughts while she leans up, bearing her weight on her elbows.

Either she's reading my mind or sharing the same uneasy feeling. "We don't have to do anything else tonight. I just want to be with you. . . . If that's okay?" she asks, her voice unsure.

Her voice is like a drug to me, the smooth sound so incredibly feminine. Pushing off from where I stand, I kick off my shoes. Moving forward, I crawl into bed next to her, taking in all the slopes of her body. Her words ring through my thoughts: *I just want to be with you, is that okay?* How could I, or any man, have a problem with that?

"That's fine," I say, trying to control my desire and anxiety over the situation. Pulling her flush against me, I rest my arm around her, kissing her along her forehead. "I don't want to leave yet, anyway," I whisper into the dark of the room.

I'm not sure who falls asleep first, or when; but what I do know is that when I wake up, I'm the only one in the bed. Before I can really panic that she's freaked out over our innocent little sleepover, I hear the faint sound of coffee brewing. Exiting her room and making my way to the kitchen, I spot her. Her long, dark hair is halfway down her back, and she's wiping the counters down. Dani never stops moving; her nerves obviously keep her going. I wonder if it's because I'm here. It means she'll actually have to deal with what's going on between us. Two mugs by the brewed pot catch my attention—a good sign. If there were only one, I'd assume she was kicking me out of her house.

I clear my throat to avoid startling her.

Turning to face me, she gives me a polite smile. "Good morning."

"How did you sleep?" I ask, staying planted where I am, not wanting to invade her space.

Tucking her hair behind her ear, she looks down at the floor in embarrassment. "Really well, actually."

Damn, she looks just as beautiful in the morning. Dani looks like she could be in a catalog with her pajama shorts and slouchy sweater. I move to pour myself coffee, unsure of how to navigate this. The silence starts to elongate.

Feeling like an idiot for not having anything to say, I stumble forward. "Thank you for the coffee." I bring the black liquid up to my mouth, savoring the hot, bitter taste.

She looks at me thoughtfully as she pours herself a cup. "Thank you for staying with me again."

"No problem." Literally. I want to say I don't think I could have left if she asked me.

Her delicate hand stirs the spoon in her mug with quick, circular motions. She's not looking at me when she says, "You don't need to break it off with Chantal."

Leaning against the counter, I pause mid-drink. "Why's that?"

Dani's still not looking at me. I set my cup back down on the counter. I'm worried this will be over before it's even started.

"Because . . . Where is this really going to go?" she asks, hesitating.

"We could date," I answer honestly.

Her eyes finally meet mine. "Date?"

"Why is that such a strange concept?"

I can see Dani's flustered, trying to find the words to express her concern regarding my suggestion.

"I was married to your brother. It's only been what, six months since he died? I still come over for family gatherings," she says incredulously.

I nod along. "All of that is true, but that's not why you're saying that or giving these lame excuses again. You're scared about what people would think."

"Aren't you?" she asks, a little less exasperated this time.

"I've told you I've wanted this for longer than I should have. I thought I had made it clear, but maybe I haven't," I answer, taking her face in my hands. "I want you. And it doesn't bother me who knows that. And just so it's out there, I let Chantal know we wouldn't be seeing each other anymore yesterday. Before I even came over." I drop my hands, wanting to put that subject to bed.

Her cheeks turn pink by my admission. She turns her body to face mine and leans against the counter, like I had a minute earlier, except she tilts her head to the ceiling in thought. Before I can move and press my lips to the hollow of her neck, she tilts her head back down.

"I'd be lying if I said I didn't want this, but I'm not ready for others to know. Especially because we don't even know where this is going yet."

"What do you want to do?"

"I'm suggesting we do what you said. Let's date, but let's keep it our secret."

I don't know how to feel about this. I'm glad she's willing to take a chance on us, but I don't like the secrecy. I understand why she wants it—I do; but I want to shout it from the rooftops and lay my claim. Let everyone know she's mine. Pushing that down, I know the right thing to do is to agree. To give her time to get used to this.

"Okay, we'll do it your way. For now."

"Thank you," she responds gratefully.

I can tell she was worried about what my reaction would be. It's something she did constantly in her marriage. Dani will learn I'm not like him soon enough. Feeling the need to kiss her, I close the gap. My lips find hers so easily, it's like they're magnetic. It's sweet and gentle, and it's quick. I want more, but now is not the time. I need her to know her body isn't what I'm after—even though it's an incredible bonus. Smiling over the rim of my coffee mug at her, I take a big gulp, loving the combination of my two favorite tastes: coffee and Dani.

"Alright, kids, I want these group projects done and turned in by Monday. Next week starts presentations," I say to my class as the bell rings.

The bustle of the hallway enters my classroom as my door opens. Dozens of preteens scurry out into the madness. Grateful for a small break, I quickly open my desk drawer to retrieve my phone. Notifications show up on my screen. A few are from the guys, and one is from my mom. None from Dani. It's been a few days since I was over at her place. I know internally she's freaking out and maybe even trying to create space. She can try all she wants—that's not happening. Dani will just be putting off the inevitable. I slide my thumb over my phone, go to the home screen, and click on Messages. Tapping on her name, I begin typing:

I hope your day is going well. Are we still on for tonight?

I begin smiling all of a sudden at the prospect of seeing her. It's strange to feel this nervous and excited. I'm in my thirties for crying out loud, and this girl makes me feel like I'm sixteen again.

Remembering the other messages waiting, I pull them up. Travis's is the most pressing:

I need your help. This is not going the way I thought it would.

Unease sits on my chest, cooling the warmth texting Dani had brought me.

I write back: **I'll come over later.**

As soon as it's sent, my phone buzzes in my hand. It's Dani.

Yes :)

Going over to Travis's before my evening with Dani will be problematic. I'm not sure how, but I can feel it. Before I can dwell on it too much, the bell rings and students filter into my room. Unfortunately, the last few hours of my workday drag on, the clock never seeming to move.

I just want to get to my friend's place so I can leave. When I do finally get there, I walk right in like I live there. Looking around the apartment, I see it's just as messy as always, not giving me an inkling of what is happening. In the same instant, Travis walks out, looking a disheveled mess.

"What happened?"

His hands go to the back of his head. "It's so much more than we thought," His voice is panicked, and he's begun pacing.

"How much more?" I ask the stupid question, knowing it must be severe, given his reaction.

"I can't do it. I'm sorry, I love you, man, but this is too risky. We could get caught. Let's just tell someone and let them handle it," he begs me.

I walk over to my friend, stopping his frantic movement. "We can't tell anyone. There are several reasons why that's a bad idea."

"You only care about one of those reasons!" he argues. "Nate, man, think this through. Think about how bad this could be if it comes out not on your terms."

Anger bristles in my chest. "Trav, if you can't handle this, tell me so I can take care of it myself."

He looks at me, disbelief etched across his features, and mumbles, "I can't believe you're still going to do this, man."

"It's not a big deal. No one needs to know. I'll be fine," I assure him.

"Isn't that what Joel said?"

I roll my eyes at the comparison, "Just help me load it all into my car."

Travis turns his back on me, heading out the door toward his storage room outside his apartment. I follow him out, grabbing all the black bags I know will be going with me. My best friend and I make several trips to load my trunk up with the painful secrets I'm trying to bury. He was right: it's worse than we originally thought. I scan the parking lot and see no one seems to have seen our sketchy behavior. When I start my car, the dashboard clock shines. *Damn! It's later than I thought.* I was supposed to be on my way to Dani's by now.

Anxiety fries my nerves. I start tapping my hand against the steering wheel, unsure of where to go. I should go home and take care of the items weighing down my car. But if I go home, I'll be late. And that's if I'm even able to leave at all. If I go to Dani's, it's not like she'll be sifting through my trunk. Still, the thought of having proof of my secrets this close to her makes me uneasy. Bitterness leaves a nasty taste in my mouth as it becomes increasingly clear that I was wrong. I had hoped this situation wouldn't affect her at all, but it already is. My eyes dart to the time. I'm thirty minutes late. Sliding my hand into my pocket, I pull out my phone. I can't call her, because she's beaten me to it. Her name flashes on my screen. Tapping the green button, guilt overflows my whole body.

"Hey, you still coming?"

Hearing her uncertain tone amplifies my regret. "Yes! I'll be there soon. I'm sorry I'm so late. Travis needed my help moving some things in his apartment, and time got away from me."

"Okay. See you soon," she says, her voice laced with understanding.

Against my better judgement, I head straight to her. When I arrive, I let myself in, and a garlic aroma is heavy in the air.

"Hi," I say lamely, taking in the scene before me. She's just in jeans and a cardigan, but the simple clothing molds to every curve of her body. Her ponytail sways as she stirs the linguini, and my fingers itch to tug her head back so I can kiss her neck.

"Hi. Glad you could make it," she says with a wink, making a joke of my tardiness.

Dani still talks to me the way she always has. I'm grateful our new setup hasn't changed that.

The events over the last few hours plague me, making me feel further from her than the couple of feet we stand apart. Closing more than the physical distance, I take her in my arms. She smells so sweet, like vanilla. Dani's arms are pliable, snaking their way around my neck. I've been waiting for tonight since I got to work this morning. Memories of the weekend danced in my head. I became worried she had or would change her mind about us. It surprises me how much I've missed her. My body melds with hers. There's no exaggeration when I say our bodies are like two puzzle pieces that fit perfectly together.

I release her, and we grab our dinner plates and head to the table. My stomach grumbles at the sight of the carbonara. I'm starving; I haven't eaten all day.

"Mmm, this smells amazing!" I tell her.

"Thank you. I remembered you liked this dish," she responds, smiling down at her plate.

I think back to the first time she made this for family dinner. Her hair was up in a messy bun—emphasis on *messy*. Loose strands of hair popped out all around. Music flowed out of a small, portable speaker in the kitchen as she bopped around cooking for us. We all had asked if we could help, but Dani refused, stating Joel would come and help her shortly. My parents and I knew that wouldn't be the case. He'd sat in the living room with us, making half-assed attempts at conversation and checking his phone constantly. After thirty minutes of that, I had marched back into the kitchen, not wanting to take no for an answer. I'd wanted to help so she wouldn't be in there by herself. Entering through the open-door frame, I smelled the hot chicken and cheese.

"I came in to help, and you're not pushing me out this time," I said with humor, trying to cushion the blow of my brother being useless.

Her quiet tone let me know exactly how disappointed she felt. "Can you grab the pan of rolls and put them in the oven while I stir in the Parmesan?"

I moved before she was done with the question. Closing the oven door, I leaned over the stove and took in a big breath. I hadn't complimented the aroma out loud yet when she said, "Wait till you taste it." Her pride was evident. Dani lifted the spoon up to me, offering me a taste. I lowered my face, and my eyes stared into hers. Her irises were deep pools of melted chocolate. I closed my mouth over the wooden spoon to taste the homemade sauce. Savoring the delectable flavors, I managed to dribble a few drops down my chin.

"Oh my god, you weren't kidding," I said with appreciation.

Dani seemed to be fixated on my mess. Her hand briefly lifted to wipe my face, but she quickly pulled back, second-guessing herself. I reached up and wiped the little bit of sauce off my chin myself. We spent the rest of the time cooking and joking around. Listening to her laugh at me, I understood why Joel fell in love with her. She was magnetic.

The gorgeous girl across from me is the same one from that day years ago. She made my chest ache for her that day, and I'd hated that I felt something for my brother's wife. As much as I loved Joel, he wasn't good for Dani. Even my parents could see it.

"How's teaching going this year?" she asks me, bringing me back to the present.

"It's going well, although now that Thanksgiving is over, the kids are all waiting for Christmas break," I respond around a big bite.

"Do you like the group of kids you have?" she inquires thoughtfully.

"I love this semester's kids! They're so funny and surprisingly kind for seventh graders. They aren't full of angst like past years," I answer.

"Middle school is such a hard time. They're still so young, but they're trying to find out who they are. I can't believe you chose this over high school," Dani responds with an outward shake of her head.

I laugh at her in surprise. "I taught high school one year. And that was enough for me to know I never wanted to do that again. Now *those* kids have attitudes!"

She makes a sound of agreement through her glass of wine. "How did the girls like you?"

I'm confused. "Fine, I guess?" I'm not sure where this is going.

"I bet they doodle hearts in their notebooks because of you. Crushing on Mr. Stephensen and all his sweaters." Dani giggles.

"Whoa, what's wrong with my sweaters?" I ask, pretending to be offended.

"Nothing. Nothing!" she assures me, still laughing. "I would have done the same if you were my teacher."

"Well, I'm glad I'm not. You'd be half my age."

I love this shift in her. She doesn't feel held back; she can say anything she wants. Our evening continues seamlessly. Stories of terrible, yet funny things students have said over my years of teaching and memories of family dynamics are shared over the cherry-wood dinner table. When dinner is over and the dishes are placed in the sink, I remember how this next to perfect night was almost derailed. My good mood begins to waver. Dani doesn't seem to notice. Turning toward me, she reaches out to hold my hand. As our fingers interlock, she continues my way until she's stepping up on her tiptoes to kiss me. Her lips, as soft as rose petals, touch mine briefly. She's an amazing kisser; I'm always left wanting more.

Dani pulls away. "Thank you for coming over tonight."

I chuckle. "You made dinner, I showed up late, and you're thanking me? Well, you're welcome. I'll come over whenever you want if I'm thanked this way!" I lean in to kiss her forehead to punctuate my sentence. "Thank you for dinner."

Her eyes have drifted closed with innocent delight. "You're welcome."

Knowing I can't leave her with dirty dishes, I roll up my sleeves and begin rinsing the plates, placing them in the dishwasher.

"Stop, you don't have to do that," she protests.

"When have I ever not helped? Or left a mess just for you to take care of?" She ignores my rhetorical questions, but she knows the answer is never. I think she knows I'd do anything for her. "Besides, it's only fair. You cooked. I can clean."

I continue rinsing plates without complaint from her. We stand in comfortable silence. Every once in a while, I peek over at her to find she's doing the same to me. When it's all said and done, the silence has changed. It's as if we don't know how to end our first technical date. Even if my car didn't need to be emptied, I wouldn't stay. I couldn't. It's not the right time, and besides, I'm not sure she would ask me to stay. Drying my hands on her towels, I look for the right words.

"It's getting late," she says, breaking me out of my thoughts.

I fail to contain my smile. "Yeah, I should head out."

We've always been able to read each other's minds; this is just another example of that connection.

"I'll walk you out." Her dainty fingers find me, interlocking with mine.

Time with her goes by so quickly. She makes me forget about everything but her. The earlier part of the evening is gone. There's a nip in the air tonight. After we get off her front porch stairs, I stop mid-step, causing the gravel to make a loud *crunch* sound. I don't want her to get too cold.

"C'mere, let's stop here. I don't want you freezing," I reveal, turning her to me instead of the car.

"It's okay, I'm always cold," Dani protests, but doesn't move, wrapping her arms tight around her torso like a blanket.

I envelop her, wanting to be as close to her as possible. Her head is resting on my chest, blocking out the cold air.

"Thanks again for dinner and for giving this a chance," I murmur.

Looking up, she doesn't say anything. She doesn't have to. She lifts up onto the balls of her feet to kiss me. Her supple lips touch mine softly. She's still easing herself into this—me and her. I'm afraid she's going to pull away, but she does the opposite instead. Dani pushes her body flush against mine with fervor. Her tongue playfully licks the tip of mine as our lips dance together. Oh, how I wish I could do this forever. I pull her bottom lip in between my teeth, and she rewards me with a low moan. Tangling her lips with mine one last time, she holds me there. Not ready for the kiss to break. I can feel the tip of her nose has gotten cold from being outside. Reluctantly, I pull away from her.

"You're getting cold like I knew you would," I say, trying to hide how heavy I'm breathing. "Go inside. I'll talk to you later."

"Okay. Drive safe; watch out for deer," she responds quietly.

Driving home takes me hardly any time at all. I'm left smiling the whole car ride. Our first date went perfectly. When I pull into my driveway, though, I'm reminded of the contents of my trunk, and the joy I feel comes to a crashing halt.

CHAPTER 14
DANI, PRESENT DAY

I'd be lying if I said I wasn't a little nervous to see Chantal. Although it hasn't been that long since we went to my parents' for Thanksgiving, it feels like so much has happened since that week. We've talked on the phone and messaged each other back and forth, but she hasn't mentioned Nathan. Curiosity has a grip on my throat, but I refuse to let it out, wanting her to bring him up on her own. Luckily, she's swinging by Tav's to grab lunch while I'm working today, so I know she'll stop in to gossip—her favorite pastime. Nerves settle into my limbs, making it hard to sit still. I'm up pacing around the room, studying an expense report when she walks right in, food already in her mouth.

"Hey!" I chime, excited to see my friend despite the possible impending conversation.

Chantal makes a sound of greeting while her mouth is busy.

"What's new?" I ask, keeping my eyes glued to the report, afraid she would see I'm desperate for specific information.

Swallowing the bite that's in her mouth, she looks at me. "Well, let's see. Nathan broke it off with me."

My eyes fly to where she is in the room. "Really?"

"Yeah, it seemed a little out of the blue to me. Have you seen him any?"

Not wanting to lie, I tell a half truth: "We've seen each other a little bit."

"Has he mentioned seeing anyone else?"

I can't get a good read on what she's feeling. This is my chance to come clean. I can just tell her now, and we can move forward. But I don't do it. Instead, I choose silence over the truth and shake my head no, not wanting to lie out loud. "Would it bother you if he had?"

"I guess I'm just confused. It's not like we were serious. I thought he was fun to date; but with him ending it so abruptly, I wasn't sure if maybe there was a hidden reason," she admits thoughtfully.

I can do nothing but clamp my mouth shut and shrug. This is fantastic. I'm the worst friend. I find my way around my desk and sit down in the creaking chair. *What am I doing?*

"Are you okay?" Chantal inquires, watching me.

"Of course. Why?" I respond, trying to hide my sudden awkwardness.

"You're acting weird," she answers, then switches gears by making plans. "Let's go out tomorrow night. I'm in the mood to let loose."

"Sounds great. I could use it too," I reply honestly for the first time.

"And I'll invite the guys!" she adds giddily.

Panic begins to rise up. "Would you really want to have Nathan there?" I try to change her mind.

"Oh please, he wouldn't bother me. Plus, it'll give him a chance to see what he's missing," she says, winking at me.

"Oh, good," is all that I can say.

After Chantal eats, she leaves my office, and I am left to sink lower in my chair to count the lies that are piling up. I'm digging myself into a hole. I started this. Why couldn't I have just been honest with her from the beginning and tell her that I liked Nathan? Placing my palms over my eyes, I block out the light and push inward, trying to find some peace. Taking a deep breath, I tell myself it's all going to be fine.

Getting ready for a night out turns out to be more fun than I remembered. Or maybe it's because my goal is to make Nathan's eyes pop out of his head without letting anyone else notice. Shimmying into my ripped jeans, I pull the waistband up over my hips to the hem of my black lace tank and pair them with my black-velvet heeled boots. Wrapping my hair around the barrel of my curling iron, I try to give my hair just enough wave to have body. When my eyes are lined with black and I've added a little pink, nude lip, I back away to assess my handiwork. Not bad. I feel sexy. I smile at the vixen in the mirror. Nathan's eyes will struggle to stay off me while his hands twitch, eager to touch me.

I check the clock, and it's perfect timing. I slip on my jacket as I head to the bar address Chantal sent me. Walking into the establishment, I see it's much nicer than the dive bar we usually go to. The sconces look polished and new, and the floor is a beautiful, finished hardwood—not splintering or uneven in color. The place feels much newer. Scanning the crowd, unable to spot my group, I walk over to the bar to get a drink before wandering around.

"Moscato, please."

The bartender nods at me in response before grabbing an empty glass from below. A firm hand comes around my hip and slides down to my thigh. Shivers flow over my skin, and I whip around to see who is touching me, half expecting it to be Nathan. I see Paul. My chest seizes.

"Hi there."

I don't know where he gets the idea that this amount of touching is okay, but I remove his hand from me.

"Hi," I say with no warmth, turning my back to him.

He doesn't take my hint. "I'm glad you came out tonight. We haven't gotten a chance to talk since your birthday," he adds, pulling his lower lip in between his teeth. Paul is good-looking, and he knows it. I get the feeling this expression usually works in his favor. Well, I'm not interested. Little hairs on my body are standing up, cautioning me he's too close.

"Where is everybody?" I inquire, wanting to move us toward them.

"They're over here," he replies, turning his head for me to follow his gaze.

Giving the bartender my attention once more, I thank him. Picking up the stemless glass, I try to distance myself from Paul despite going to the same table. The closer I get to our group, the better I see him. Nathan's eyes are already on me, and he's doing nothing to disguise what he's thinking. With each click of my heels on the hardwood, the more on fire I feel. I picked this outfit explicitly to rile him up, but I wasn't anticipating for it to happen so quickly, nor for it to have an effect on *me*. His usually warm irises have turned dark as he takes me in from my head to my toes. I can feel where his eyes land as if they're his hands, and right now, I wish they were.

"Hey, guys," I greet the table, making sure not to give all of my attention to Nathan. I sit down in the closest open seat, and he's diagonal from me, too far away to be suspicious. I mentally cheer. Hellos circle around me while Chantal switches seats with Paul to sit next to me despite his protests. Relief floods me when he finally agrees.

"Fine, this seat has a better view, anyways," he retorts as he takes her old chair directly across from me. This guy is such a creep.

Conversation engulfs the table. Travis, Nathan, and Paul go back and forth over old college stories and share embarrassing antics about the situations they'd get into. Their laughter is contagious. Listening to these stories, I allow my gaze to wander over to Nathan. I picture him in his early twenties at school. I've seen the pictures of him at Maureen and Pat's house, and he looks almost the same: he's wearing dark jeans and a Henley shirt, with his brown hair longer and pushed back in the front. I can see how enamored the girls at his college would have been.

He must feel my gaze, because his eyes move to meet mine. There is an aggressive tone to them, like they're silently staking claim. I want to drive him mad. I lift my glass to take a drink, gliding my tongue over my bottom lip after I swallow the sweet white wine. He casts his gaze down to my mouth, while I tenderly wipe my thumb achingly slowly against my lips to wipe off any residue. My ears are ringing. I can't hear anything in the bar but my own heartbeat as he has taken up my sole focus. I'm playing a dangerous game. I haven't looked away from this gorgeous man yet, and anybody could be noticing by now. Closing my eyes, I tilt my head up, twisting my neck around and faking a stretch before I return my attention to the group.

I open my eyes, and Chantal turns to me. "Let's go dance!"

Finishing off my glass, I scoot my seat away from the table, following her toward the throng of bodies. "Pour Some Sugar on Me" filters through the speakers. It gets substantially louder the closer we get to the dance floor. Weaving our way around people, I let my body feel the music, causing my hips to sway. Chantal feels it too. We're holding each other's hands as we dance, belting out the lyrics. Songs begin to roll into one another. When it shifts to a slow song, we're both laughing. It feels like we just got out here, but based on the sweat on the back of my neck, I'd say otherwise.

"I'm having so much fun!" I shout over the music.

"I know! Want to do one more song?" Chantal asks.

"Not yet, this one is a slow song. Let's go back and get another drink."

We must have put on quite a show, because when we arrive back at the table, the guys' chairs are all turned toward the dance floor.

"Like what you see, boys?" Chantal flirts.

"You guys looked great out there," Travis answers her quickly, slipping his arm around her playfully.

Even though most of their attention is on us, it didn't stop other girls from showing up to ask them to dance. In spite of the men declining, the most beautiful girl in the group pulled out a chair next to Nathan and proceeded to sit down, giving him an eyeful of cleavage she strategically pushed up in the process. My chest tingles with jealousy, and I can't look away. I'm surprised he can't feel me burning a hole in the side of his face. I'm annoyed that he's listening to whatever she has to say, and I'm angry that she can give him attention like this in public. Looking down at the table, I aim to refresh my mind. I see the empty glasses on the table and remember I was coming to get another drink. I happen to spot a full glass next to my empty one.

Pettiness makes me smile, and I use this to interrupt their *important* conversation, "Is this for me?"

Nathan turns his whole body toward me, giving me the full scope of his gaze. "Yes, I got you another one." He flashes me a smile, and I melt.

Bar Crawl Barbie looks irritated that he turned away. "Thank you," I reply, taking a drink.

Nathan surprises us both by getting out of his seat and moving to stand beside me. My eyes roam our group. No one notices anything strange about the act.

"Are you trying to kill me?" he mumbles beside me.

"What?"

"Looking the way you do. Dancing how you were. Was your goal to kill me? Or for me to kill everyone else so they wouldn't gawk?" he asks again, his voice deep and seductive.

"I'm not dressed any different than your friend over there," I argue.

Nathan chuckles. "I hadn't noticed. I was too busy looking at you."

"Sure you were. Didn't seem that way when she first came over." The hurt of seeing another girl getting to be with him out in the open returns.

He makes a *tsk-tsk* sound. "Dani, have you always been so jealous?"

I'm being a brat, and I know it. I can't help it, so I ignore him.

Nathan continues more sincerely, "I was telling her I'm here with somebody, then came to stand next to you." He leans over, bumping my shoulder with his.

I think about his accurate accusation of jealousy and the truth behind it. "I'm not, by the way," I answer his earlier question, tucking my hair behind my ear in embarrassment over my admission.

"Not what?"

"Usually jealous. That's umm . . . never been an issue before," I explain before taking another drink.

Nathan doesn't say anything. He just leans back on his heels and ponders what I've said. I've just admitted he's the only person I've felt jealous over, including my marriage.

Feeling insecure over how much I've shared, I don't wait for a response on the matter. "I'm over being here. Do you want to leave?"

"Tell me about it. I only came tonight because I knew you would be here," he responds. "Let's go. I'll drive us to my house," he finishes.

"No! That's too obvious. You leave first, then in a couple minutes, I'll leave and meet you there."

"Doesn't that seem like too much? Do you really have to leave after me?" he asks, disappointed.

"It's fine. I don't want people to know yet," I explain.

His mood has changed to somber because of me. "I'll see you soon, then."

I almost reach out for his hand to stop him and apologize, but reign myself in. Fifteen long minutes pass before I'm finally out the door. I've made it three feet from my Camry when Paul calls my name. Annoyance rattles through me. What does he want?

I don't stop my trek, but I grant him the courtesy of a backward glance. He's jogging toward me. "Just checking to make sure you're okay to drive."

"Thank you for checking, but I can make it home on my own."

"Are you sure? I don't mind driving. We could even go to my place." He flashes me his most charming smile while his hand seeks out my waist again.

I step back against my car, warning signs are going off. I need to be direct. "No thank you, Paul. I'm not interested in you like that." I open my door, slipping inside quickly. It's alarming how he doesn't move away from my car now that I'm in it. Bringing the engine to life, I step on the gas, trying to get to my much-needed destination as quickly as possible. Pulling into Nathan's driveway, I jump out of the car the second it's off. Letting his front door slam behind me, I search for him.

"What took you so long? What's wrong?" The last question rolls right out as soon as he sees my face. And I go right into his welcoming and safe arms.

"Nothing, it's nothing. Thank you for letting me come over," I mumble against his chest.

"You are always welcome here."

"Can I stay the night?" I ask, trying not to beg. I'm not sure if this is right or how he'll feel about me inviting myself to stay.

"Done," he says simply, punctuating the word with a kiss on the top of my head. "I'll give you a few minutes. Go grab a shirt of mine to sleep in."

I scurry back to his room. It's much bigger than mine. This isn't the first time I've been in it, but it's the first time I'll be staying in it. Nathan's room is what you would picture a guy's room to be: it has dark navy accents and is overall bare of *things*. I scan the bed; it's neat. I can't wait to sleep. I'm more tired than I expected.

I reach for a brass handle and pull open one of his drawers. It takes me a few tries, but I eventually find his shirts. The first shirt I find is the one I go with. It has some type of design on the back; I don't pay too much attention to it. Slipping off my boots, I throw them in the corner of the room. The rest of my clothes join them on the floor. I only notice his shirt isn't as long as it seems once it's on me. Rifling through more drawers, I pull a pair of boxers on after I take off my panties. Nathan's clothes smell like him; it's soothing.

I peek into the adjoining bathroom, and I'm pleasantly surprised by how clean it is. Throwing my hair up in a messy bun, I want to wash the makeup off my face. Turning the water on, I wait for it to warm up. Splashing the water on my face, I make do with the soap that's on the counter. Rinsing the suds and makeup off, I pat my face dry and quickly exit the bathroom. I'm sure it's not a big deal, but he never said I could go in there. Closing the door exactly how it was, I hear a knock on the bedroom door.

"Come in."

Nathan's steps slow when he sees me in his clothes. He puts something on the bed and walks over to me.

I look down at the options I chose and ask, "Is this okay? I didn't know if anything was off-limits. I also used your bathroom to take off my makeup."

He comes toward me, turning me around to face the big mirror on the wall while he wraps his arms around my stomach. "So beautiful," he whispers, leaning his head onto mine as we make eye contact in the mirror.

I tilt my head more, and he gifts me a trail of kisses up and down my neck. I'm getting the feeling he prefers me in this hair up, no makeup look. Nathan is smoothing over all the cracks Joel has made over the years and unintentionally providing comfort for his disturbing friend's behavior. The pressure from his mouth on my neck is mesmerizing. I begin to feel his tongue caress a thin line. I grip his wrist and nudge it down my torso, past his boxers. His big hand cups me at the same time. That, coupled with the madness his mouth is wreaking—I could almost come undone.

Laying my head back on his shoulder, words slip out of my mouth, "Oh my god, Nate." My breathing is erratic, and I'm desperate for more contact than what he's giving me. Twisting to catch his lips, I kiss and nip at him, silently urging him on. In a flash, he pulls himself away from me.

"Why did you stop?"

His breath is coming out unevenly while he roughly rubs his face with his hand. "I didn't want to get carried away."

"You weren't."

"I just—" He stops what he was going to say to change his explanation. "We've got time. I don't want to rush you."

"I was the one pushing it further." I can't help but feel a little rejected.

I'm not sure what else to say. Nathan walks back over to grab what he set down. Sitting on the edge of the bed, he turns over a small, open box in his hands. It's a deck of cards.

"I was thinking we could play a game," he states with uncertainty.

Oh yeah, that sounds like just as much fun as fooling around, I think. He's trying to protect both of us. He's been clear he's felt things for me longer than I probably am aware, and I was married to his baby brother. If this goes wrong, nothing in our lives will be the same. "Sure."

Climbing into Nathan's queen-size bed, I take the deck from him and shuffle it until I'm satisfied. He stands up and unbuckles his pants, wanting to get undressed. Pushing his jeans down his bare, muscled legs, he exposes his blue boxer-briefs. I can only be distracted by how snug and perfectly they fit on his thighs until he takes off his shirt and haphazardly tosses it at his hamper. Nathan climbs into the bed, waiting for me to deal. Well, this just seems unfair.

We end up playing several games of crazy eights. Despite the distraction that Nathan's breathtaking shirtlessness was providing, we have a good time goofing off. I'm not sure how long we play or how late it is, but at some point, we end up falling asleep lying down facing each other with his arm over my side while he lightly scratches my back. He makes me feel cherished and protected. It makes me wonder what would have happened had I met him first.

CHAPTER 15
DANI, PRESENT DAY

I can see my breath as I exhale. Wrapping myself tighter in my peacoat, I continue my trek up to Maureen and Pat's, a warm dish of sweet potatoes in my hands. Opening the door, I hear Pat's voice first.

"You'll need to get used to the idea of her dating. She's not married anymore," his voice is low but stern with truth.

"She needs to grieve longer than this!" Maureen's voice is contradictory to his.

I've walked into a secret conversation about me. I hang on to the door tightly, not wanting it to close. This way, I have an exit if I need it, and they don't know I've heard them.

"This is all hypothetical. Who's to say she's even dating now?" my father-in-law retorts.

"But if she is, that's her choice. She knows what is right for *her*," Nathan's voice rings clear while defending me. I didn't know he was here; his car wasn't in the driveway. My stomach is in my throat from embarrassment over him having been involved in it.

161

I hear a dramatic scoff. I'm assuming it's my *loving* mother-in-law, "Of course you would say that."

This is so uncomfortable it's painful! I'm frozen still, halfway in the house. Do I break up this conversation, or listen for more?

"She's family, Maur. End of story," Pat interjects.

I let that be the end and close the door loudly, letting them know I'm within earshot. Anxiety fills my belly, making my heart race. I feel like I'm walking into a bear's den. Soothing the lines on my face, I step into the kitchen where everyone is congregated. "Hi, guys," I say lamely.

"Hey."

"Hi."

"Hey."

A mixture of greetings come out too quickly.

"Here are the sweet potatoes. I'll go put them on the table." I'm trying to keep my voice level, but the boxy kitchen walls feel like they're closing in on me. I attempt to walk out of the room at a normal pace. When I've reached the dining table, I take a deep breath. Air fills my lungs, warding off the suffocation I was feeling.

Nathan comes out, laying napkins on the side of each plate. I'm sure it's just a ruse to talk to me. "How much of that did you hear?"

"Enough. How'd you know I heard any?" I ask, watching him move around the table.

"They didn't notice, but I could see it on your face. I'm sorry you heard any of it."

"How often do you guys talk about me like that?" I spill out, worried about the answer.

His expression answers for me. "Hardly ever, honestly. I know it probably doesn't seem like it, based on what you heard." Nathan pauses, making sure he chooses the right words it seems. "It's just that—"

Before he can continue, his parents walk out carrying food. "We can talk about this later," he mumbles.

They set food all around the table. Spoons clatter around the room with dishes being dug into. Disappointment nags at me; I want to know what Nathan was going to say.

"Oh, Nathan! The new neighbors across the street, the Joneses, their daughter, Amanda, is about your age!" Maureen gushes.

"Cool, I guess?" he responds, unsure why.

Oh no. I can sense where this is going.

"Well, you should ask her out. She's a teacher, too, and very pretty!"

"Mmm, I don't think so," is all he says before taking a bite.

"Why not? You're not dating anyone." Her tone is filled with accusation.

My eyes take in the side of his face before I realize I'm paying way too close attention to the situation. I pull my focus away and set it to anywhere but him. Pat has been watching me. I force the fakest smile of my life as I push a big forkful of food in my mouth to keep it busy.

"I'm just not interested," Nathan answers with nonchalance.

"Nonsense. I'll give you her number."

"Maureen, lay off, will ya?" Pat is always the one to diffuse the Maureen bomb. No one else wants to jump on that grenade.

Even Joel avoided it as best as possible, schmoozing his mother and playing into the fact he was her baby. Her words ring in my head like an alarm: *She will need to grieve longer than this. She will need to grieve longer than this.*

What will happen if they find out about Nathan and me? Will we even last long enough for me to worry about that? Sadness at that possibility grips me. *How will Maureen and Pat react? And if I were to date someone else, would I be exiled from the only family I have close to me?* Memories of the loneliness I felt after Joel's death creep in.

Sensing someone is trying to get my attention, I gladly snap out of my own thoughts. "I'm sorry, what?"

Nathan looks at me. "I was asking if you could give me a ride home after dinner."

"I'm not sure if that's necessary. Dad could give you a ride home," Maureen answers before me.

"Dani will already be going in that direction to get home. Why would Dad drop me off just to come back here? Doesn't that seem inconvenient?" His voice has taken on an annoyed edge since the beginning of the dinner.

I use this moment to speak up, "Yeah, it's no problem."

"All right, it's settled then," she responds, tight-lipped.

My sweet father-in-law jumps in, always wanting to smooth everything out, "The funniest thing happened at the grocery store . . ."

The story ends with another customer accidentally knocking down a pyramid of apples. Nothing that extraordinary, but that's Pat. He'll tell any story or joke to change the subject onto something more pleasant. Dinner, despite the tension, is delicious. Even with all the awkward arguing, it's still better than being with my parents. So, I suffer through it with a grain of salt.

Packing up our leftovers in separate bags, I watch as Maureen not-so-secretly slips a folded-up phone number into Nathan's bag. We walk down the driveway together, and I have to fight the urge to lean into him for comfort. He's quickly becoming my solace in many ways. It scares me.

As soon as the Camry is out of the driveway, his hand is on my thigh. It's an easy yet effective touch to let me know he's there when I'm ready.

"So, what were you going to say before your parents came into the dining room? You guys don't usually talk behind my back, it's just . . . Just what?" I say, reciting his words.

"My dad happened to make a silly comment about us bringing dates to dinner, and my mom jumped on it. That was all." His fingers squeeze my leg lightly—his way of saying *don't worry about it.*

That's all I do. The car rolls to a stop at a red light. I close my eyes, taking a moment to myself. Opening them up, I ask what's on my mind, "What do you think they would say if they knew?"

"I'm not sure, but what I do know is that it doesn't concern me enough to stop."

His voice finds its way through my body, settling my nerves. I feel like I'm on a roller coaster that's just reached the top. I know the descent is going to be chaotic, but I can't for the life of me get off now.

"You know, when you offered to help me, I thought you'd actually be helping," I say to Chantal, who's behind me.

"I am helping!"

I twist my body around, careful not to fall off the ladder I'm standing on.

"I'm keeping you company. Admit it, this would be boring if I wasn't here," she sing-songs.

Reaching forward to shelve supplies, I respond, "Okay, valid point."

"How are you? I feel like we haven't hung out in a while."

I play dumb, even though I've been feeling the disconnect too. "Really? It hasn't been that long."

"You look great, like life is returning to your face. Could it be a man?" she questions, wagging her eyebrows.

"No," I answer frantically. "Just me, myself, and I. How're you doing?"

"Eh, fine. I guess."

She seems like something's wrong. I know if I push, she'll spill it. I'm about to pry when my phone dings.

Still on the ladder, I ask, "Will you check that for me?"

I inch my body back down off the ladder, and it takes her a little longer than I expected to answer me. "It's Nathan. That's weird—he wants to know if you want to go with him to a tattoo appointment this weekend," she responds, waiting for me to give an answer.

"Yeah, maybe," I answer aloud, trying to sound indifferent.

"What's your password? I can respond for you." Chantal gets ahead of me.

Off the top of my head, I'm not sure what our thread of text messages looks like. I'm suddenly thankful I put a lock on my phone. "That's okay, I'll just answer him later."

Chantal sits back in her seat. "So have you guys been hanging out more?"

"Yeah, a little bit," the same lie as a few weeks ago slips out. "That's not uncommon for us, though." I wouldn't normally explain myself like this, and based on the look she's giving me, the same thing just crossed her mind.

But she doesn't question me about it. "I wonder what he's going to get."

"I'll let you know when I find out," I respond, not thinking.

"So, you are going to go, then?" Chantal eyes me carefully, unable to hide her surprise.

"Should I not?"

"If you want to go, you should go."

Not sure of what else to say, I try to lighten the mood: "Maybe I'll get one while I'm there."

"Pfft, yeah okay," she says, stressing the vowels.

"Hey! I've thought about it, but nothing stands out as important enough to be on my body forever," I respond in defense.

"I just can't see you all tatted."

I laugh. "It's not like I'm scheduling an appointment to cover my entire body."

"I know, I know. I don't know why I'm acting shocked; you'd chicken out before you got one, anyways."

I roll my eyes at her. "Well, if I decide to get one, will you go with me? And make sure I don't chicken out?"

Chantal hesitates for a moment, pondering. "You promise?"

Holding up my fist, pinky out, I offer it to her. "Promise."

Christmas seems right around the corner. The temperature outside keeps dropping, and people are in a frenzy driving around getting any and all early shopping done. I consider whether or not I should be getting Nathan a Christmas present. Any other year, I normally would, but this year has different circumstances. We're in uncharted territory. A couple ideas come to me, but they're all trivial. I don't want to give Nathan a meaningless gift. But I'm also not sure what I want it to mean. This will have to be something I wait on until I can put more thought into it.

When I arrive at the tattoo parlor, the heavily inked woman behind the front counter points me in the direction of the room Nathan is in. Although it's unnecessary; I would have been able to find him myself. His deep voice bellows from the room down the hall. The first thing I see when I reach the room is the artist delicately peeling the stencil off Nathan's broad back. The purple lines of the stencil add even more definition to his muscles.

"You've got company," the stranger says to him, catching my movement in the doorway. "Come in, I won't bite." He lets out a raspy laugh. He sounds like he's a smoker.

Nathan turns around to face me and smiles, his dimples becoming visible. I've been caught in the doorway staring. It shouldn't be as big of a deal, but for some reason, I feel embarrassed, like a kid that was caught with her hand in the cookie jar.

"Sorry! I don't know why I got hung up right there," I admit.

Nathan walks over to the mirrors to check the placement. Looking more closely, I see it's what looks like a Viking warrior. I remember the conversation with Chantal. Maybe I should text her what it is, but I know I'm not going to.

"What made you decide on this?" My body moves closer, wanting to get a better look at it or him.

"My ancestry." I can hear the smile in his voice before he turns to face me, giving me a chaste kiss on the corner of my mouth. A small part of me wants to be mad at his public display of affection, but he chose a shop far enough where no one knows us, so I let it go. Besides, another part of me liked the feel of him doing it somewhere that wasn't private.

"You ready?" the tattoo artist asks, his machine already buzzing.

"Let's do it." Nathan straddles the seat to give open access to his back.

The vibration of the handheld tattoo gun is incredibly intimidating. I hold Nathan's hand, all the while knowing this is more about having physical contact and less about his comfort. He doesn't seem phased by the tiny needle going over and over again on his skin. I watch the process in fascination.

"Thank you for inviting me to come with you," I tell him.

His thumb rubs circles on my hand as he pulls it up to his mouth. "I would say you're welcome, but it was more for me."

We hardly speak after that. I'm too invested watching the artist work, and he's too busy guiding his hand leisurely up and down the side of my thigh. I can barely think straight. The subtle movement gives the butterflies in my stomach wings.

The man whose name I never learn goes over tattoo care as he's bandaging Nathan. It all sounds pretty straightforward. The artist made it clear I might have to help him clean it, since it's in a difficult place to reach. Nathan and I end up agreeing to meet back at his place. We make a deal that I'll grab dinner while he gets the correct soap and ointment for his new ink.

The smell from the Chinese food I've picked up is wafting through my car, causing my mouth to water. I'm starving. I drive as quickly as I can to his house. I don't beat him home, though. Grabbing the food, I run into the house and trip on a rogue shoe that's by the front door. Like a newborn baby foal, I lose my balance and slip. I accidentally bang my elbow on the way down and end up yelling and dropping the food everywhere. I have hot fried rice and General Tso's sauce all over the bottom part of my sweater, sleeves, and somehow my hair.

I hear heavy footsteps. "What happened?"

I can't even answer, because seriously, what the hell happened?

"Just leave the food there; we'll call in pizza," he says, reaching out for my hand to help me step over the mess I've made. "You can take a shower." I follow his lead down the hall to the master bathroom. My eyes scan the floor-to-ceiling tile. I'll never get used to how beautiful it is and that he did it himself.

I groan. "Thank you. Do you mind getting me a towel?" I ask, noticing the towel rack is empty.

"I'll be right back."

Taking off my shoes first, I can't bring myself to look in the mirror. Nathan comes back and lays a towel and some of his clothes on the vanity. I hadn't even thought about what I would wear, but the thought fades.

"You can give me your clothes when you get out, and I'll throw them in the laundry for you."

An idea comes over me. "You don't need to wait," I respond, slowly stripping off my sweater.

The air around me chills my skin, causing goosebumps. Lowering the dirty sweater from my arms, I search his face. Nathan's eyes slowly descend. He's never seen me without a shirt. I'm still wearing a bra, but still. This feels more intimate than him seeing me in a bathing suit. This time, he's seeing what's his. I just hope he doesn't pull away again. I wouldn't be able to take it. My eyes don't leave his face as I fumble with my jeans before pushing them down to my ankles. Standing up, I'm glad I decided to wear pretty panties. The emerald-green thong makes my skin look smooth and elegant. His cheeks have a pink flush to them. I know he said we had time, but I'm tired of waiting. Thankfully, he doesn't make me. Nathan inches closer to me, his hands circling behind my back, unclasping the demi bra. The barely-there lace falls quickly, exposing my breasts.

The rough inhale he takes lets me know how affected he is by me. His mouth hovers over mine, not quite making contact. He's drawing this out. Nathan runs his fingertips down my back around my rib cage to cup my chest. My nipples ache at the feel of his calloused fingers over them. I can't take it anymore.

Reaching up on my tiptoes, I kiss him, entwining my arms around his neck. His big hands travel down my torso until they reach my hips. He squeezes so hard I whimper. His mouth tastes so good, and I feel like I'm in a trance. This kiss tells me how much he's been holding himself back from me. His tongue caresses mine before he bites my lips. Nathan's hands move to my butt so he can lift me up to his chest. Wrapping my legs around his waist, I feel ignited. This position puts me above him, and I gladly take control. I twist my hands in his hair, and on the sides of his neck, I pour everything I've felt for this man into my kiss.

Nathan sets me down on the sink, breaking contact for a millisecond so he can slide off his shirt. I reach out to touch his chest, marveling at how painstakingly beautiful he is. I rip at his jeans, guiding them down until they're at his knees. I need more. Reading my mind or my body, he lowers his hand between my legs. Even over the fabric, his touch makes my eyes close. But then he pulls his hand away, and I'm left cold.

"Nate," is all I get out.

His deft fingers return, slipping past my panties, finding the most delicate side of me. He's only just begun sinking in, and I feel the rubber band that is my body wind tighter and tighter with each movement he makes. Nathan swallows my moans, leaning down to kiss and lick at my mouth while his hand invades me.

"More, more, I need more," I moan into his mouth.

Nathan withdraws, pulling me from the sink and whirling me into his adjoining bedroom. He lowers us to the bed, and I frantically push at his boxers, freeing him. Pulling my panties to the side, he eases himself in, allowing my body to get used to his intrusion. It's too much; I feel my body stretching to take him in. But it's not enough.

Making sure not to mess with the bandage on his back, my nails dig into his flawless skin, pulling him in closer. He stifles his groan, and his hands clench the bedsheets while I circle my hips underneath him, making him lose his mind. Our breaths quicken, as does his pace. I want to unpack and live in this moment. My eyelids close, feeling too heavy to stay open. Pressure builds within my body, begging to be released. Nathan's expert movements push me higher and higher, shattering me in the process. I lie weak beneath him when he shudders through his release.

Bliss. Pure, euphoric bliss. Nothing will be able to knock this smile off my face. Somehow in the post-sex haze, Nathan rolls off me and I onto him. My head is in the crook of his shoulder, where I lay with my eyes closed, going over what just took place.

"Well, I'm glad I didn't turn the shower on yet. All the hot water would be gone." I giggle playfully.

He sits up and looks down at my naked body. "Yeah."

He doesn't have any of the flirty attitude I'm used to. He feels a tad restrained again.

"You okay?" I ask carefully, sitting up with him.

"Yeah, why don't you hop in the shower, and I'll call for food."

Placing my chin on his shoulder, I try to entice him. "Or, you could shower with me and call after."

There's something in his expression that makes me nervous. He scans my face, searching for something. I can't tell. He inches forward and kisses my forehead and then the tip of my nose. "That's okay. I've got some things I can do while you're in there." He declines, standing up to slip his pants back on.

"Okay."

I'm confused and a little hurt by the rejection. I enter the bathroom wanting to wash the remaining food off of me. Stepping into the waterfall of hot water, I lather soap over my body. I wish I could have left the remnants of him on me longer. It feels wrong for me to wash away the evidence of our lovemaking. My smile from before comes back as I recall his skillful lips and what he felt like when he let go. It's a shame it's taken us this long to allow ourselves to feel this. A lightbulb flicks on in my brain. That must be why he was acting weird. This is the first time we've gone past the line. Cutting the water off, I step out of the walk-in shower to dry myself off.

When I'm mostly dry and dressed in a pair of his sweatpants and a long-sleeved T-shirt, I exit his room. I don't see Nathan anywhere, but I do see the food still lying by the front door. I search for paper towels, but the roll is empty. Typical guy. Remembering he keeps the rolls in the garage, I open his kitchen door that leads into his garage. I scan the room before finding them down the stairs. Black bags are in my way. Moving them, I grab two rolls just to be sure I have enough. Then, I hear something behind me. I turn around, and Nathan is standing at the door.

"What're you doing in here?" he asks with a gruff tone.

"Grabbing paper towels. You were out of them in the kitchen."

He looks down at the bags I've moved. "Are you going through my stuff? Get out of the garage. Don't touch my things!" he says in a rush.

My throat swells. "You can't be serious," I respond, my voice small. Walking up the small staircase back into the house, I put the rolls on the table and face him.

"Do not go in my garage." His voice is raised.

Nathan stomps angrily to the back of the house. I stand in the middle of the invisible havoc as I listen to my heart creak and break open. He regrets what we did. That's what this is. What it has to be. Nothing else makes sense. Tears burn my eyes, making my vision blurry. But I refuse to let them fall. They can wait until I'm out of his house away from him.

Making a dash for it, I leave the same way I came—a mess. Tears warm my cheeks better than the heat in my car. I'm so embarrassed. Tonight meant everything to me, but I was the only one. *How could I be so stupid? Was this just a conquest to him? Maybe I pushed him too hard.* He didn't seem that bothered about it, though. I think back to the way he looked at me with such hunger as his fingers buried themselves in me while I moaned for him. I physically shake the thought from my head. It doesn't matter how good it was.

As I step foot into my dark and empty house, my stomach growls. It dawns on me that I didn't eat dinner. Despite the noises my stomach is making, I don't have an appetite. I don't bother turning any lights on as I go further into the house. Making it to my bedroom, I crawl into my desolate bed. The sheets are cold; it seems fitting. Pulling the buzzing phone from my sweatpants, I see several missed calls from Nathan. My face feels sticky and tight from crying. Taking a deep breath, I wipe my face and decide to save what little dignity I have.

Opening our text messages, I begin typing; **It's okay. You don't have to explain. Let's forget about it.**

Setting my phone on the empty side of the bed beside me, I hear it vibrate once more. I ignore the text that's just come in. I'm sure it's from him, but I don't care to read it right now. Lying down, I smell his eucalyptus shampoo in my damp hair and his Gain laundry detergent on my—*his* clothes. Oh my god, we have each other's clothes. I'll worry about exchanging them later. I can't possibly add that concern to my plate tonight. An hour ago, I thought I'd be spooned in his strong arms as I fell asleep and maybe even woken up with morning sex. But reality is a cruel, cruel joke. Instead, I smell like the man who rocked my world, then crushed it. *How am I going to fall asleep like this?*

CHAPTER 16
DANI, PRESENT DAY

A cluster of burnt orange and light pink dances across the sky, filtering through my blinds. The colors usually are beautiful, but this morning, they fall flat. I managed to fall asleep last night around one in the morning. The calls and incessant texts faded an hour before that. With six hours of sleep under my belt, I decide it's time to face the music. Grabbing my phone from the empty side of the bed where I left it, I see seventeen unread text messages, eight missed calls, and two voicemails. My eyes sting from the bright light on my phone and the lack of sleep. I move past the voicemails. I can't bear to listen to them. I know they'll be half-assed apologies, and I'll fall for his sexy voice. Going through the messages, they're all from him, except one. I tap Chantal's name first.

What're your plans for this week?

I'll respond later. Nathan's are next, and I'm ashamed to say how eager I am to read them.

Call me please.

I'm so sorry.

I overreacted.

Dani answer your phone.

Please.

I didn't mean it.

I'm so so sorry.

Give me another chance.

Please forgive me.

Please pick up the phone.

I'm begging you.

Let me know you got home okay. I just want to know you're safe.

And so on. The rest are pretty much the same. I'm surprised he didn't drive over here after I left, although I'm glad he didn't. I'm not sure what triggered his reaction last night, but I need some space to wrap my head around it. I don't feel quite as sad as I did, which feels like a step in the right direction. I'm just overall disappointed. Reading his words again, I get hung up on his last text. Guilt slowly washes over me. His brother died in a car accident, leaving us waiting. I should have been more sensitive to that, even while I was ignoring him. I don't call him, still not ready to hear his voice, but I type quickly.

I'm home. Sorry if I worried you.

Staring at the message, my finger hovers over the send button. I don't owe him a response. But I send it anyway. I know I will feel worse if I say nothing at all.

Time passes, and I receive no response. It's just as well. *I wouldn't have answered, anyway,* I tell myself. Pride sits in the corner of every room I'm in, licking its wounds.

Around lunchtime, Maureen and Pat's home phone calls me. I'm definitely not in the mood for chitchat, but I don't know if it's important or if they need something.

I reluctantly answer, "Hello?"

"I'm coming over," my lover's voice fills my ear, shocking my system, before he hangs up not needing a response.

My body buzzes already reacting to the man on the phone. Damn him! He's tricked me. He knew I wouldn't answer his calls, so he called me on his parent's phone.

I need to make sure I look okay. I hate that I care. Rushing to the bathroom, I rake my fingers through my hair before guiding it into a ponytail. I'm still in his clothes from last night. I go to my room and begin pulling out a pair of blue jeans and my lounge sweatshirt. After I get dressed, I go over my appearance in my mirror. I don't look the best, but honestly, anything feels better than the idea of him seeing me in his clothes looking a mess.

When he arrives, Nathan walks right in like usual, but with more hesitancy. I'm sitting on my couch, pretending to be invested in some British reality show. Little does he know I've only just turned it on and have no idea what's happening. He sits down a cushion's length away from me, coat still on.

"Thank you for letting me stop by," he says, sounding nervous.

I keep my eyes forward on the TV and aim to sound unaffected, "Didn't seem like I had a choice."

"You always have a choice. You could have locked the door."

Is he serious? I couldn't lock him out if I tried. I just rushed around my room making sure I looked at least half decent before he showed up. "What do you want, Nathan? Why are you here?" My real feelings edge through my tone. The anger doesn't come close to the anguish in my stomach. I turn to face him, and that's when I see it. The exhaustion. He doesn't look like he slept any better than I did.

"I'm so sorry I flipped out on you last night. I was out of line. We had an amazing night, and I ruined it." His red eyes stare back at me.

"Why did you?"

"Being with you like that made me nervous. I had a lot going on in my head, and I took it out on you. It will never happen again."

I can tell he's being truthful, but there's more he's not letting me in on. I can feel it, and I'm not sure how much I want to push him.

"Can I have another chance, please?" he begs. "When I came back out and you were gone, I got so worried. I knew I had messed up, and I was scared of what you were thinking."

I give him my honesty. "I was thinking you regretted sleeping with me."

"No, not for a second," he refutes, scooting forward toward me. "Last night was perfect. You were perfect."

All of his words sound like ear candy. I want to believe him, but could I allow him back in my bed again?

Nathan's voice is low, "Dani, I'm sorry I hurt you." His facial features are scrunched together. His discomfort over the situation eases mine.

"Don't do it again." My resolve weakens, and I sit up, going to him.

Nathan pulls me the rest of the way onto his lap, and I go willingly. His arms tighten around my body while I take his face in my hands. "I mean it. Don't do it again," I repeat myself.

"Never again," he says in agreement. His eyes are full of lust as he stares at my mouth.

Leaning down, I take what is mine and kiss him with slow, shallow laps of my tongue. His hands waste no time exploring my bare back under my sweatshirt. Goosebumps rise against Nathan's cold fingers, and I wiggle against the chill. Breaking out of his arms, I stand up in front of him. His wide eyes look up at me, dazed. I hold out my hand, and Nathan takes it gratefully. A coy smile plays on my lips as I lead him down to my room and allow him to apologize more than once.

With the holidays being only a few days away, it's Tav's patrons' favorite time around the restaurant. Skinny Christmas trees are placed in corners and garland twirls around the railings. Looking up, I see the beautiful blanket of twinkling lights covering the ceiling. It reminds me of my wedding reception. They are the same lights we had that night too. I smile at the memory, relieved that no grief follows.

"What're you over there smiling about?" Chantal asks.

"Nothing. I just remembered something," I say more to myself.

"Next time, remind me I don't want to work the holiday shifts," she groans. "I'll be going on vacation."

"Suit yourself."

Tonight will be busy. It seems counterintuitive, given how close to Christmas it is. But people have family visiting in for the holidays and would rather not cook. Plus, this week starts our holiday parties. Chantal always jokes about work, but truth be told, she loves it here. This place wouldn't run as smoothly without her. And she knows it.

I've been walking around with this lump in my pocket, and it is not working for me. I leave my staff and head back to my office, needing to deposit my jacket and its contents. Removing the black box from my pocket, I readjust the green ribbon it's adorned with, setting it in my desk drawer. It'll wait there until tonight when I see him. I instantly become giddy. Once I decided what it was that I wanted to give Nathan for Christmas, the days dragged on at a snail's pace. I just hope he likes it.

Coming out of my office to stretch my legs, I see Phyllis before anyone else. She's in her festive red jumpsuit tonight with a multicolored lightbulb headband where the lights flicker. She sips her cocktail, looking unbothered.

"Have you put your name in for the raffle yet, Ms. Phyllis?"

"Only about a dozen times," she answers me with a lift of her drink in cheers. "Are you all done with your shopping?"

"Finished this morning and got almost everything wrapped." The holiday spirit emanates from me.

I've always loved giving gifts. That's why I brought Nathan's gift tonight; because I can't wait another day. Knowing I'll see him after work, I grabbed it when I left for Tav's.

There is a tingling sensation on the back of my neck. Twisting my head, I search the crowded room. I feel his presence before I see him. I'm amazed how in tune with someone you can be. I spot him weaving through people, aiming for the table nearest to us. *Never wanting to be far from me*, I think, biting my lip to keep from smiling. I'm a little surprised he came in. It isn't totally unlike him to stop by, but Nathan hadn't mentioned it beforehand. My heart flutters in my chest at the sight of him. I'm falling in love. The thought stops me in my tracks. That can't be. It's too soon.

Nathan waves at me across the two tables between us, then mouths, *You look pretty.* It's impossible to contain the flush that rushes up my neck and rests on my cheeks.

"Did someone turn the heat up in here?" Phyllis's raspy voice breaks me out of what felt like a private moment.

"Huh?"

"You and what's-his-name makin' eyes at each other."

"We might need to cut you off if you keep spouting crazy ideas, Phyllis," I respond, deflecting.

"Uh-huh. I'm old; I'm not blind," she says pointing her bony finger.

After that, I keep myself moving, making my way around the busy restaurant and checking in with anybody who might need help. Everyone is doing great. Letting out a relieved sigh, I accept there is not a whole lot I need to do.

Jenna, one of my younger waitresses, finds me. "Table five wants to talk to the manager."

The poor girl looks nervous, but I know the table. Following her out, I spot them.

"Why are you worrying my waitress?" I zero in on Travis and Nathan. I turn to look at Jenna. "It's okay, I know them. They try to make me wait on them every time they're here."

"We wanted to say hi," Travis claims.

"Hi," Nathan cuts in, his voice deep and drenched in sex.

The hairs on my body stand straight up, begging for him to touch me. My voice betrays me by shaking. "Hi! Now, *Jenna* will take good care of you both."

I guide the young girl forward, walking away. Every nerve in my body is on and firing. I'd like to dump a bucket of water on my head to cool off, but I'm afraid I would short circuit.

The music that filters through Tav's is practically nonexistent when I'm in the back office. I don't hear the busyness of the front, but the soft noise of the kitchen close by does filter in. I like the quiet. It allows me to focus on my tasks and get everything I can done. Over the next hour, a couple of my waitresses come back to vent about bad tippers or other crappy customers. I let them get it out and send them on their way.

I hear a knock on my door, but no one immediately comes in. What could it be this time? Instead of a disgruntled employee, Nathan rushes in. My cheeks practically rise up to meet my eyes, involuntarily beaming at him. "Hey."

"I'm sorry if this isn't allowed," his voice comes out husky while he strides around my desk. "I just couldn't possibly wait until tonight." Grabbing my arms, he guides me up into his.

Our lips meet in between us, and it's a slow and meaningful kiss before it builds and becomes frenzied. His hands go into my hair, lightly pulling on the tresses, and I want nothing more in this moment than to take him on my desk. But my dream is just that, a dream. Breaking the kiss, my erratic heart threatens to beat out of my chest.

"I'm glad you came back here. I have something for you, and I couldn't wait, either. Or, more like didn't want to." I'm breathless. Opening the drawer, I pull out the box. I'm suddenly nervous about how he'll take it. His dimples give away his excitement while he eyes me cautiously. Sliding the green ribbon off, he opens the top and just studies it. Nathan says nothing for four very long seconds. Insecurity sets in. This was a mistake. I feel like I've been cut open and am left vulnerable for him to see.

I'm the first to break the silence, "If you don't like it, that's okay."

He finally looks at me. "Not like it? I love it! I can't believe you're giving this to me," he exclaims. I follow his movements as he slides the old watch out of the box and wraps the brown leather around his wrist, fastening it. Giving the watch to him was much easier this time than the first. He reaches forward, thanking me with a tangle of his lips, and then he's gone.

Hours later, the party has died down, and closing time looms. I'm making my final lap around the restaurant, double-checking certain areas. I stop by Chantal to see how her night has been going.

"The usual," she says, annoyed, while she avoids meeting my eyes.

"Okay, well, I'm going home. Are you okay?"

Chantal doesn't answer me. "Got it. Thought it was interesting Nathan had Joel's watch on when he left." She says with no actual interest.

I feel like I'm in a trance, answering without a physical question. "I gave it to him as a Christmas gift."

"I figured. He seemed to disappear for a while." Her tone is loaded with suggestion.

"He came back to say goodbye. I happened to have it with me. So, I gave it to him early," I rebut. I'm swimming in a pool of dread, trying to buy my time. She doesn't question me any further.

We're getting sloppy. That's two people who have noticed odd behavior tonight. We need to be more careful. What would have happened if she had heard us? Nathan and I don't know where this is going yet. My mind is going a mile a minute. I attempt to let it all go for a different day. All I want is Nathan, so I head to the home I've stayed at twice this week.

The following night, we swap Nathan's house for mine. I was content to stay, but he decided traditions needed to be resurrected.

"I can't believe you never built a gingerbread house when you were a kid," Nathan chides me while he squeezes icing on the corners of the cookies.

"Well then, you'll be shocked to know I hardly watched any Christmas movies, either," I admit back to him. "It wasn't my parents' thing, doing stuff like this with me." I don't mean for it to sound as sad as it did, but Nathan picks up on it nonetheless.

"They missed out," he says with a wink.

I've come to enjoy being home with him, either at my house or his. Simple acts, like building a gingerbread house together, hold more weight. That's just Nathan's way. Everything is easy, but it's meaningful.

He runs his finger along the cookie to smooth out the icing and presses the last piece into its place. "Now we can decorate it."

I feel like a little kid, enthusiastic about how my side will turn out. Designing the snow-covered rooftop, the icing doesn't adhere the way I thought it would. I now understand why he was using his finger. Mimicking his trick, I rub my finger over the icing and am surprised by how much better it works for me. Opening the little pouch of candies, I sprinkle the glittery snowflakes on the fake snow.

I end up absentmindedly sucking the sugar off my fingertips. "Oh my god! You should try this."

Nathan laughs at my naivety. "I know, it's good, right?"

I lift the packet to his open mouth and squeeze as hard as I can. It explodes with a pop, getting icing everywhere. Thick icing covers his mouth and chin. He looks ridiculous, and I can't help but belly laugh at the image.

"Think this is funny?" he asks, lunging for me and kissing all over my face to transfer his mess.

I'm still laughing as I protest. I catch him midway over me and bring his face down to mine. I kiss his sugar-coated lips, and he tastes decadent. The warmth from our mouths smears the white goo across the two of us. I'm trying to be careful where I place my hands because they were caught in the explosion, too, and I'm not sure he wants the icing in his hair or on his clothes. The idea of having to clean each other up is tempting. The doorbell brings us to an unfortunate stop. Pulling away, I compose myself as best I can. When I get to the door, Nathan follows, trying to catch me.

"You still have icing all over your mouth!" He laughs, although it's still covering his face.

Opening the door, we both freeze. Chantal stands there staring between the two of us. "I knew it!" she spews at us and then turns away to leave.

Desperate to explain myself, I follow her to her car. "Please, please talk to me."

"You've been lying to me."

Word vomit spills out, "I'm so sorry! I wanted to tell you so many times."

"But you didn't. How long has this been going on?" She's eerily calm.

"After Thanksgiving." I spill all the lies I've told. "But . . . we kissed on Halloween."

She looks at me thinking, connecting all the dots. "That's why he broke up with me?"

"Yes. Chantal, I never wanted to hurt—" Tears prickle my eyes as she looks at me disgusted.

"Yeah, yeah, that's what they all say."

"Please don't say anything. We're not telling people yet." I beg.

"Unbelievable." She's unable to mask the hurt. "You know I gave you chance after chance to be honest with me about how you felt about him, and you still chose to lie."

"I know! I was wrong. I was worried about what you would think," I cry.

"Well, congratulations, Dani. Now I just think you're a liar," Chantal says before slamming her door in my face and driving off.

I linger in the cold for a minute longer, staring at where her car just was. Shuffling my feet, I enter my house. The heat from inside feels too hot on my cold cheeks. I rest the weight of my body on the wooden door and just stare at Nathan, who's been waiting for me.

"You okay?"

Am I? I'm pretty sure my best friend hates me. Her reaction was valid, though. I had been lying for a very long time; and, truth be told, I don't know how I would have reacted had I found this out. I worry this will change everything. The mood inside has already shifted so much; we're no longer in the Christmas spirit. Not wanting to add to it, I shrug at his question. "Guess we'll see tomorrow."

It never ceases to amaze me how early my mom is willing to call me and complain about something I'm doing. Huddled over a steaming cup of coffee, I listen to her go on and on about the benefits of water versus coffee. Disregarding the fact that it's 7:15 a.m., she's forced me to beat the sun up with this phone call. I drink the coffee.

"But anyways, Merry Christmas, dear," she says with a sigh.

"Merry Christmas, Mom."

"Your father and I wished you could have come up since you don't have anyone anymore." But what she really wants to say is "since I'm all alone." Being alone is unfathomable to Cindy Davis.

"I'm not alone. I have Joel's family," I say quietly, hoping not to wake the naked man in my bed. Nope, definitely not alone. I smile to myself as I sip my coffee.

"Those people aren't your real family. You don't have any real ties to them anymore. Joel's dead honey. Us—we're your family," she explains.

I inwardly groan. My mother's problem is she truly believes she's being helpful yet doesn't have enough compassion to know she just insulted me. I'm not sure I'm awake enough to pick this fight. "We've been over this."

"But I have someone I want you to meet. His name is Devon—" she practically croons.

"No," I interject midsentence.

She ignores me. "He's a doctor."

"No. I will not have you set me up."

"Please just think about it. Maybe you could move back home," she suggests, like it's the simplest thing.

"Mom, my life is here. I have family and friends here." *Although my best friend isn't speaking to me*, I don't say out loud.

My floor creaks, telling me Nathan is coming down the hallway. He enters my kitchen half-dressed and rubbing his eyes. The sight of him wakes me up more than the coffee. "I'll talk to you later, okay? I've got to go, Mom," I hang up the phone with my gaze still on him. "Did I wake you?"

"It's okay. What did your mom want?" His sleepy voice might be my favorite. Nathan moves about my kitchen to pour himself coffee, already comfortable in my space.

"She's found me a doctor to marry." Sarcasm spills off my tongue.

A yawn mixed with laughter echoes from his chest. "What about a teacher?"

My heart jumps into my throat. "What?"

"It was a joke," he warns. "A bad joke. So, did you mention you were seeing anyone?"

"No. Why would I?" I'm confused where this is going.

"She's your mom. I figured because she doesn't live down here it would be okay if you told her."

"Not my mom. I couldn't give her any sliver of information without her being able to weasel it all out of me."

"Chantal knows now. I don't see why we can't tell people."

"And Chantal's mad, Nathan. How is that a good example?"

He rolls his eyes. "She'll get over it."

"I'm not ready for everyone to know. This was not specifically about Chantal," I argue.

His voice is stern. "You're not the only one in this relationship."

"Don't you think I know that? I was also married just six months ago." My chest grows tight while our argument builds.

"I'm tired of keeping my feelings for you hidden. I'm tired of being a secret," Nathan confesses, the muscles in his shoulders bulging with tension.

"Maybe we should stop this, then, before it gets too serious."

Hurt is etched across his face, his eyes cast down at me. "We both know it isn't that simple. We're more than that."

I shrug, acting unaffected by his admission, pushing my walls back up—the same walls he took so much care chiseling down.

"Are you willing to toss us away that quickly?" Nathan criticizes.

"I think I jumped into this too quickly. I need to take a step back and get some clarity."

"What am I supposed to do? Wait for you to be ready?" he asks, his anger rising with volume.

"I'm not asking you to do that. You could call that Amanda girl," I say, adding the final nail in the coffin.

"Yeah, maybe I'll do that!" he contests, storming off to get dressed.

I'm frozen in my kitchen as I listen to Nathan pack his things. Panic is coursing through me. I can feel it with every frantic beat of my heart. The worst part is, I did not mean a word I said. I felt like a caged animal being backed into a corner with no other choice. My legs are cemented to my chair, and I'm silently screaming at them to move. *Move and tell him you're sorry! You don't mean any of it!* But they don't. They rest against the wood, not caring that I've just pushed him away because I'm scared. Like the coward I am, I wait to see if he'll say anything else. He doesn't.

Once he's dressed, he walks out of my house without a goodbye or even glance in my direction. With the slam of the door, my tears fall, and I'm left wondering if this is really better than if people knew.

CHAPTER 17
DANI, PRESENT DAY

I plant myself down on the ground, trying to get comfortable and set my thermos on the stone ledge in front of me.

"Well, I've certainly made a mess of things lately," I talk to the ground.

I'm a mess. It's been over a week since Nathan or Chantal have spoken to me. Silence fills the space around me. I don't know what I expected coming here, but for some reason, silence isn't it. I'm too in my head. Maybe if I keep talking out loud, it'll help me.

"What am I going to do, Joel? What should I do?" I ask him, feeling defeated. "If you were here, I know what you'd tell me." I chuckle at the thought and deepen my voice, "Babe, you're worrying about things that don't matter. What do you want?"

I sit in stillness, thinking about that question and all it's possible answers. That was just like him, to never worry about other people's opinions. I look around the cemetery: the trees are bare, and the grass has turned brown. Everything here looks depressing. It looks like I've been feeling. The winter chill has picked up since Christmas. Tilting my head up toward the gray sky, I see tiny snowflakes begin to fall.

I look back at the smooth stone and talk to the inanimate object. "It wasn't supposed to be like this. I wasn't supposed to feel anything at all." The freezing air prickles my face as I'm overcome with regret. "I'm sorry, maybe the anniversary of our wedding isn't the best choice to come here and tell you, but I love your brother." The tightness in my shoulders ease with the weight of my secret being removed from them. "Maybe this was what I needed. I needed to tell you." I sigh. "Thank you for listening. You know, as the day approached, I didn't know what I would do, but I'm glad I came here."

My hair whips around my face as the wind picks up, I raise my wrist to check the time. I have to go, or I'll be late. I feel like I've only just gotten here, but the time tells me I've been here almost an hour. It's a shame. Normally, I wouldn't want to linger around the cemetery, but I feel at peace right in this moment. I reluctantly push myself off the ground and get ready to leave. Maggie will only wait for so long.

It's always stumped me how Maggie's room contradicts itself. It's made to look decorated and homey, but I feel like I'm put on a stage. It's stuffy, yet there is a slight draft. And it always starts the same. Maggie's good about getting me talking even when I don't know where to start.

"How are you?" Her monotone question feels loaded.

Crossing my legs, I move a throw pillow from the corner of the couch over my stomach and wrap my arms around it. It's something I've been doing since I started therapy, but I didn't notice until she pointed it out to me. "It's like armor you're holding on to, shielding yourself," she told me.

"I went to see Joel today. It would have been our fourth wedding anniversary," I answer.

"What did you talk about?"

"Nathan, mostly," I tell her, recalling the visit. Maggie isn't surprised. She has picked up on my feelings toward him. She doesn't say anything, patiently waiting to see if I have more to say. "We're not talking," I finally add.

"I'm so sorry to hear that. What happened?" she asks with compassion.

"I pushed him away." The truth flows out of me. "He practically begged me to be open with everyone about him and our relationship. And I couldn't do it." Pent-up tears slide down my cheeks.

Maggie tucks a loose, gray strand of hair behind her ear as she scribbles on the notepad in her lap. When she stops, her eyes meet mine, to make sure I'm listening. "Have you considered the depth of which you were living in Joel's world? I mean, you had mentioned earlier in our visits not feeling like your own person because you were so focused on him and his needs."

I sit with her question, replaying the last four years of my life. It's not the first time I've done it, but this time is the first where I feel like I'm watching a movie. I'm removed from the chaos instead of reliving the pain, fear, and grief over again.

Maggie continues, "What do you want in your life right now?"

"I want to be with Nathan, but—" I admit for the first time aloud. The tears dissipate, drying on my face.

"No buts. Why can't you let yourself have this?" she asks, forcing me to reflect.

"It's only been six months since my husband died. It's too soon, and with his brother, people would lose their minds."

"You know, I have a lot of clients who are going through the same thing. Clients who are going through a divorce or who have lost a loved one. They're all feeling it too. How will it look if they move on, and what's the right amount of time to grieve? You are not alone in feeling like this. There is no rule book for grieving, Dani. No one has the right to tell you what you should feel or shouldn't do. Especially because they weren't involved in your marriage to begin with," she states with soft precision.

Her words give me strength as our session continues. "But I keep pushing him away. What if this was the last time?" My worry is evident.

"Then that is something you'll have to face," her soft voice is honest. "You won't know how he feels until you try to talk to him. He may surprise you."

When I enter my house after my therapy session, I stand in the middle of the living room and absorb what my life looks like. I'm not surprised that the rooms feel emptier without him. Nathan always brightened the space he occupied. This house was no different. I'm certain one of the main reasons Joel and I bought it was his brother's excitement during the first walk-through and his ability to paint a wonderful picture of what our life could look like here. Warm, amber eyes danced as he spoke of backyard parties, babies, a swing set, and sunsets on the porch. I clearly remember that exact moment: it was the first time I admitted to myself we were changing. Nathan and I looked at one another longer and more frequently.

Pacing around, I'm unsure of what move I should make next. I swallow my nerves and dial Nathan's number but hang up on the second ring. *How am I going to do this?* I have no idea what I'll say, or what to do if he pushes me away. My cell phone dings, and my heart rate gallops. He's probably wondering why I called. As I stare down at the screen, my heart sinks. It's not him. It's a mass text from Travis.

Party at my place tonight. Bring whoever.

I manage to wipe away the hopelessness and look at this as a good thing. This is my chance to see him in person. I get ready with as much patience as I can muster, slipping on my white, off-the-shoulder top that fits me like a glove. I bring something my mother ingrained in me to fruition: if you have to apologize, look your best while you do it. I slide a pink gloss over my lips—my last touch before I'm ready. Butterflies sit in my stomach waiting for takeoff.

Determined to fix this divide I've caused between the two most important people in my life, I hastily jump into my car. Turning the key in the ignition, the car just clicks. The only other sound I hear is of my heart dropping to my stomach. This can't be happening. Laying my head on the steering wheel, I keep turning the key, hoping the car will magically roar to life. I feel beaten down when it doesn't. Calling Nathan isn't an option. I need to make up with him first before I try to ask him for any favors. Grasping at straws, I resort to calling Pat. He picks up on the first ring and agrees right away.

After some time, he pulls up in his old station wagon, and my worries are alleviated.

"I come with a gift," he says, holding a car battery.

"Thank you. You're a lifesaver," I say gratefully.

"Well, don't you look dolled up." His words are almost lost underneath my car's hood as he unhooks my dead battery.

Getting approval from the most fatherly figure in my life makes me feel validated. "There is a party tonight."

"That must be where Nathan was going."

I hang on to his words, needing to know more. "Oh, did Nathan mention he was going?" I inquire, feigning no real interest.

"He was dressed up, so I suppose," his hands move, working in the belly of the engine.

"Cool. Maybe I'll see him there."

"Ya know, I'm glad you two have each other, as friends," he says thoughtfully.

"He's a good guy."

"And you, you're a wonderful girl. I'm not going to stand here and pretend I know what all Joel put you through when he was alive, because I don't. Maureen and I have our suspicions, but I'm sure it's only a little accurate. You deserve more than what he gave you, and I know I'm not the only Stephensen man to tell you that," he stares at me, making his point clear.

Today has been a whirlwind day, but I feel more ready to face whatever comes. I've been so worried and naive about this whole thing. I only hope I haven't screwed it up for good. I reflect on Pat's words. I should be happy. I deserve to be happy! Nathan was always helpful and compassionate from the very beginning, even when I was married to his brother. And in some ways, he was a better partner than Joel. That's never changed, even after Joel's death. He helped me grieve and shared some of his hurt so I wouldn't feel so alone.

When Pat clicks the new hunk of metal in place, he signals me to start the car. Nervous it's not going to work, I close my eyes in anticipation. My old girl roars, causing me to turn the corners of my mouth upward.

"Thank you, thank you, thank you!" I exclaim, bouncing out of the car.

"No problem, kiddo. I know you normally ask Nate for help, but I was happy to be called this time. I hope you guys can work out whatever is going on," he tells me, sharing that he knows a lot more than he lets on.

I pull up to Travis's building. Cars are packed in the parking lot and spilling onto the grass. Circling around the neighborhood, I park in the vacant, gravel lot behind his place. Not many people know about it. There are only a handful of cars in the lot when I get to it, but I recognize a few: Chantal's black mustang and Paul's Jeep wrangler. Great, maybe I can make amends with two people tonight.

The closer I get to the apartment complex, the louder the music becomes. I'm a little surprised the cops haven't been called with complaints. My hand vibrates from the bass when I reach the door's handle. When I slip inside, the smell of alcohol and sweaty bodies hits me in the face. The whole scene reminds me of a college party. I toss my coat on the back of a chair and head into the kitchen to grab a drink to ease my nerves. Tapping the keg, I fill my cup until it's half full. I see a few familiar faces and smile, saying hi. It's taking every ounce of effort I have not to scour my surroundings for Nathan and Chantal. Instead, I sit back, watching the party unfold, wanting to blend in like a fixture of the room.

I notice the furniture has all been moved out of the way to make space for people to dance. Normally, I would be in the throng of them, but without my bestie, I'm not in a dancing mood. A tall body with brown hair is dancing very intimately with someone. Her hand is delicately over his shoulders while his hands squeeze her butt, pulling her closer to him. My eyes refuse to leave the back of his head, willing him to turn around. I can't swallow around the large lump that's formed in my throat. Please don't be, please don't be. As the couple twists and turns, the lump dissipates. It's not him; it's a stranger. Letting out a ragged breath, I gulp my beer.

I quickly become bored with waiting. Getting up to move around the room, I mingle as I go. I catch a glimpse of Paul talking to someone in the kitchen, but I don't dare get close to his vicinity. He is not who I want to be around tonight. Chantal comes into view first. I attempt to get close to her, but she evades me every time. She makes it simple for me to understand she doesn't want to speak to me. I'm torn between pursuing her further or granting her space. Ultimately, I choose the latter.

I don't want to chase her down and hold her hostage in a conversation she isn't ready to be a part of. I'm left praying it doesn't last forever.

Travis breaks me out of my tiny pity party, throwing himself into an awkward hug with my arms by my side. He's already drunk, and I'm about to be if I don't get away from his fumes.

"Glad you could make it," he slurs.

"Wouldn't miss it," I lie. "Who's all here?" I ask, fishing for information, since I haven't seen Nathan.

He's no longer looking at me and instead is undressing the redhead across the room with his eyes. "The usual group," Travis mumbles.

"Hey, the place looks great. Everything looks the same, though. I thought Nathan helped you move some things?" I remember when he was late.

Travis looks back at me startled, his focus intently on me. "He told you about that?"

I'm puzzled by his reaction. "Yeah, why wouldn't he?"

"Do you know if he told anyone else?" He looks around as if he's afraid someone might hear.

"I'm really confused. Why is this a big deal?" I ask, noticing he's started to sweat. "Are you okay?"

Travis crushes the rest of his beer as the barely dressed redhead struts over, distracting him, ruining any chance I have of getting answers. She giggles while she leans over and sticks her tongue in his ear. The fact that I'm present for this does not deter her.

Excusing myself, I walk around the party aimlessly. There is absolutely no sign of Nathan. My desperation gets the best of me, and I start asking people if they've seen him. But no one has because he's not here. The fluttering butterflies that flew in my stomach earlier are dead and have turned to cement blocks. I'm leaving. There is no point in me being here anymore.

Finding the chair I laid my coat on proves to be quite difficult. When I finally find it, I realize I must have walked by it several times. There's a dozen coats on top of mine, so I have to dig for it. Once it's in my arms, Paul seizes the last moment of opportunity to speak to me before I leave.

"You leaving already?"

"Yes, got a big day tomorrow," I lie.

"Here, I'll walk you out." He opens the door.

I plead, "No, that's okay! You don't have to."

"I want to," he insists.

As we cross the backyard, Paul does all the talking. About what, I have no idea. I'm not even listening. It's weird he hasn't noticed. I come to the conclusion that he really enjoys the sound of his own voice. It's fine for now because I don't have anything to add. I've really grown to dislike being around him. Everything he does feels slimy to me; the charm he portrays seems incredibly insincere and manipulative.

I manage to get a step ahead of him, trying to open my door fast, but he catches up with me. Maneuvering my keys in my hand, I try to signal my desire to leave as Paul rambles on. I want to get out of here. This night has been a colossal waste, and I feel worse than before, if that's even possible. He's leaning on my car, not taking any social cues. Annoyed by his presence, I'm yet again not listening to what he has to say. Paul misreads my body language and moves in closer, trying to kiss me.

My hands immediately go up to his chest. "Paul, I don't see you like that."

"Oh, stop playing hard to get," his arms coil around me, constricting my movement.

"I'm not playing anything. We've been over this. You and I aren't going to happen," I tell him, my irritation clear. "I've got to go."

Turning my back on him, I open my driver door, anxious to leave. Paul moves lightning quick, opening my back door and tugging me back.

He shoves me down in the backseat before I realize what's going on. He's moved on top of me and sloppily kisses my face.

"Stop! Paul, stop! No!" I try to shout, but he covers my mouth with his hand.

"Stop being a tease, Dani," he slurs angrily. He moves his other hand down my stomach to the top of my jeans. Tears begin to slide down my temples, dampening my hair, while I beg the universe to stop this. I'm kicking with all my might, bucking my body to get him off me, but he's much bigger than I am. His body doesn't budge. His gross, unwanted fingers slip underneath my jeans to stroke what's not his.

"You feel so warm on my hand," he whispers by my neck.

Vomit rises in my throat. His mouth runs across my chest. I'm trying to pry his hand off my mouth so I can scream, but nothing is working for me. I shake my head violently, attempting to move his hand even slightly. Paul laughs at my fight as his fingers scrape past my underwear, and I feel him pushing into me through his jeans. He must be distracted, though, because his pressure on my mouth lets up. I tilt my face up and down, crushing my teeth down on his hand as hard as I can. Paul screams at my assault. He looks down at his broken skin, then slaps me across my face. The slap echoes through the car.

"What is going on? Get off her!" Chantal yells, running to the car. "Are you okay?" Her voice is frantic as she yanks him by the arm out of the back seat. Paul falls to the ground but pushes up quickly before he bolts from the scene.

Chantal carefully helps me out of the car, keeping her hands on me to make sure I can walk or don't fall apart. I'm not sure which. "I need to go home." My voice sounds weak.

"Here, I'll drive you." She coaxes me into my passenger seat, then walks around to the driver side.

I don't argue. I sit beside her, silently crying while my body aches and my face stings. Occasionally, Chantal looks over at me, checking that I'm all in one piece.

"It is going to be okay. We're almost to your house. I'll wait until Nathan gets there," she says, aiming to comfort me.

My chest squeezes. "You don't need to do that."

"I'm not just going to leave you."

"We're not together anymore," I explain, turning my face away from her.

"Why not?" She sounds surprised by my admission.

"He didn't want to hide anymore." The tears fall harder than before. She pulls into my driveway and hugs me over the console. "Why are you being so nice to me right now?"

"Because something awful just happened to you, and you're still my best friend," she admits, stroking my hair. "Do you even know what I was the maddest at?"

I'm not sure what the right answer is—there's so many options. Silence fills the car. "That you kept it from me. I don't care that you're dating Nathan! I care that you lied, that you felt you couldn't tell me."

"I'm sorry. I regret not telling you the first time. I really messed up," I whimper.

"Water under the bridge. Let's get you cleaned up," she says, releasing me.

Standing in my bathroom, I stare at the sad girl looking at me in the mirror. Makeup runs down her tear-stained face. I feel worn down, like I could fall asleep the instant I close my eyes. Running over the events that transpired, I wonder if there is anything I could have done differently. But it's futile. The blame is solely on Paul. I did not ask for this nor give him any invitation. Showering will make me feel a little bit saner, but I don't know if I have it in me. But then I picture his hands and mouth on me, and all I want is to wash him away.

Turning the spray on, I wait till it heats up. Stepping into the shower, I sit myself down on the floor and let the scalding water pour over me. It burns, but it's healing. My tears get lost in the cascade of water, and I try not to think of anything. I'm not sure how long I sit for, but I don't get out until the water goes tepid. I hear Chantal in my living room talking on the phone. Her voice hushes as I exit the main bathroom. "Where are you? You need to be here now."

Nothing feels real tonight. My moves are sluggish as I get dressed. I'm clothed in one of Nathan's shirts he left by accident. I lift the neck up to my nose, breathing it in. His scent lingers, bringing me peace and heartache. Crawling into bed, my eyes drift closed, and images of Nathan's smiling face come to me, making it much easier to fall asleep.

CHAPTER 18
DANI, PRESENT DAY

Loud songbirds chirp outside my window, waking me up. Don't they know it's January? My body aches from the tension I've been holding all night, and my eyes burn, feeling scratchy. And, thanks to the annoying, winged creatures, a headache is brewing. I feel like I'm suffering through the hangover from hell. The only silver lining is I didn't actually overdo it last night, so that means I won't be throwing up.

I snap my eyelids shut as tight as I can, silently refusing to get out of bed. Reaching out my arm, I rub the empty stretch of bed. I don't feel Chantal next to me. I must have been asleep when she left. I don't know what I'm more grateful for: that she was there to stop Paul last night, or that she's forgiven me. I begin working up the courage to get up, and I hear rustling nearby. Stretching, I slowly sit up and am surprised to see Nathan perched on the edge of my dresser in what I assume were his clothes from yesterday. He's dressed in a white button-up with the sleeves pushed up, showcasing his defined forearms, and gray slacks. His hair is disheveled like he spent the night running his hands through it. His eyes are dark with shadows lurking behind them while he examines me from far away.

"What are you doing here?" I know full well Chantal had to have called him.

He doesn't even answer the question. "Are you okay?"

"I'm fine," I lie.

"When you feel up to it, we'll go to the police station."

"What for?" I stare at Nathan, taking him all in. My body craves him, but I keep myself planted in my bed.

"You'll need to give them a statement, file a restraining order, or something," he explains.

"I'm not doing any of that. It's over. Paul"—saying his name hurts—"*he's* gone. He's not stupid enough to do anything else."

Nathan looks at me dumbfounded. His gaze focuses somewhere near my cheek, and I see him clench his jaw. The lines on his flawless face grow harsher. I know this isn't what he wants. Ignoring the soreness I feel in my body, I get out of bed. Walking right past him, I go into my bathroom. Staring at myself in the mirror, I see what had his focus. There is spotty bruising on my face near my mouth. Tears threaten to fall, but I push them down. Not again; I did enough crying last night. Nathan comes in and moves up behind me, gauging my reaction, but I can no longer look at it while he's here. I don't want him to see like this.

Meeting his eyes in the mirror, his clothes gather my attention again. "Where were you? Why are you dressed up?" He wasn't there when I looked for him, but he was somewhere nice. His appearance shows that.

His reluctance to answer is telling. I pester him with a look that says I'm waiting before he delivers a crushing blow: "On a date."

I was out looking for you, and you were on a date, I want to scream at him. But I don't. This is my own fault. My body feels like it's about to crumble beneath me, and I grip the sink to anchor me to it so I won't fall. "With who?"

"Amanda," he says with no emotion to the name or girl.

"I bet your mom is thrilled," I retort with baseless anger.

He spins me around so we're facing each other. His hands are on my hips as he speaks, "I was trying to get over you. You pushed me away. Remember?" He pins me with his question. "There is no use. For me, it will always be you," Nathan says, his voice getting softer as he continues.

Reaching up, he cups my face, and I wince at the contact. He pulls his hand back like it's been burned and stares at the marks. "I'm so sorry." His eyes turn red with guilt.

I step closer, wanting to comfort him. "No. We're not doing this, Nathan. You weren't there, so there is nothing you could have done." We're so close now, I can smell mint on his breath. His eyes flicker down and go wide. Suddenly feeling insecure, I follow his gaze and mentally scold myself. I forgot I slept in his shirt. Of course he'd see me like this. Groaning, I lay my head on his chest, ultimately giving up on any distance, and wanting to touch him. His arms wrap around me like a warm security blanket. "I wanted to be comfortable, and it smelled like you," I explain tentatively.

Nathan lowers his head, kissing me with just the right amount of passion and comfort. I helplessly slide into his arms, pouring my apology for all the times I pushed him away into my kiss. When our tempo fades, he holds me close and promises, "No one will ever hurt you again. I'll make sure of it." The angry fire builds in him so quickly.

"You can't protect me from everything." I try to reason with him.

He angles my chin up so I meet him eye to eye. "Watch me." His tone is dangerous as if he's threatening anyone who could have overheard us.

I'm not some delicate flower; I'm not going to fall apart. But you'd think otherwise by how Nathan's been watching me like a hawk. I scrambled to come up with an excuse to go into work last-minute just to get a break from his surveillance. No one has seen or talked to Paul. I don't really care where he is as long as it's far from me. I think Nathan might have tried to talk to him, but he'd never tell me if he did. Nor would I want to know what he had to say. For Paul's sake, he should steer clear of him.

The light bruising around my mouth has faded, so it's almost like it never happened. Almost. Stepping foot in my office, I take a breath of relief, thankful I'm not stuck at home. Things feel normal here. Nathan made me take a few days off work so I could feel better and relax. Chantal agreed to come in and take care of a few things so nothing would fall behind. I see a stack of mail on my desk. Shrugging my jacket off, I let it fall to the floor. I pick up the pile of envelopes and comb through them. For some reason, this has always been able to distract me. I toss the acquired junk mail and begin looking at and organizing the bills in order of due date. When that's all done, Chantal barges in, causing me to jump.

"Sorry, I didn't mean to scare you."

I turn back to what I was doing. "It's okay."

"Nathan said he was going to try to keep you home for a little longer. What happened?" she asks, already implying it's probably my fault. She knows me too well.

"You guys in cahoots about where I am at all times now?" Chantal ignores my question, pinning me with a look. I go on, "He's breathing down my neck. It has already been four days since I was last here. I needed a little space."

She responds, understanding, "I get it. Really. We're just worried about you."

"Well, thank you, guys. You both are so important to me, but I'm okay. I promise."

"I take it you guys are back together now?"

My sheepish smile answers for me. "Yes. We're not exactly broadcasting our relationship, but we're not hiding, either."

"What do you think Maureen is going to say?" she asks, scrunching up her nose.

"That is one conversation I wish we didn't ever have to have," I answer honestly.

"You guys will get through it. Oh hey, before I forget. Let's do a girls' night. We could do Wednesday night? We're both off."

"That's perfect! It's a school night for Nathan, so he'll hardly miss me." I say it, knowing that is not true. He's admitted he sleeps better when I'm there. And based on how we migrate toward each other at night until our limbs are entwined, I'm led to believe he will definitely notice the absence. Oh well, he will have to be okay. I need my friend time, especially after our big fight.

Sweat beads and runs down into my hairline, dampening it while the sound of our breath fills the room. My head rests on Nathan's bare chest, and my heart rate slowly descends. Every time we make love, it feels better than the last. He sighs underneath me as his fingers sweep through my hair.

"I feel like I could lie here forever," my voice comes out breathy, the way it always does after he brings me to orgasm.

"You're telling me. I've got a beautiful, naked woman lying next to me after we just had mind-blowing sex." I laugh at his perspective. "I'm going to take a nap. Nothing could get me up," he says, pleased with himself.

"No, you can't," I argue. Nathan closes his eyes in protest, and I giggle more at him. "Travis asked for you to come over, remember?" I try pushing his side to roll him over, but it's no use.

"Travis would understand," he says, rolling over onto his stomach and burying his face in the pillow.

Sitting up straighter, I throw my leg over his side, straddling his back. Bending down, I whisper in his ear, "Look at it like this. The sooner you get back, the sooner we'll go again. Maybe even in the shower, or the kitchen counter. The possibilities are endless."

I shriek as he spins his body to lay on his back so he's facing me. "Now we're talking." He pulls me down to kiss him.

His tongue flicks its way into my mouth, tasting me. I tug on his hair, making him groan. It's so easy to get wrapped up in him. I don't want to stop, but we both have things to do today. I pull back. "No, no. You're trying to distract me. You still have to go. Save it for later." I smack his butt like a football player when he stands up.

Nathan grabs whatever clothes he finds on the floor. He looks at me with the devilish grin I've become fond of. "Fine, you win. But you are not safe when I get back."

I change the subject to Travis. "What does he need help with today?"

"I'm not sure, actually. Maybe his car?" he says while he pulls the shirt down over his head.

"He was acting weird at his party the other night. I noticed his apartment didn't look any different, and he was acting really frantic over you telling me you had moved things," I recall the brief conversation.

"That's weird," is all Nathans says.

"Did I misunderstand? Did you not move anything?" I notice his movements have slowed, and it seems like he is taking his time finding an answer. Suddenly, I feel strange over being the only one naked. Getting up out of bed, I search for my clothes, slipping on my panties when I find them.

"I was moving things for him he didn't want anymore. That was it. So maybe he was confused over your question."

"That makes the most sense." I nod, thinking out loud while I slip on my shirt. "I don't know, he just seemed really freaked out."

"If it will make you feel any better, I'll ask him about it. But other than that, don't stress over it. Seriously." He pins me with another look.

"You're right," I say, finding my jeans on the floor and sliding them up my hips, much to Nathan's chagrin. "Don't forget: Wednesday I'll be with Chantal for the night."

"I know. I'm glad you two have worked things out, but I'm bummed it takes you out of our bed, though." He's pouting, and it's the most adorable thing. He said our bed. I love the way that sounds. Our vocabulary has begun to change to show a little more permanence, using *we* and *our*. I am not sure if this is something Nathan has noticed, but I definitely have.

I've been at Chantal's for an hour, and I already have green goop covering my face while she has a moisturizing sheet mask over hers. The girl works fast. Bowls of snacks and dip lay sporadically on her coffee table between us. The wine in our glasses decreases as the time goes on.

"You know I have to ask: who is better?" she chuckles into her hand.

I know what she's asking, but I play dumb, hoping she'll reconsider her question. "Who is better at what?"

She does not. "Who is better in bed, Joel or Nathan?"

Blushing at the question, I know the answer immediately. I don't even have to think about it. Nathan's ability to read and work my body is like nothing I've ever experienced before. He moves and touches me with such appreciation, it feels like he's afraid he'll never get the chance again. "I'm not answering that," I say over my wine glass, avoiding her stare.

"Oh, come on!" she dares.

"It isn't right that I can even answer that question," I say, mortified. "I'll allow them to have their privacy."

"It's a shame I didn't have a go at him." She smirks.

"Ha, ha," I respond sarcastically.

"All right," she says, elongating each word. "Well, give me something. I mean, are you going to move in together?"

I shake my head vehemently. "No, it's way too soon." *Isn't it?*

"But aren't you over at his place all the time, or him at yours?" she asks, wrestling with logic.

I think about the question. "Yes, but we like splitting it between the two places. As of right now, it works for us."

Chantal smiles while she scoops dip onto her chip. "As long as my best friend's happy."

I was worried how it would be with us after we made up. Could I talk to her about Nathan? Or would I have to tiptoe around the subject? I'm grateful it is the former. Chantal helps me think things through, always giving me a different angle. And doesn't allow me to run from an issue.

Leaning forward, I grab a dark-burgundy polish and begin painting my nails. The color is beautiful and makes my hands look more feline. Chantal pours herself a little more wine, then puts on a movie we've watched at least three times before. It's something we've learned over the years we love to do: re-watch movies and quote them together as the scenes roll on, laughing at each other in the process. This feels like the first real step of our fight being over. I'm fully relaxed with my best friend.

The next day, I leave right from Chantal's place to go to work. It was the evening we both needed, but it would be a lie to say I didn't miss sleeping in Nathan's firm arms. I roll my eyes at myself. I'm acting like a schoolgirl. One night without him is not a big deal. When I arrive at Tav's, the first order of business is going through the books, making sure everything matches up.

I'm about halfway through when Jenna walks in with a large vase filled with a dozen long-stemmed, white roses. "Hi, these are for you," she chirps.

Standing up from my chair, I can't help but feel excited over the disruption. I help her set the vase on the corner of my desk, surprised by how heavy they are, and snatch the card from its holder.

She talks to me while I read. "These flowers are beautiful."

There is never a moment I don't think of you. —Nathan

My teeth sink into my bottom lip as my eyes flutter closed. Help me, I'm in deep with this man.

"I take it these are from your boyfriend? It was the guy at my table during the holiday party, right?" she inquires.

Jenna is one of many who have already put two and two together regarding mine and Nathan's relationship. I'm a little surprised it doesn't bother me as much as I thought it would. "Yes. He just wanted to let me know he was thinking of me," I beam, wanting to brag.

"Wow! You are a lucky lady."

When Jenna leaves, I type a quick text to Nathan letting him know I received his gift and that the feeling is mutual. The rest of my afternoon becomes wasted with daydreams of all the possible futures we could share together. Each dream is better than the last. Being open with him feels light years better than hiding. I'm disappointed we lost any time because I was scared. Nathan is worth all the risks, and only we decide where this goes. From all our time we have shared, I've learned that as long as he is by my side guiding me out of the dark, nothing can knock me down. He opens my eyes to my own strength and provides me with a sense of security. Because when we're together, nothing could go wrong.

CHAPTER 19
NATHAN, PRESENT DAY

There is a fiery rage deep in the pit of my stomach that has been burning since the night of the party. I can still hear the panic in Chantal's voice when she called to tell me what happened. *Something happened to Dani. Where are you? You need to be here now.* Her words ring over and over again in my head. I immediately left my lame attempt at a date, needing to get to her. I know it could have been worse, but nothing prepared me for seeing how sad and broken she looked while she slept. Dani's eyebrows were pinched together on her forehead, and she held her hands up under her chin, like she was ready to fight her attacker. Not to mention the blotchy, purple bruise on her cheek. I don't think I slept a wink as I paced around her house and popped into her bedroom to check on her.

How could Paul have done this? We've been friends since middle school. I know he has always been forward with women, but this is thoughtless. He attacked someone. And not just anyone—Dani. I have absolutely no respect for him anymore. I called the guys after I arrived to check on her and told them what had happened. Everyone agreed to shun him; not one of us would be friends with a predator.

The urge to find Paul and rip him limb from limb is only increasing with each passing day, which is why I'm driving to the gym right now. Travis mentioned he saw his car in the parking lot. My imagination paints pictures of Paul's disgusting hands on her while she begs him to stop. It has me seeing red. My hands tighten around the steering wheel, and my knuckles turn white. He's lucky if I don't kill him.

When I enter the gym, it's with purpose. I don't stop to talk to anyone. I don't even bother checking in. As I scan the expansive workout room, my steps never falter. He's not in here. I keep moving, heading to the locker rooms. I allow the door to fall shut behind me, but no sounds filter through the space. My feet carry me down the rows of lockers, but I don't see anyone until the second to last row. I spot him getting dressed. Paul doesn't see me coming. He's fiddling with his phone when I grab him by the shirt and slam his body against his open locker.

"What the hell, man?" he yells at me.

"What the hell kind of man attacks a woman?" I seethe, throwing his words back at him. "You will never go near Dani again. Do you understand me?"

His voice fills with venom as he laughs at me. "Oh, so this is what this is about? Don't tell me you're screwing her." Taking my silence as confirmation, he continues, "She must really want to stay in the family. Jumping brother to brother like that."

I push my forearm over his neck, watching him struggle to pull it away. "Keep it up, Paul. See if I don't beat your ass right here." I'm half hoping he makes me.

He raises his hands in a mock surrender. "I'm sorry man, truly, I get it! The way she felt underneath me, begging, I would have nailed her too."

Paul mocking the assault and the pain he's caused makes me lose control. My fist slams against his mouth, causing his head to ricochet off the metal locker. Paul regains his composure faster than anticipated and lunges at me. He takes me to the ground, but I roll from underneath him, pushing his body down to the floor in the process. I'm up on my knees quickly, raining my fists onto his cowardly face. Paul's mouth sputters with blood, but this doesn't touch the pain I wish to inflict.

Blinded by anger and leftover fear from that night, I don't see his arm swing at me. He lands two jabs on my ribs, knocking the wind out of my lungs. Gasping for air, I look down and see for the first time how much blood is on the floor. It's more than I originally thought. I glance at his split face, that, along with my hand, is pooling blood underneath us. I can't be caught here in this mess. And I can only assume what people have heard, although no one has come to check.

I grab the collar of his shirt and lift him up so he can hear me whisper, "This was only a warning. If I see you anywhere near her again, it will be much worse for you." I ignore his scowl as he wipes the blood from his mouth with the back of his hand.

Throwing him back to the ground, I leave as quickly as I can, not wanting to draw attention to myself. Paul can clean up his mess; I'm not doing that for him anymore. When I ease into my driver's seat, my heart is still beating against my battered ribcage. My mind is distracted while I drive. I can't focus on anything, and my hands tap on the wheel as I drive out of there. My energy rivals a bear locked in a cage, and I need it to calm down. Dani will be leaving for work soon, but that's okay—I just need to see her, to touch her. Her elegant hands and delicate temperament are always able to effortlessly diffuse the bomb inside of me. I don't think she's aware of her gift.

I pull up behind her as she opens her car door. Her brow creases, wondering what I'm doing here, and she waits for me. Turning the key to cut the engine, I step out into the January air. Ice crunches underneath my feet. She looks gorgeous as she stands there in her navy winter coat, hair down over her shoulders. The white snow behind her gives her a soft halo.

"Hi," she says, smiling at me while she closes her door and then leaning up against it. "To what do I owe the pleasure?" As I approach her, she notices my scraped and bleeding knuckles. "Oh my god, what happened? Are you okay?"

"I'm better now," I say, reaching for her chin to kiss her sweet lips. My body melts into hers. Pushing her against the car, I take, and take, and take. My tongue strokes hers, making me feel renewed. Yes, I'm much better now, finally at ease with my lips slow against hers.

"What happened?" Her voice comes out breathy and distracted.

"I had a conversation with Paul." Her eyes go wide, and her body stiffens. "He will not go near you again," I assure her.

"You didn't need to do that. What if you get in trouble because of this?" she asks, concerned.

"He needed to pay. I was not going to let him walk around scot-free. Trust me, he got the bare minimum." I chuckle as I replay the sound of his jaw on my fist. When she still doesn't seem happy, I regain her focus by stroking her hair out of her face. "Hey, look at me. You're mine to protect. It kills me that I wasn't there to stop it." My voice grows more tender. "If anything more would have happened to you, I would never forgive myself. I love you, Dani. I always have. Even when you were with my brother, it killed me having you so close but out of reach." My admission rolls off my tongue with ease. Her breath catches, her eyes are full, but the dam never breaks. I don't expect a response. I don't need her to be in love with me right now. I know her feelings for me are real.

Dani reaches up to touch my face. "I love you, Nathan." Her voice rings clear. Her lips brush against mine. "Take me inside."

"But you were leaving to go to work."

She takes my hand, leading me down her walkway. "I don't care. I'm the boss. I can be a little late."

The second her front door closes behind us, she's kicked off her shoes and shed her coat on the floor. I watch her quickness, following suit. Her hands fly to my shirt, sliding it up over my head, while her lips wreak havoc on my throat. Her fingertips against my stomach make me tremble. She lets out a yelp when I grab her by the waist, hoisting her up. Dani's long legs wrap around me. It's hard to concentrate on my steps with her coveting my body like this. Her lips are everywhere, from my jaw to my neck, to my ears, to my shoulders. Her nails scrape at my back.

"W-we have to slow down, or I won't make it to your bed," I stutter breathlessly.

Whipping off her shirt, she throws it by my feet. "I can't wait another second. Here is good," her voice is heady.

Dani tugs me down to the floor as she bites my bottom lip. I'm positioned over her, and her legs are spread to accommodate me. I trace a finger over the swells of her breasts, dipping my fingertip underneath the lacey cup and pulling it down to expose her. Lowering my head, I take one in my mouth hungrily. Dani arches into the pleasure, giving me permission to take more. I move to the other side, kissing up and down her breast before lightly nipping at its peak. She moans beneath me.

I lift myself up, keeping my eyes trained down at her. Her nipples are hard and red from my invasion. Dark brown eyes stare up at me expectantly. I unbutton her pants and pull them down her creamy thighs, her panties included. She kicks them off her ankles while I sit back, tugging mine down. All that bare, olive skin makes me want to sink my teeth into her. She's intoxicating. I slide into her in one long stroke. Dani shivers at my entry, pulling my mouth down to hers. And I have to still myself to savor the sheer intensity of it.

"Oh my god," Dani mumbles into my mouth.

I swallow her sounds as I slowly move over her. My hands are greedy as I splay them over her waist, squeezing and pulling her closer to me with every thrust. Nothing has ever been this good; nothing after her will ever be this good. With every touch, I'm marking her as mine.

I move down her jaw, licking and biting her neck; it's something I've learned she loves. My mouth clamps around the top of her shoulder, and I hold her against me while she chases her mountain peak. Her arms wrap around my shoulders, clinging to me for leverage as she writhes underneath me. I can tell she's close by how rigid her body has gotten. I slow our momentum, making sure to hit every inch of her. Dani lets out a sob as her body squeezes mine in release. The sensation sends me over the edge, causing heat to build in my legs until it erupts from me.

I collapse on top of her, unable to bear the weight of my own body any longer. Her warm skin welcomes me, and I listen intently to her heart race in her chest. She only gets better with time. It occurs to me this afternoon tryst happened because she loves me. And that's what I've always wanted.

I normally stop by my parents' after work. It's not an uncommon thing, but it's starting to feel more inconvenient these days, since I'm rushing to get home and see Dani.

My mom greets me with a kiss on the cheek while her hands are busy mashing a meatloaf together. "Hi, honey."

"Hi. Hey, Dad," I say as he walks in with a newspaper.

"Hey, son. That smells great," he tells my mom as he looks over her shoulder. "Are you staying for dinner tonight?"

"No thanks, I have plans."

"You going out with Amanda again?" my mom asks, not hiding her bias.

"No, Mom. That wasn't going to work, and you know it," I reply.

"I was just trying to help you."

"What have you got going on tonight?" my dad asks.

I bend my fingers, cracking my knuckles, mustering up the courage. It's now or never. "I'm having dinner . . . with Dani."

"That's great." Dad smiles at me, not surprised.

My mom stands as still as a statue. "Do you really think this is appropriate, Nathan?"

"We can't keep doing this dance, Mom," I plead, exasperated.

Her voice rises in disbelief, "I agree, so stop this, please. Your brother would hate this! She is his wife."

"No, she was his wife. If Joel were still here, this wouldn't even be a conversation right now, and you know it. He was my best friend, and if he could see me now, he would see how much I love her. He would want me to be happy." My dad's face lights up with approval.

My mom whips her head around to face me. "Love her?"

"Yes, I love her. And she is not the monster you treat her like."

"That girl has weaseled her way into both my boys' lives, and look where Joel ended up." She sneers.

My fists clench, attempting to control my anger. I don't have the chance to defend Dani before my father jumps in, "Oh, Maur. That is not fair! Joel's demons were entirely his own. Dani was an innocent bystander that got swept away in his wake."

"Look, I'm not asking you to like it. I'm just telling you we're together."

"Think about this. Where is this honestly going?" Her voice is softer than before. She's trying to manipulate me by getting in my head and making me doubt what I feel for Dani. But I won't let her.

"I don't know. But as long as she wants me, I'll always be there for her," I say with certainty.

Standing up, I'm about to walk out. My dad stops me and speaks with authority, letting my mom know where he stands. "You both deserve each other." His smile is contagious. It makes my visit feel like it wasn't a total loss. He pats my back with approval while mom stays silent on the matter.

I decide I've gotten all I can from this conversation. I jump in the car and pull the door closed at my side, longing to get home to Dani; she'll be there soon. *Home.* This is the first time I've noticed I attribute that word to her. The weather outside contradicts the affection I feel in my bones. The sky looks eerie and gray with an impending storm. Travis calls me at the same time that thought crosses my mind.

"Hello?"

"Hey. Have you found a new home for the bags?"

"No." And it's really starting to concern me, especially with how often Dani is at my house now. "It was more than we were both prepared for, remember?"

"Well, you need to get rid of it," Travis tells me.

"Thank you!" Sarcasm is laden in my voice. "I wasn't aware. You know, I distinctly remember having my help bail on me. Otherwise, this wouldn't be so bad for me right now."

"I'm not going to apologize for making sure I'm not involved in this madness. You made your own choice. I was just calling to check on you. See if maybe you finally decide to stop this, especially now that you have Dani," he blasts at me.

"I do have Dani," I agree with him. "But you almost tipped her off the other night, and I don't know if she would forgive me if she were to find out. So, the next time you're about to say something stupid, don't."

"You're starting to act like Joel. Do you really think she's been through what she has and won't be able to tell you're acting strange? She's not blind." I can't find the right words to argue with him. "Whatever, man. Like I said, I just wanted to make sure you were okay," he says, ending the call offended.

I'm nothing like Joel. My mind declares war on itself. *This is entirely different. But I'm still keeping secrets. That's because it is better if she doesn't know. Shouldn't that be for her to decide? I'm protecting her. She doesn't want to be protected.* My thoughts ping-pong back and forth. Everything is coming full circle, and I'm not sure what the right answer is anymore. Maybe Travis is right. This needs to end. This can't just be on me anymore. I mean, really, who is this helping?

When I get home and see Dani's car already there, a surge of excitement fills me. All this talk of her today has me missing my girl. As I enter the house, it is dead quiet. I search every room, but there is no trace of her. Desperation kicks in. and I dial her phone number. A faint ringing sound plays. *She's here, but where is she? Is this some sort of game?* I continue toward the sound like a cat stalking a mouse. I can tell I've gotten closer because the volume grows. My chest seizes with panic when I realize she's in my garage again. I open the door, and Dani's standing there, shoulders hunched, and my black bags are torn open. My eyes feel as big as my head as I watch her confusion turn to betrayal. When her eyes finally lift and make their way to me, all I see is pain. Tears flow from her eyes like waterfalls.

"Please tell me this is a joke," she croaks.

My chest aches, and suddenly, no possible explanation seems good enough to justify what she must be thinking. My silence on the matter infuriates her. She kicks the open bags over, scattering packaged and unpackaged needles and various-sized bags of pills across my garage floor.

Finally finding my voice, I all but scream, "Let me explain!"

Her tears haven't stopped, but she stands there like ice. "No need. I let Joel do that enough to know the explanations never really matter."

CHAPTER 20
DANI, PRESENT DAY

I have gone back in time. That is the only explanation. I've somehow stumbled into a time machine and have gone back two years. I'm standing still, staring at Nathan, daring him to say something—anything. He looks fear-ridden; he hasn't blinked the entire time. It feels like we stand there suspended in time for several minutes, neither one of us speaking. I swallow the lump lodged in my throat and shoulder past him into the house. Am I really going through this all over again? He grabs my elbow, stopping me in my tracks. How could he do this? He knows exactly what I went through with Joel.

"You don't understand." He seems to respond to my unspoken thoughts.

Fat tears slide down my face as my body melts to his voice. There's hesitation in my movements, and he sees it. Nathan pulls me to him, wrapping his arms around me tightly. "I'm not doing it. Any of it. The drugs aren't mine," he says with authority.

I steal a look up at him. "Wh-what?" Please let this be true. I want to believe what he's saying, but I've been burned by this before.

He holds my gaze, moving his hands to my sides and still grips me, like he's afraid I'll slip away. "I swear to you, none of it is mine. I couldn't do that to you."

His admission feels real. I know as soon as he's finished speaking that I believe him. Nathan wouldn't do this to me. I back out of his arms but still hold his hands. A giant weight is relieved from my shoulders before confusion sets in.

"I don't understand. There were bagfuls in there," I state, remembering the unfortunate scene. "Whose is it?"

His hands squeeze mine. "It was all Joel's."

"That doesn't make any sense."

"His problem was bigger than we knew, clearly," Nathan waves his arm out to signal the damage.

"Why would you have all of this now?"

"He told me where he kept the things he didn't want to bring home."

"What he didn't want me to find." I utter the words he doesn't.

He nods. "I was trying to get rid of it all so no one would know. I didn't want Joel's or your name to be drug through the mud anymore because of this. I definitely didn't want you to have to handle this and be put through more pain because of him."

I hear his explanation and believe him again. Yet, something sticks out like a sore thumb. "Why would Joel tell you where his stuff was?" I ask the question and am suddenly scared of the answer. I'm met with silence, and the truth slaps me in the face so hard, I almost think I hear it. I take a forced step back, dropping his hands. "How long did you know he was using?" It's a direct question he can't get away from.

"The whole time."

Daggers pierce my back into my heart. I close my eyes from the blinding pain. I feel like a silly little pawn on a chess board. "The whole time?" I repeat his words. "You knew the whole time and didn't warn me or try to help me?" I choke out.

"Wait, I did help," he tries to defend himself.

"Only when I asked for it. Only when I called begging. How could you have kept this from me? You knew what it was like for me during that time, and you just allowed me to feel alone through it all." I bite back the sob, but it doesn't stop the sound from my throat.

"No, no, it wasn't like that." Nathan moves toward me, but I dodge him.

"Oh yeah, what was it like? Because I was the only one at home with him not understanding what was going on or how to help him. All the while you knew the whole time and had the audacity to act surprised when I first called on you!" I yell at him. "I felt so alone, like I was helping him by myself. And you let me." My voice crumbles as I recall the last few years.

"I wanted to tell you," he all but whispers.

"But you didn't. I don't know what's worse, if you had been doing it, too, or you knowing and never telling me," I hurl at him.

"Let me find the safest way to get rid of the drugs, and then we can get through this."

"I don't think we can."

His eyes penetrate mine. "Don't say that."

"I felt there was nothing that could come between us, but that's gone now." My chest aches with a sob wanting to break free.

"I'm so sorry, Dani." Soft tears glide down his cheeks, and I can tell he's trying to keep himself planted where he is instead of coming to me. It almost makes me go to him, take him in my arms, and comfort him. But I will not put myself back in this position.

"Me too. I never thought you'd hurt me like this." Just like his brother. I feel completely destroyed. The hurt aches through my chest and down my limbs like I was hit by a train. I'd almost prefer that reality to this one. Reluctantly, I turn to leave, knowing that this is the end. My steps echo in my ears as they leave his house for the last time.

My days roll into nights, and I begin to feel like a zombie. I'm unable to pay attention to things around me. I feel empty and alone. It's no one's fault but my own. And what did I expect? I fell in love with my husband's brother—this is my karma. I'm not sure who I'm angrier at, him or me. I'm at a complete loss of what to do now. In a strange turn of events, I decide to call my mother, desperate for some kind of comfort. While the phone rings, I question my decision.

My mother answers on the second ring, "Hi, sweetie."

"Hey, Mom," my voice sounds as lifeless as I feel.

"To what do I owe the pleasure of this call?"

I honestly don't know, but I keep that thought to myself. "I just wanted to hear your voice, I guess."

"Are you okay? You sound upset." She sounds more accusatory than concerned.

"I'm fine," I lie. "What are you up to today?" I ask, wanting a distraction from my misery.

"Well, I have a spa appointment in a few hours."

"That sounds amazing."

"Oh, Dani, you should come up for the weekend, and I'll make you an appointment. We can have a mother-daughter day at the spa! How about it? Massages, sauna, and nails," she says, enticing me.

It does sound perfect. And time away might serve me well. Yeah, my parents can drive me crazy, but I'm dying to be somewhere that won't remind me of Nathan.

"I can be up there tomorrow," I answer, suddenly grateful for the getaway.

"Oh, okay. Great!" my mother responds, clearly surprised.

I smile for the first time in a week. "Thanks, Mom. See you soon. I have to get ready for work."

Hanging up the phone, I'm eager to pack my bag now, but I reign myself in. *It can wait till tomorrow; don't rush. It'll only make the time feel slower*, I tell myself. Getting ready for work is a breeze when I don't care about anything. I don't blow-dry my hair or put makeup on. What's the point? I'm not looking good for anyone, nor do I feel up for trying to keep up with appearances.

That doesn't stop Chantal from pestering me about it after I hole myself away in my office.

She eyes me warily. "I thought you said you were handling the breakup."

"I am. I'm great." I stare down at my desk, continuing to fill out tax information.

I hear her blow out a breath. "You're doing great? Really? 'Cause normally, you wouldn't come to work looking like this." She moves her hand in my direction.

"Hey," I respond, wounded.

"You know what I mean. Not wearing makeup is one thing—you don't wear enough to really tell a difference—but you never let your hair look a mess like this. If you come in with it wet, it's at least in a bun or something."

"I didn't have time to do anything to it," I offer the excuse. "Oh, before I forget, can you cover another one of my shifts?"

She looks at me thoughtfully. "I am not sure wallowing in bed is the right answer anymore."

"That isn't what I'm doing. I'm going to get away—go up and stay with my parents."

"Is going to your parents' really the best idea?" Chantal asks.

"Honestly, I don't know. But it's better than being here right now. Everything reminds me of him. I just need to get my head straight."

"I get it. It makes sense." She sighs. "Well, of course, I'll always help however you need. It's just crazy. Feels like déjà vu, everything happening for a second time. He really knew about it from the beginning?"

I nod my head, staring down at the keyboard distracted, no longer sure what I am doing.

"Well, maybe he was really trying to protect you, you know, like he said," Chantal tiptoes around the statement, avoiding meeting my betrayed eyes.

"That wasn't for him to decide. He left me in the dark and made me feel like I was suffering alone."

"Are you sure it's over, for good?"

"It has to be," I say firmly. Although, as the words slip past my tongue, memories of Nathan surface: the way he was always so gentle and caring, the way his fingertips felt against my bare skin. The memories are so strong, I can almost smell him, like he's standing right in front of me.

She frowns, and disappointment lies heavy in her voice. "It's a shame. I'm sorry, I thought he was going to be it for you."

"Me too. I'll be fine. It's not the first time a Stephensen's disappointed me," I mutter, trying to make light of the situation, but it falls on deaf ears. "Excuse me, I'll be right back."

Chantal flicks her eyes up to watch me leave but doesn't say anything. I leave her at the booth as I head to the bathroom. As soon as my boot hits the tile floor, I can't control the tears that fall. Leaning against the door, I sink down. Covering my face with my hands, I try to regain my composure, but it's having the opposite effect. I cry harder. Stifling the sound, I let the tears fall, coating the sleeves of my sweater. I cry at all the memories of Nathan: the way his lips felt on mine, how handsome his provocative smile was when he wanted me, the way he gave me goosebumps with a simple look or touch, and all the ways he made me feel safe.

The silver lining of all this is I at least have Chantal again. I'm not sure what I would do without her. It's true. If she hadn't forgiven me after I lied to her and then I found out about this, it would be adding a second dagger in my chest. I'd be an inconsolable mess. I just need to get through tonight, and then tomorrow, I'm driving far away from here. That's it, just a few hours—I can do it. I give myself the saddest pep talk while I sit on a dirty, public bathroom floor. Literally picking myself up off the ground, I leave the bathroom and the tears behind, hoping I can get through tonight quickly.

I can't remember the last time I woke up this early. The kitchen clock reads 5:00 a.m. I'm exhausted, but restless. There's no point in going back to bed to only stare at the ceiling for a few more hours. I get ready, trying to take my time and not rush through the mundane routines. If I leave too early, my mother will ask why. I take a hot, extra-long shower and make sure to cook and eat breakfast. But it's no use; I'm still ready by 6:30 a.m. Screw it, I'm leaving now. I toss my duffel bag into the car and begin the six-hour drive.

The solitude feels quite refreshing compared to the stark loneliness I was feeling at my house. I notice I'm halfway there when I see a red bed and breakfast sign. My phone jolts my attention away to check the caller ID. It's Nathan. *Are you kidding me? This is exactly what I was getting away from.* I let my phone ring several times until it goes silent. He can leave me a message that I won't listen to. As if to mock me, my phone pings, letting me know there is a new message. And I can't help but want to know what he has to say. I take the first exit I see and pull into a gas station. I refilled the tank an hour ago, but I'm desperate to get out of the car and away from my cell phone.

Its blinking notification makes the car feel confined, suffocating me with all the possibilities of what he could have said. Lifting the nozzle, I squeeze the handle and fill any empty space in the gas tank. I go as far as to walk around the gold body of my Camry several times, distracting myself from my desire to hear his deep vibrato. When I feel my head is on straight and my resolve is strong, I climb back into the car. The rest of the ride feels a little more solemn. As the tires roll down the interstate, my mind does the same, running through more memories of Nathan and I together. Mentally berating myself for getting caught in this situation, I'm taken aback by my lack of tears at the moment. I'm like a statue, sitting still with no emotion. Maybe this is a good sign.

When I pull up to my childhood home, a place I never thought I'd visit for comfort, I breathe easy. As I step past the heavy front door, its weight closes itself with a thud behind me. My mother, hearing the noise, walks out of the den with a scowl. "Oh, it's you. What time is it?" She checks her thin Swarovski watch.

"It's one," I reply.

"You're here early. We weren't expecting you just yet. How was your drive?" I want to read into her words, but there isn't any malice in them.

In this moment, I'm thankful I hadn't cried in the car. She would have been able to tell. "It was easy," I answer plainly. I'm not sure what comes over me, but I hug her fiercely, surprising us both.

Her tentative voice is right by my ear. "I'm glad you came home."

Her arms are wrapped around my back like limp noodles. Feeling embarrassed, I fight the urge to apologize. I just caught her off-guard. She doesn't like sharing her feelings. *It's fine*, I tell myself again, not needing to dwell on it.

"Now, are you ready to spend the next few hours in heaven?"

"Yes, I need this," I respond honestly.

"Okay, they have us at six, but that's okay! I'll call and have them move us up. Do you want to take your bag upstairs and change?" She says, eyeing me up and down.

"Why?"

"Well, your clothes might be okay to travel in, but that's not the kind of thing anyone would show up in," she mutters, eyeing my oversized sweatshirt.

I sigh. "Mom, we're going to the spa. We'll be changing into robes there. What would be the point of me changing my outfit, just to change out of it into a robe?"

"Fine, forget I said anything," she feigns hurt.

Lying on the warm, blanketed table, the masseuse begins rubbing and pushing at my muscles with a purpose. My eyes flutter closed from the sensation. This feels amazing. I could fall asleep for the next hour, but I don't want to miss any of this. Her thumbs circle in one sore spot near my shoulder and work out the kinks. "You feel tight right in through here," she says to me, touching my upper back. "Have you been really stressed?"

That's the understatement of the year. Where would I even begin? "You could say that." My voice comes out sleepy.

The rest of the hour goes by all too quickly. I want to ask her to keep going, that I'll pay the difference, but she has other clients. Standing up to slip my fluffy robe back on, my neck and shoulders feel loose. Wow, I hadn't realized they were so tense until now. The masseuse points me in the direction of the manicurists where my mother is sitting. Moving to the station beside her, I look at the colors they offer.

"How was your massage?"

"Amazing. I didn't want to leave the table." I chuckle to myself. "How was yours?"

"I had a massage the other day when we were on the phone. I got a facial instead. I love the lady who does mine." She pauses, and I think we're done talking until the nail techs come over. "What's going on?"

I look over at her, confused. "Well, I was thinking of going with the purple. Is that too much?" I ask, staring at the color again, unsure.

"No, that is not what I meant. Why are you here?" she continues.

"Because I wanted to see you," I answer, hoping she buys it.

"You have never just come up spur of the moment like this before," she pesters.

Nodding hello to the woman who sits down in front of me, I aim for a pleasant tone. "I thought a trip away sounded nice."

My mother, on the other hand, doesn't care about the employees hearing us. "Danielle." Her gaze pins me, demanding answers.

I offer my hands to the nail tech to file and buff them as needed. "Couldn't I have wanted to see my mother?" I silently beg for her to drop it one last time.

But it is useless. "Yes, but that is not what brought you here, so spill it."

"Fine." I rack my brain trying to decide how much information I want to divulge and how exactly to share it. "I was dating someone." The words form on my lips before spilling out without a second thought. "And he was wonderful. Being with him felt too good to be true, and it turned out it was. I came up here to get away from the constant reminders of him. Although it hasn't made a difference." I look down at my nails, not wanting to see—or, more accurately, feel—any more shame.

Mom's softness in this moment stuns me. "I had no idea you were dating someone."

"Not many people did. I was afraid it was too soon," I mutter.

"That is nobody's business but yours," she sticks her nose up with her words.

I laugh at the irony of her statement—the statement I've heard over and over again. "That's what Nathan kept telling me." Letting his beautiful name rest on my tongue leaves a sour taste in my mouth. Suddenly, I realize I just made a grave mistake.

My mother's body swiftly turns in her chair to face me directly, not caring that she's pulled away from her manicure. "What? The guy you were seeing was Nathan?"

"Please don't," I say quietly, not wanting to cause a scene. I knew I shouldn't have said anything.

She mocks zipping her lips together and throwing away the key. Cindy Davis has always been one for the dramatic. We sit in awkward silence while the nail tech paints my nails in smooth strokes.

"How did this happen? I mean, I'm not that shocked. He seemed as smitten as Joel at your wedding." Her observation sends a shot to my chest. I close my eyes on its impact.

"Mom," I warn in forced politeness as I look back and smile at the tech. "Can we do this later?"

She is able to keep her questions to herself while our manicures are touched up. But I see from the way she's biting her cheek and avoiding eye contact, more and more questions are forming. Great. I know I won't be able to hold them off forever.

Proving my point, the second we get inside her car, they're unloaded on me.

"Nathan? The teacher? How serious was it? Did you say 'I love you'? What happened?" Her voice comes out rushed.

I roll my eyes toward the sky. "This is exactly what I was trying to avoid and why I came up here." I continue because I know she won't stop otherwise, "Yes, I love him, okay, but it doesn't matter. It's over with. Now, can we move on?"

"I didn't know it was a crime to ask my daughter questions about her dating life," she pouts, making me the bad guy.

My eyes roll twice as hard as the last time. "It's not. I thought I made it clear I'm in pain right now. I'm so miserable that I came up here."

"That doesn't seem fair."

"Why not?" Everything feels like it's boiling over. Years of hurt and resentment pour out. "It shouldn't be a shock that I don't like coming back. You've tried controlling me my whole life and put me down with your insensitive comments. Moving to Virginia gave me freedom—the freedom to do whatever I wanted without worrying about your backlash."

"I was only trying to protect you from making any mistakes."

I rub my temples to soothe my anger. "Why is everyone taking it upon themselves to protect me this way?" I all but scream, my eyes tingling with unshed tears.

"Okay, okay, I get it. I will stop interfering and offering my comments that are obviously not wanted. Sheesh, it's not that big of a deal."

"It is to me," my voice breaks like a defeated child.

"Okay." Cindy Davis, always one to get the last word.

We ride together silently until we get to the house. Even though this conversation didn't go as planned, it still feels like a small win. I can tell she's hurt by it, but I won't apologize for the truth. Hopefully, this honest moment between us will bridge the gap to one another. When we pull up the looped driveway, she puts the car in park in front of the house.

Reaching for my door, my mother speaks up, extending an olive branch. "The purple you picked isn't too much, by the way." This is her trying, for I know it's too dark of a color for her liking.

I smile at her in thanks. "Thank you for taking me today. I actually enjoyed it. Most of it."

"Me too. You know I'm here if you want to talk about it." She squeezes my arm. It's the only affection she knows how to offer.

This is the nicest conversation we have had, and I feel guilty I'm bracing myself for the petty comment that's sure to come, but never does.

Coming down from my room at the sound of a doorbell, I smell teriyaki and ginger. My father brings in bags of Chinese food and rests them on the counter. I get plates and cutlery out of the cabinets and drawers and take them to the dining room table. As we pile our food on our plates and sit sporadically, everything feels the same as when I was a kid. My father hardly speaks, and Mom talks about her latest trip planned with the occasional question kicked off to me. I don't mind it tonight, though. My mind is in another place. I push the lo mein and sesame chicken around my plate with the fork. Food has become lackluster, making me lose my appetite. I wonder what Nathan is doing right now, but I push the thought down. *It is of no concern to me, and I don't care anyways,* I remind myself.

I've been in a daze. Looking up from my plate, I hadn't realized anyone had left the table. My father is gone—probably in his office, where he always is. My mom is moving about the kitchen putting food in the refrigerator. I stand up, not wanting to put off the inevitable, and scrap my untouched food into the trash. I rinse it before putting it into the dishwasher and notice my mom watching me.

"Just wasn't hungry," I answer the question in the air.

Her voice is full of sympathy. "I understand."

"I think I'm going to go to bed."

"Wait," she says, stepping forward. I stop in my tracks, waiting for her to continue. My mom comes closer, hugging me tighter than before with an awkward pat on the back. "I love you. I hope you'll visit more often now."

I want to suggest they can come visit me, but I'll take the baby steps. Dropping her arms, she waltzes out of the room, not needing a response. I climb the stairs one at a time, each step forward feeling heavier than the last.

When I lie down in my bed, my muscles feel soothed from my massage. I think about what all my mom has said today, the way she's surprised me, and is trying. I want to tell someone. Sitting up, I reach for my phone. Muscle memory has me typing in Nathan's name. The voicemail notification from earlier today pops up. Longing gets the better of me. Maybe if I just hear his voice . . .

I press the sideways triangle. "Dani." The gravelly voice rakes through my body.

Immediately stopping the message, I set my phone down with deep regret. I'm not strong enough for this yet. I force myself to lie down again, pushing it off for another time. Sleep evades me, like I knew it would. I'm left staring at the blank ceiling all night unable to find any rest. This heartache is exhausting. It's like I'm grieving a loss all over again, but this time, he's still here.

In the morning, I pour myself a large thermos of coffee to keep me alert on my trek home. I thank my mom for the weekend and promise her we'll talk more than once every few months. She doesn't say anything about my loungewear attire for the drive, showing me another good sign for our relationship. When I hit the road, I feel only slightly better than I did when I came. I want to stay, but I know I can't. I can't run from this anymore. It's time for me to move on.

CHAPTER 21
DANI, PRESENT DAY

My arms are loaded down with plastic bags full of groceries. I struggle to lift them. Summoning all the strength I have, I get the bags inside to the kitchen counters. Heaving out a sigh, I slip my weak limbs out of the handles, taking inventory of the indentations across my forearms. As I put the bags' contents away, I scan the room. This house is a mess. Sweaters are left wherever, shoes are strewn about, and there are dirty dishes left on countertops. How could I have left the house like this when I went to my parents? *Well, you were preoccupied with . . . other things*, my brain reminds me. Well, not anymore.

Forgetting the remainder of groceries, I begin piling dishes in the sink and walk around gathering clothes. When I toss the clothes in my hamper, my doorbell rings. I mentally go through the list of people it could be. Not Chantal; she's working. Couldn't be Nathan; it's a school day. I doubt Pat would come over, and I haven't seen Paul since the attack. Must be a neighbor. Opening my front door, I couldn't be more off base.

Shocked is an understatement. "Maureen?"

"May I come in?" Pat's not with her. We've never been alone like this before, nor has she ever come over by herself. She seems uncomfortable with being here.

"Yes, of course," I say, holding the door open and moving out of her way. We walk back into the recently tidied living room, and I'm feeling a little grateful I picked up in the first place. I don't know why she is here or how long this will take. *Do we sit?* I decide to follow her lead. Her eyes roam about the room, avoiding me, until she ultimately sits. So, this will not be quick.

"I tried coming yesterday, but you were not here," she says matter-of-factly.

"I was with my parents," I answer, somewhat confused. Why would she come here? "Is everything okay?"

"I know about you and Nathan." Her voice is as flat as her stare, holding no emotion.

I realize I'm terrified of this woman. Not that she would hurt me physically, but I've been on the receiving end of her meanness long enough to know it's a painful place to be. "Oh."

"It probably doesn't come as a shock to you that I didn't like it."

"Can I stop you? There is no me and Nathan anymore. We don't have to do this." I say, moving my hand between the two of us. "If this is you kicking me out of the family, then—"

Maureen scoffs, "The guys would never allow that." Realizing how her tone came across, she continues, "He told me what he did. How he kept it from you. Not only that, but that Joel's lies went deeper than you—*we* thought," she corrects herself, looking down in shame. "I'm sorry." It's the first time she's ever acknowledged that I was a victim in this situation, not the cause.

"Thank you," I respond robotically, shocked this conversation is taking place. *What made her even decide to talk to me about this?* If she can come over here and so very clearly bite the bullet, then so can I. Taking a leap, I ask, "Maureen, why do you dislike me so much? You have to admit, this is practically the most pleasant conversation you and I have ever exchanged."

My mother-in-law wrings her hands, taking her time thinking of the answer. When she begins, her voice comes out shaky and slow, like she's speaking about a secret she's never told. "Joel wanted you more than anything he had ever wanted before, but Nathan—Nathan was hypnotized by you immediately. I could tell after our dinner together when we met you. His eyes followed you around the room, and he hung on to your every word. I didn't want you to come in between my boys. I was afraid." A tear slides gracefully down her cheek when she shares the truth. "And then hating you . . . it just became habit."

I never thought I would know the reason. I always figured it was because I *stole* her baby. Her admission has me floored. We sit in silence as I take on the weight of her words. "I would have never done that to Joel, to Nathan, or to you. I wouldn't have pitted them against each other." Even though Nathan's and my feelings started long ago, nothing would have happened. I was committed to Joel.

"I'm sorry, Dani." She says my name with kindness instead of her usual contempt.

"Was this why you came over?"

Maureen wipes under her eye to keep herself from crying. "I wanted to get it all out and ask if you were coming to dinner," she asks with a half laugh. I can find the humor behind it; we're sitting here talking about our tumultuous relationship and then switch to a dinner party.

"Probably not," I answer sadly.

Maureen stands up and moves to the door, getting ready to leave. "Before I go, I just wanted to say, Nathan has never been as happy as he has been the last few months. I'm certain that has everything to do with you. And there is no judgment in my words right now; it's just the truth. I love my boys, but only one is alive. And I want to see him happy. With whoever that may be."

I don't have anything to add, so I settle in the moment and fight the urge to break in front of her. She walks out, and I close the door behind her. I'm left questioning everything that has happened in the last five years. Nothing is what it seemed. Joel had lied to me almost our whole relationship, my mother-in-law's hatred had more to do with habit at this point, and Nathan had feelings for me from the very start. *What am I to do with this information?*

I walk aimlessly around my house with no actual plan, dumbfounded by the recent chain of events. *What does all this mean? Where do I go from here?* I search for my phone, finding it in the kitchen. I swipe it from the counter and go sit on my couch, pulling my legs up in a protected position. No one is here or after me, but what I'm about to do will hurt me nonetheless. I need to feel secure. There are three voicemails on my phone I haven't listened to. The first two are from the night I left his place in a hurry. I play those first.

His voice fills the space around me, and I close my eyes, trapping the tears in.

"Hey, please come back. I'm sorry I snapped at you. I don't know what that was. I know that was uncool, and not like me at all. Come back so we can talk about it."

I click delete and press the next one.

"Dani, you're not answering any of my calls or texts, and I get it! I was a jerk for no reason. I'm so sorry. Please just let me know you are home and that you are safe. Please."

Nathan sounds alarmed, like he had been pacing around his house. He begs at the end of the message, and it's nice to be reminded I wasn't the only one hurting. I click delete again and move on to the last one. It's from two days ago.

"Dani." His voice comes out broken, and I have to stop the message for a minute so I can get control of my racing heart. "I know why you are avoiding me, and I don't blame you. But you have to know everything I did, I did for you. I'm sorry I wasn't one hundred percent honest. I thought I was doing the right thing. If I could do it over again, I would tell you the truth. I wish you could forgive me, but I know why you can't. It's just—" his voice cracks with sorrow, and there is a long pause. I think the message is over, but it continues. "I'm dying over here. I love you so much—more than I ever thought I would love anyone. And I miss you. I can't eat. I can't sleep. This house feels barren without you in it. You were always it for me, Dani. I'm sorry I ruined it. I shouldn't have called. This wasn't fair to you. I just wish I could re-do it all."

When the message fades out, the floodgates have broken, and I'm left in a puddle of myself. I listen to his last message over and over and over again, soaking in his heartbreak, listening for anything I may have missed the first or second time. I feel like an addict who has just gotten her fix. Every time I listen, it hurts but not as much as going without it does. Is it possible for someone to withstand this much heartache in one year? Thinking about his message, I realize he's right. The house feels desolate without him. Nathan helped me make this house feel like a home after Joel. And now that he's gone, I'm back at square one.

I scrub my face with my hands, drying my tear-stained face. *Well, there goes my makeup,* I think, tilting my face toward the ceiling in exasperation. I don't have time for this. I have to leave for work soon. I was already ready when I ruined my face. I wash the smeared mascara off me over my bathroom sink, hoping the redness in my eyes will wash away with it. It reminds me of Nathan and I on his bathroom sink. The images pierce through me: his hands lifting me up to sit on the vanity, the way his scent tantalized me while he kissed me. It was only a month ago, and yet it feels so much longer than that. I leave the bathroom quickly, wanting to leave the memories in there. Checking the clock, I throw on my coat and grab my keys to leave for work. It's not time for me to leave yet, but that seems to be a new habit I'm forming. It's just what I do when I can't stand to be alone in this house with all the painful reminders of the two men I've ever loved.

Work doesn't distract me like I need it to. I'm not only caught up with work, I'm ahead of schedule since I've been coming in early or staying late. So, I've been helping my staff with whatever I can. I've bussed a few tables, taken drink orders, brought food to tables, and seated customers so the hostess could have a break to text her boyfriend. I spot her leaning up against the back wall by the kitchen biting her lip, all giddy. I sigh as I watch the teenager, thinking to myself, *soak it in while you can.*

I eventually end up behind the bar helping my bartender, David, serve drinks. We fall into a nice groove. I cover the left side of the bar while he covers the right. Like clockwork, Phyllis shows up, but instead of sitting at the bar, she chooses a bar top table and waves her hand at me to come over. I nod at Jenna, who was about to come greet her, letting her know I'd wait on Phyllis tonight.

"What'll it be, Phyl?" I ask her, my hand on my hip as I lean on one of the chairs at her table.

"Vodka Cranberry. Doctor says I need to drink more juice."

"I don't think that's what they meant."

Phyllis just winks at me, and I leave to go back to the bar to make the simple drink. I pour cranberry juice, then the Smirnoff vodka—her favorite—and deliver it to her waiting hands.

"That's all I need right now, hun. I'm just watching the game." Phyllis dismisses me, and her eyes are on the screen overhead. It's a football game. I'm not paying enough attention to tell who's playing.

I walk the five steps back to the bar when David says, "I got it from here. Thanks, boss."

"Okay, cool. I'll just go back to my office then." I look away, not wanting to seem disappointed.

My eyes roam around the room, taking in everything. No one looks busy enough to offer help; they have it under control. That should make me happy. But as I walk back to my isolated office and close the door, it makes me anything but. I'm left alone to think about the state of my life. Widowed, lied to, living in a house I've been neglected in. Maybe I should move. This could be where the healing could start. The idea becomes more appealing as I contemplate it. The jilted home has too many painful memories from Joel and now Nathan. It was already something I had thought about before we broke up. I can afford it myself, but seriously, three bedrooms? It's too big for just one person. I like this idea. Moving papers around on my desk, I grab a Post-it and make a note to look into this more when I'm off. I'm sticking the Post-it in my pocket when Chantal barges in.

"Hey, Phyllis is asking for you," she says, her hands on the doorframe and handle.

"Got it, I'm coming," I reply, walking out with her.

When I reach her, she's on her second drink, but there's a third in front of her.

"Sit with me," her raspy voice fills the space between us.

I pull out a chair and angle it at the television she's watching. "I didn't think you liked football."

Lifting her glass to her mouth, she says, "I don't. But I bet my friend Eugene that his Cowboys would lose, and they did."

I laugh under my breath at her explanation. I want to be her when I get older.

"Here, take this," she offers me the third drink.

"I can't drink this. I'm working."

"So what? You're the boss." She pushes it in front of me. "You have been moping around for two weeks. Let this cheer you up."

"I have not been moping," I say, offended.

Phyllis rolls her eyes, annoyed by my blatant denial. "Yes, you have! You have looked miserable every day you've been here."

"All I'm hearing is that maybe you shouldn't be here every day."

She ignores me. "Did it not work out with the brother?"

At the mention of Nathan, I pick the rose-colored drink up and take a large gulp, saying to hell with the rules. "Nope."

"Why's that?"

I stare down at the glass, twirling it in my hands and thinking about her question. "There were secrets. I don't do secrets. Joel had enough for me, and I'm not interested."

Phyllis leans in a little, forcing me to look up at her. "Were his secrets selfish, like his brother's?"

I flash back to our argument, what Maureen admitted, and his messages. "No," unbearable honesty flows from my lips.

She pats my arm softly while she shakes her head. "I understand, darlin'. It can be hard to forgive at first."

I finish the ill-advised drink, unsure if the alcohol or my loneliness is making me share. "Serves me right, anyways, getting involved with him. What kind of person dates their dead husband's family?"

"We're all connected in one way or another. It doesn't matter what that link in the chain is. It's not like he was your brother." She bumps her shoulder into me as she jokes. "C'mon, Dani, don't shame yourself for finding love and moving on. Yes, you and Nathan were connected through Joel, but that was at first. You both love each other; everyone can see that it's different. Look at us—we were connected through Tav's, and now we send holiday and birthday cards every year."

I listen to Phyllis ramble on until she gets distracted by the next game that has taken up the screen. In all fairness, I hadn't thought about it like that. Her perspective of the situation definitely gives me new context. I sit with her as the chatter around the restaurant hums in my ears. I no longer hear her, or anyone in particular, as I dwell in the mess I find myself in again.

The next day, I pick up Chantal from her house. She comes barreling out, and it reminds me of being picked up by friends in high school. I smile at the thought. Cruising down the highway, we're not far from our destination. It only takes about twenty minutes to get there, and she hasn't stopped talking the entire time. She's so nervous. I decided what we would do today after talking to the all-wise, all-knowing Phyllis last night.

"I think it's funny I'm the calm one and you're the one being a chicken right now." I chuckle, eyes on the road.

"I am *not* a chicken! I just didn't realize you were going to make me get one too. What will I even get?" she asks herself in disbelief.

I pull into the parking lot and shut the car off. "Whatever you want. Pick from their predrawn list, I don't know. You don't have to get one if you don't want." My excitement spills over into my voice.

I practically drag Chantal into the tattoo shop with me. The first thing I notice when we walk in is the smell. It's clean. It smells like soap and disinfectant, like a weird, artistic hospital. The second is that the setup is different from the shop I went to with Nathan. We sit in their waiting area, listening to the crooning of their machines, waiting anxiously to be taken back. Luckily, I called yesterday and set up an appointment with an artist named Mike. There is another man sitting against the opposite wall from us. This will clearly not be his first time. Colorful ink adorns the bigger chunks of his arms and neck. Mike comes out with a loud clap of his hands in greeting, dressed in a faded black band T-shirt.

"Dani?" he asks, making sure I'm his next appointment. I nod my head, unable to speak from my sudden jitters. He ushers us back to his alcove in between two other makeshift rooms. His space isn't as small as I anticipated. Mike points to the two drawings he did in different sizes, leaving me to debate how adventurous I want to be.

I figured it was a simple design when I called him, but I'm in awe of how perfect he made it based on my description over the phone. "I like this one," I say, holding out the slightly bigger option.

"Alright lady, where do you want it?" He says *lady* with the same ease as he said my name.

I point an inch below the very bottom point of my thumb, "Right here, on the outer edge of my wrist."

I sit in the pleather chair and am shockingly calm now. Mike takes his time prepping my tattoo. He picks out a razor and starts shaving my wrist. When it's hairless, he very strategically places the quarter-sized purple stencil on my wrist. It's cold against my skin. Smoothing it out, he slowly peels the thin paper off. I watch every step, excited to finally say I have a tattoo. It looks exactly how I envisioned. With my arm by my side, I get up to look at it in the mirror, biting my lip from excitement.

Chantal moves closer, lifting my arm herself so she can see it. "It's so cute. I love it."

Mike starts his tattoo gun, and the loud buzzing intimidates both Chantal and me. "You going next, cutie?" He eyes my friend as I sit back down in his chair, getting comfortable.

She giggles. The sound tells me she's afraid, but a stranger wouldn't know. "I don't know about that. Maybe."

As he goes to work tracing the purple lines and leaving them black, it doesn't hurt quite as much as I anticipate. It feels like tiny bee stings. It's not something I would sign up for for hours, but for small work like this, it seems doable. Mike continues working closer to the edge of my wrist, and, damn, does it hurt more there. I look at Chantal, hoping to strike up a conversation; instead, I find her distracted by her phone, looking upset.

"What's wrong?"

As soon as she hears my voice, she slides her phone in her pocket and looks up at me. It came off too panicked for me not to notice. "Nothing."

"It definitely was something. Who are you texting?" I ask, staring down at her jeans like I'll be able to tell through the denim.

"It was Nathan," she answers, clearly feeling guilty.

"It's okay. I'm not expecting you to write him off, Chantal." I would never do that.

She avoids eye contact, so I turn my attention back to my arm, wanting to see how much is done. Not as much as I thought. I didn't realize he would have to go over the same lines again to make sure the ink takes. "He's miserable and looks worse," she tells the back of my head.

I don't know whether her insight makes me happy or sad. Of course, I like that I'm not the only one in pain. But having listened to his messages, I already know how miserable he is. His voice alone gave it away. No, I want Nathan to be happy. He's been through just as much as I have. And the tragic void I'm feeling after this year? I wouldn't wish that on him.

"He deserves it a little bit though, right?" she says as I turn back to her, sensing her attempt at easing my discomfort of the subject.

But she has it wrong. I don't want him to feel this way. "Right," I mumble, forcing a smile.

Fifteen minutes later, Mike is wiping my arm with a dry paper towel that feels like a Brillo pad to get excess ink off me. How could this be the worst part of being tattooed? Tattooing is technically being stabbed over and over again with tiny needles, and I would take that over the dry, sandpaper texture that is his paper towel. Gazing down at my arm, I try not to squeal.

I can't look away from the little rope that's twisted into a knot. "This is perfect!"

After I get a good, long look at my wrist, Mike finishes by bandaging it up. "Leave that on for a few hours. When you take it off, it needs to be cleaned."

"Got it."

"Your turn," he turns his eyes to Chantal, who sits down and asks for the first thing she can think of. A rose with a long stem. They flirt the entire time she's in her chair. But I give her credit; the thin lines look pretty and feminine on the inside of her bicep. I'm able to sit quietly without being bothered. Their attention is on only each other. I look at the dainty rope on my wrist through the clear saran wrap bandage. I feel elated I went through with it. I'm sure no one thought I would. While my fingers feather over the permanent black lines, I still feel hollow. And unfortunately, I know the only thing that's going to fix it.

CHAPTER 22
DANI, PRESENT DAY

The air has stilled, removing the worst of the chill. I take it as a good sign. Despite that, I pull my coat tighter around me, hoping to ease my nerves. The cold ground crunches beneath my feet, letting anyone close to my vicinity know that someone is coming. Although, as my gaze roams the space in front of me, it seems I'm the only one visiting. My steps come to a stop, and I reach out, lightly touching the stone in acknowledgement. It's the third Thursday of the month; he's supposed to be here. I pull my phone out of my pocket, tapping the screen. I'm right; he should be here. It's after school hours.

I shove down my disappointment and stand there waiting. Minutes slowly pass. The wind has started to pick up, making my nose drip from the cold. So much for my good sign. I could go to his house and see if he's there, or I could go home and forget I even came here. I know my next move before I've given it much thought. I'll do whatever it takes.

As I turn around slowly, my bones feel stiff from the frigid air. My steps falter, freezing me where I stand.

Nathan stands a few yards away from me, unmoving. He has dark circles under his brown eyes—eyes that are staring at me. His eyebrows are raised in surprise; he doesn't know why I'm here. Nathan doesn't walk any closer to me. He's waiting for me to handle the situation in front of us. Because up to this point, I've ignored any attempt he's taken to talk to me, practically shunning him. Chantal was right. He doesn't look like himself. He is still just as handsome as before, but looking at the man in front of me makes me want to weep. He looks like a shell of a person. My body moves toward him on its own accord, wanting desperately to make it better.

Nathan watches me get closer to him. "What are you doing here?"

"I came to find you."

My honesty shakes him. "Well, you found me."

"I did," I say simply, watching him, unsure what to say. "How are you doing?" The trivial question rolls off my tongue.

"How am I?" Nathan sounds hoarse. "Dani, I'm in agony."

His pain vibrates through me, and I'm shell-shocked. I suddenly have no words to offer him. He tries to walk around me, but I catch him, grabbing his hands. The single touch causes electric currents to race through my every nerve. God, I have missed him. The heat of his touch mixed with the scent of his tea tree shampoo is sending me into withdrawal. Urgency washes over me, and I'm unable to keep the little distance we have.

Standing on my tiptoes, I pull him down to my level, brushing my lips across his. They're warm and hesitant. I'm about to pull away when his full lips part for me, and his hand snakes it's way around the back of my neck. Nathan presses his body into mine, and I hold onto him like a buoy in the middle of the ocean. The kiss is hedonic, causing a fire to burn low in my belly. But then, Nathan rips his mouth from mine.

"I'm sorry. I shouldn't have done that," he says, looking down at me.

I watch the rise and fall of his chest, cursing the absence of his mouth. "Why?" I ask, too breathless.

"Because we're not together anymore. And, and . . . I'd rather just be friends than go through this heartache all over again." Nathan releases me from his arms and steps away.

My heart drops in my chest. "Is that really what you want?"

Nathan doesn't answer me, choosing not to lie. "It's how it should be. You have a hard enough time with the fact that Joel was my brother."

I cross the small distance he put between us and reach my hands up to either side of his neck so he'll focus. "Not anymore. You were a better husband to me than my actual husband. I should have been paying attention to that the last few months instead of hurting us both. I'm sorry I didn't see that sooner. We're tethered together, Nathan. That's all that matters. I don't care how anymore."

"Are you sure?" he whispers across my face.

"Yes."

Nathan rests his forehead on mine and closes his eyes like he's deep in thought. "I don't ever want to be apart from you again."

"I know. The last two weeks have been the longest of my life," I admit to him.

"It's been a few weeks for you, five years for me."

I stare up at him, soaking in his sadness. I decide to share my own secret. "I often wish I had met you first."

Nathan raises my hand, feathering a kiss on my wrist. My sleeve inches up in the process, showcasing the top of my small tattoo. His thumb lightly glides across it. "I like it on you."

He bends down to kiss me once more. "Okay." I shake him off with a laugh. "I want to go get my hair cut. You spend your time here. I'll see you after. Do you want to do my house tonight?"

Nathan kisses my forehead, unable to stop himself. "Sounds perfect. Why are you cutting your hair?" he asks while he tugs on the ends like a little boy on the playground.

"It's time for a change. I'm starting a new chapter of my life." I smile at him lovingly.

"Okay then. I can't wait to see it," he says, swatting my butt playfully.

My once long, flowy tresses now end right past my shoulders. Gabrielle, the stylist working her magic on me, blow-dries my hair with a round brush. She pulls the strands of hair smooth and slightly tucks the ends under. The bristles of the brush and hot air are calming against my scalp and shoulders. I can't stop looking at my new do in the mirror. It's a nice change. I feel made anew, and I hope Nathan likes it. When Gabrielle is done, I shake my head, loving how much lighter it is and how the ends dance around me.

I'm eager to get home and settle more between Nathan and me. Leaving the salon, I hope he hasn't beaten me home. I want to change into something sexier to surprise him. I wonder if he's missed me the same way I have missed him. Shaking my head at the thought, I laugh to myself. Using context clues, our kiss for example, it is very clear he has.

Pulling into the empty driveway, I mentally fist pump. *Good, he's not here yet. I still have time.* I already have the lingerie picked out in my mind. Excitement dances in my bones. Sprinting into my home, I close the door behind me, stopping for a split second. *Didn't I lock that when I left?* I have to be less careless. Feeling pressed for time, I start stripping as I walk down the hallway. I'm in my bra and jeans when I get to my room. I dig through my drawers until I find my lacy blue slip. I can't wait for him to see me in this, already picturing his calloused hands yanking it up my hips.

A loud crashing sound shakes me out of my imagination. Tossing the slip on my bed, I walk out toward the living room. I see books and DVDs have fallen from a shelf. It doesn't make sense that they would have fallen on their own. Puzzled, I pass the kitchen to pick up the mess when something slams me into the wall, smacking my head against it. I'm certain there are stars circling above my head. My eyes struggle to focus, and I'm not sure what has just happened. I feel chilled hands run up my sides, and a sick feeling weighs on me. While I get my bearings, a voice echoes in my ears.

"I've missed you."

Paul's angular face comes into view, and I push him off of me just to get slammed into the wall again. I let out a cry, and the fear sets in. "What're you doing here?" I croak.

He gropes my breast with his face inches from mine, watching my mouth as he talks. "I came to see my best girl—isn't it obvious?"

My body is rigid against his unwanted hands. "Just go. Leave, and no one has to know you were here. Please don't do this."

"I was right, I like it when you beg," he says more to himself.

Gripping my chin, he forces my head still, lowering his lips to kiss me. I twist my neck trying to get out of it, but his hand crushes my jaw. Tears prickle my eyelashes. I have to get out of this on my own because I don't know when Nathan will get here. And I'm not sure how much I can take. Swallowing my disgust, I kiss him back just enough for him to part his lips. When his lips intertwine with mine, I bite. Hard. Blood gushes in my mouth like a popped water balloon. Paul stumbles back, screaming in pain. I run on shaky legs to my bedroom, slamming and locking my door. Where is my phone? I find it under my sweater on my dresser. Slow steps and a menacing laugh filter in through the cracks in the door.

"You're going to regret that," he sneers.

I begin to call 911 when he starts slamming his body against the door with all his might. The act shakes the fragile room I'm held captive in. I'm a trapped mouse with nowhere to go. The doorframe splinters, and I drop my phone, hoping whoever picks up will be able to hear the struggle that is taking place.

"Did you really think this door would keep me out?" He stalks toward me. With every step, I move backward until I'm against the wall.

I try to escape him, but the walls feel like they're moving in. "Paul, please. Don't hurt me," I speak loudly, wanting the operator to hear. He lunges at me, grabbing my hair in his fist. It's then I notice the knife in his grasp. I close my eyes and attempt to swallow around the knot of fear in my throat. What is he going to do to me? I hear my front door open and close.

"Nathan, Pau—" I try to yell, but he yanks my head back and covers my mouth with the blade.

Moving me closer toward the broken door frame, he whispers, "Call him back here."

I vehemently shake my head no. Paul let's go of my hair and wraps his arm around my stomach, moving the knife against my neck.

"Where are you?" Nathan has a lightness in his voice. He thinks I'm playing a game.

Paul huffs in annoyance, pushing me out and down the hallway. Nathan smiles at me until he notices the knife at my throat. He doesn't say anything right away, but he keeps his eyes on me.

"Hey buddy, how ya been?" Paul asks.

"Are you okay?" His question is directed at me. Worry creases his brow. I can tell it's taking everything in him to remain calm in this moment.

I'm about to answer him when the sharp edge bites into my flesh. I let out a groan in protest. Nathan moves forward wanting to save me but is forced to halt, not wanting to put me in jeopardy. It hurts more than the blade against my throat that he has to see me this way.

"I'll tell you when you can speak," Paul says, kissing my damp cheek with entirely too much intimacy.

Tears stream down my face without control, falling onto my bare flesh. I stand as still and silent as I can.

"You don't have to do this. Let her go. Don't hurt her," Nathan pleads with the mad man, his hands in fists by his sides.

Sirens begin to sound off outside. They're in the distance but seem to be getting closer. Paul lowers his weapon just slightly as his gaze sweeps outside. I feel the change in him. He's distracted. Nathan gives me a quick tilt of his head, telling me to get out of the way as quickly as I can. Blue lights flash against the white walls, capturing more of Paul's attention.

I spring into step, moving away from Paul. Nathan tackles him to the ground in the same instant, and the knife drops in the process. I skirt around them, picking it up. Everything suddenly feels like it's in slow motion. Nathan pounds his white-knuckled fist into Paul's bleeding face over and over again. I stand above them, holding a knife. The police officers rush in and pull Nathan off Paul's limp body.

I find my voice in that moment, knocking the events back into real time. "Stop! No! It's him," I say, pointing to the man on the floor, getting the police to release Nathan.

He rushes to me. "Are you okay?" His thumbs wipe the wetness from under my eyes. "I'm so sorry it took me so long to get here."

I hug him tighter, never wanting to let go. "When this is all over, take me to your house. I don't want to be here anymore. This place only carries pain now."

"This couldn't be a worse time for this," he says, looking down at my hands in his, "but, move in with me. We could—"

"Yes."

"Yes?" he reiterates, confused.

"You make me feel safe. I have not felt at home without you. I don't care if it doesn't look like the right time. It *is* the right time."

CHAPTER 22

DANI, PRESENT DAY

CHAPTER 23
DANI, PRESENT DAY

A tickling sensation runs across my bare stomach, waking me up from my unconsciousness. My eyes flutter open. My current view is different from my old bedroom. It still takes me a moment to remember I'm not in my house anymore.

Nathan's bed faces a giant window overlooking the tall trees in his backyard. I prefer this layout. It feels dreamy. I can't wait for it to rain or snow so I can lie in bed to watch it. It's early; the sun isn't even all the way up yet. The sun leaks through the limbs of the trees, casting haunting shadows on the ground.

I feel a rough hand pass over my stomach to my hip. Nathan lies behind me, spooning me. His fingertips graze up over my stomach, back down to my hips, and eventually to my thighs, sending a thrill to my belly. His lips travel lightly over my shoulders, and I can't tell if he's just appreciating me being near or if he knows I'm awake. I savor his touch, either way. His movements are languid, and a low, waking groan escapes me.

"I could get used to waking up like this," I mutter the words.

"Get used to it. You live here now." I hear the smile in his voice.

I roll over to face him but close my eyes, still too tired to wake up.

"What's on the agenda for today?" His deft fingers push the hair back from my face continuously.

"You mean besides you?" I reply sleepily. He snickers at my joke, but I answer him, "Unpack the rest of my things."

"And get a dog."

That wakes me up. "What? What do we need a dog for?" I yawn, stretching in my new bed. My arms go up overhead, and my fingertips barely reach the headboard.

"Other than being great companions, for protection," he says obviously. "You need a guard dog. You still jump at the faintest sounds around you. It'll help you feel safer."

Moving into the crook of his arm, I nestle in. "I feel safe enough. I have you."

I moved in a month ago. I was lucky: my Realtor managed to get me an offer on the house five days after listing. We had moved some of my things over to Nathan's house after the cops took our statements from that night, and it's been wonderful living here. He never makes me feel like I'm intruding on his space and always reassures me this is my home now. Nathan is right, though; I'm still jumpy. And I'm sure it would help put him at ease if we had a dog. He might not feel obligated to check every room before I enter it. I'm optimistic this will all pass. It helps that Paul is rotting in a jail cell where he can't get to me.

Nathan nibbles on my jawline, making it hard to breathe. And I know the dog business is put to bed for now. "Well, Chantal and my mom will be over later to help you with whatever you need while I'm at work."

I nudge his chest. I want him to listen to me. "I don't think that's necessary. I can be home alone." He glances at me with a knowing look, forcing me to relent. "Okay, fine. Thank you for asking them," I say more sweetly.

Nathan moves over me, and my legs spread to accommodate his broad body. Mornings have become my favorite time of day. I'm not an early riser, but when my day begins with his gentle touch and the way he sinks himself into me, how could this not be preferred?

Bringing boxes in from his empty garage, there are no black bags in sight. Nathan got rid of them like he said he would, and I didn't ask how. I didn't want to know. I explain to Chantal and Maureen where things need to go inside and what needs to be taken to the dump. I decided early on I wanted a clean break. I got rid of most of my things, seeing as Nathan already had the majority of it, anyways. I'm mainly just keeping my clothes. As the three of us mill about the house, I happen to stop and take in this moment. I never thought this could have been possible for me: a future with Nathan, Chantal forgiving me, and Maureen being okay with it and working to be kinder.

"You okay?" Chantal comes out of a room in the back seeing me standing still in the middle of the house.

"I'm perfect," I beam. "You guys don't need to be here. Honestly, I think it's time for me to try to be alone in the house."

"Are you sure?" she asks, sounding anything but.

"Yes, I'm sure."

"Fine, but if you change your mind, call me. Or just come over!" Chantal negotiates.

"Deal."

"Hey, she's giving us the boot. Let's give the girl some space," my best friend says to my former mother-in-law.

"Okay, I just have a box of tampons and other bathroom stuff," Maureen says, looking through it. "Let me put it in the master bath, and I'll get out of your hair."

Watching them leave, I thank the two women and close the door. It doesn't take me very long to put away my belongings in the drawers Nathan emptied for me. Afterward, I decide to clean up and redecorate a little. Giving his—*our*—place a little feng shui, making it feel new to both of us. When the living room is rearranged to my liking, I sit down suddenly out of breath. That took more energy than I thought possible. It took more time than I noticed, too, because Nathan walks in with a grin covering his face.

"You're in a good mood," I tell him, thinking out loud.

"Of course I am. I get to come home to you. I ordered pizza on the way home. I hope you're in the mood for that. Hey! You moved stuff around," he says, his eyes moving around the room. "I love it. It looks more open this way." Nathan comes to my side and kisses me on the head. "What picture is that?"

I follow his gaze, landing on the one family photo I have. "It's my parents and me at the beach when I was nine. I found it when I was unpacking today. That was the best vacation I had as a child. Dad wasn't on his phone the entire time, and my mom was focused on me. But not in the way she normally would be. It was the first time I felt like I was allowed to be a kid."

Nathan listens thoughtfully, without judgement. "You were a cute kid. I hope our children look like you."

Frozen in place, his words ring in my ear. *Is this fear? No, I don't think so. Maybe surprise?* "Our children?" I recite his words back to him.

"I'm yours, Dani. And my children will be yours. And you'll be a terrific mom when the time comes. We're tethered together, remember, through it all." His words soothe and reassure me.

Abruptly, my mind connects two inconspicuous conversations I've had today. Maureen saying *tampons*, and Nathan saying *our children*. My lips stop moving, focused on one thought: *when was my last period?*

"What's wrong? You look like you just saw a ghost," he says, snapping me out of it.

I refrain from running, but I walk backward as I talk: "I got distracted. I have to go to the bathroom."

Closing the bathroom door, I find my box of tampons, remembering another pregnancy test should be in there. It's the last one of a pack of two. The first one I took at Joel's funeral. It's buried at the bottom, but I eventually find it. Ripping the thick wrapper off of the test, I turn the faucet on for added help. I sit down on the cold porcelain, unsure of what I'm hoping for.

My hand shakes holding the stick between my legs. I empty as much of my bladder as I can. I don't know how much it actually needs. I pull the activated test out from under me, push the cap back on, and set it on the counter. Turning my back, I leave the urine-coated stick on the sink and pace around the small, tiled room. The doorbell rings, making me jump. It must be the pizza.

I hear Nathan's voice in the background. "I got it!"

I lean back, eyeing the pregnancy test, and I see it: two vertical, pink lines. Positive.

My hand goes to my belly instinctively as I picture my growing body in the next few months, Nathan holding our baby, and the future. I grip the positive test in my hand and go in search of him, hoping he meant what he said just minutes ago.

I find him already in the kitchen with a mouthful of pizza. With shaking hands, I lay the stick on the counter next to the warm pizza box. I watch his face as he looks down at it, his eyes going wide and taking in the pink lines. I'm relieved when a smile dances across his face like he's just won the World Series.

Nathan turns toward me at the same time I reach up and pull him by the back of the neck down to meet me. Our lips lock, and I'm filled with another layer of love.

Holding me up with one arm, he moves his free hand to come around and rest on our growing babe. Nathan laughs into my mouth and sets me back down to really look at me.

"I will love this baby just as much as I love you!" he boasts triumphantly before he kisses me again, one hand firmly on my stomach.

Nathan has always made loving me seem so effortless. Even a year ago, if I was being honest with myself, this is the life I would have dreamed of. He is who I want this with. I love him. I always have. Opening my mouth, I elongate his affection, savoring the taste of marinara on his tongue. It's my favorite flavor: Nathan mixed with anything else.

Printed in the USA
CPSIA information can be obtained
at www.ICGtesting.com
LVHW031040161223
766668LV00025B/126

9 781637 552803